DEATH MATCH

By the same author

The Rebel series:
CANNON FODDER
THE DIE-HARDS

The Submarine series:
THE WOLF PACK
OPERATION DEATH WATCH
CONVOY TO CATASTROPHE
FIRE IN THE WEST
FLIGHT TO THE REICH

The Wotan series:
DEATH RIDE
SLAUGHTER AT SALERNO
MARCH OR DIE
THE OUTCASTS
THE HESS ASSAULT

The Stuka Squadron series:
THE BLACK KNIGHTS
THE HAWKS OF DEATH
THE TANKBUSTERS
BLOOD MISSION

DEATH MATCH

LEO KESSLER

C

CENTURY

LONDON MELBOURNE AUCKLAND JOHANNESBURG

Copyright © Leo Kessler 1988

First published in Great Britain in 1988 by
Century Hutchinson Ltd
Brookmount House, 62–65 Chandos Place
London WC2N 4NW

Century Hutchinson South Africa (Pty) Ltd
PO Box 337, Bergvlei, 2012 South Africa

Century Hutchinson Australia Pty Ltd
PO Box 496, 16–22 Church Street, Hawthorn
Victoria 3122, Australia

Century Hutchinson New Zealand Limited
PO Box 40–086, Glenfield, Auckland 10, New Zealand

ISBN 0 7126 1907 0

Photoset, printed and bound in Great Britain by
WBC Bristol and Maesteg

BOOK ONE

The Decision

CHAPTER 1

'*Here they come!*' the purple-faced Grenadier yelled above the howl of the wind that came straight from the Arctic Circle. Eyes narrowed to slits under glistening, ice-heavy eyebrows he peered into no-man's-land.

King Bull, commander of the newly formed 'Goulash-Cannon Company',* threw the old potato sack from his massive shoulders and stamped to his feet in the snow-filled hollow. 'Took their frigging time,' he grumbled. He pulled out his flatman, took a hearty swig, shuddered, and stared through the howling white gloom across the awesome steppe, bare of any tree.

Behind him the odds and sods from King Bull's cookhouse company, hastily chased from their ovens, armed and thrown into the line to bolster up the Fourth Grenadiers' defences, stared to their front, nervously fingering their weapons. All of them, even the thickest 'pearl-diver',† knew that the whole of the front in Central Russia had broken down. The German Army was in full retreat in this terrible winter of 1942. The Red Army could not be far behind these beaten wretches now trudging towards them.

Like slow white ghosts, the first dim shapes filtered out of the howling gloom of the snowstorm. Backs bent like those of infinitely weary old men, they trudged over the deep frozen snow. More and more appeared. There was no attempt at cohesion, order, military discipline. These were broken men. Even some of their NCOs seemed to have thrown their weapons away. The 'Iron Division', which in 1941 had almost reached Moscow itself, was a spent force.

* Horse-drawn mobile ovens.
† Nickname for dish-washers.

Most of this first wave reaching the Fourth Grenadiers' lines seemed to be wounded, the ones who could still walk being helped by exhausted, grey-faced comrades. Others were towed on makeshift sleds – a barn door, a ladder, even army blankets – by bent, gasping *panje* ponies.

Karl Carstens's handsome face grew sombre. The biting cold, even the fact that he was suffering from the 'thin shits' again (they all were), were forgotten momentarily, as he viewed this terrible spectacle. For three long years, he and the other two Rebels – Polack and Ami* – had been longing for the breakdown of Hitler's hated empire. But even in his wildest dreams he had never thought that the *Wehrmacht*, which had carved out a *Reich* of blood and terror for its Führer, would fall apart just like this. How confidently had the army marched into Russia the previous summer, sweeping all before it, destroying tremendous Popov armies! Now these survivors of that once victorious *Wehrmacht* were finished, at the end of their tether, good solely for the military knackers' yard.

Next to Karl, his running mate Ami breathed out hard, the breath wreathing his pinched, purple face like smoke. '*Jesus, Mary, Joseph!*' he exclaimed in his thickest Rhenish accent, completely awed by the spectacle, 'just look at the poor shits on them sledges. Some of them'll tighten up their assholes for good before this day is out, I'll be bound, comrades.'

'Wish something'd tighten up my asshole for me,' Polack, the third of the Rebels groaned, holding his stomach with hands like steam shovels. 'I swear my guts are gonna explode at any moment . . . An' I've got the wet farts agen.'

'*Schnauze!*' King Bull snapped, as the first of the wounded started to stagger and fall into their dugouts. 'Can't hear mesen frigging think. You, Grenadier!' He pointed at Karl. 'Signal the Pill that we've got a whole bunch o' wounded here. One green flare should do it. *Los!*'

* See *The Rebels* for further details.

'*Jawohl, Oberfeld,*' Karl answered, raising the clumsy-looking flare pistol with which he would alert the Fourth's grey-haired medical officer, nicknamed the 'Pill', to the arrival of the Iron Division's wounded. He pressed the trigger. There was a soft plop. Crack! Directly above their heads, the flare exploded, colouring the white gloom an unreal green; while the men of the Fourth began to help the new arrivals.

'What was it like, comrade?' Ami asked one grey ghost whose wild and demented stare showed he had experienced something unbelievably terrible out there in the snowy waste. He handed the man his water bottle, filled with hot ersatz coffee. 'Have a slug o' nigger sweat first.'

With clawlike trembling hands the man seized the flask and took a deep gulp, the colour returning to his wan cheeks almost immediately. 'Terrible,' he choked, as others staggered by unseeingly as if in some awful nightmare, 'terrible. . . . The Ivans are everywhere. Hundreds of them . . . *thousands.* We cut them down with the machine-guns by the score. But still they kept on coming . . .' The man was on the verge of tears. 'We couldn't do . . .' His words died away helplessly, the saliva trickling from suddenly slack lips.

'Go on,' Ami urged, still holding the 'nigger sweat' at the ready.

But the man from the Iron Division was no longer listening. Weakly he pushed the Grenadier to one side and started after the others, muttering, 'Got to get on. Thousands of them. Cut them down . . . still they kept on coming. Got to get on.' Then he was gone, disappearing into the snowstorm, still repeating that dread litany of doom, leaving the Three Rebels staring at each other in silent bewilderment . . .

Five minutes later, after the last of the first wave from the shattered Iron Division had passed through the 'Goulash-Cannon Company's' positions, the scream rang out breaking the brooding white silence. It was loud, piercing and completely hysterical. It raised the small hairs at the backs of

their cropped, lice-ridden heads with startling eerie suddenness.

'What in the name of Sweet Jesus was *that*?' King Bull
exclaimed, peering into the gloom, face suddenly white and
drawn. 'Did you hear –' He stopped short and cocked his
head to one side, while the others waited intently, nerves
ticking electrically. 'Horses,' King Bull declared. 'I swear I
can hear horses' hooves!'

'*Cossacks!*' someone quavered. 'It could be the Cossacks,
Oberfeld?'

King Bull swung round on the soldier, eyes blazing with
sudden rage. 'Will you just knock it off, arse-with-ears!' he
exploded. 'You hash-slingers are wetting yer drawers as it is.
Don't frigging well make it no worse.' He was businesslike
again suddenly. '*You, you* and *you*, Carstens,' he nodded at the
Three Rebels. 'Get your lazy butts over there and find out
what's going on.' When the three of them seemed to hesitate,
he cried, 'Go on . . . we'll cover you. See what's making that
shitting noise. It's getting on my tits. *Los!*'

Reluctantly the three friends clambered out of their holes,
unslinging their rifles as they did so, while the others
crouched lower in their slit-trenches, clearly expecting a
horde of screaming savage Cossack horsemen to come
charging at their position in the very next moment. Even
King Bull dropped back into his trench, clicking off the safety
catch of the machine pistol that hung from his massive
shoulders as he did so.

'Why is it always us –' Ami began miserably, as they started
to trudge into the white whirling gloom, but Karl cut him off
with a curt, 'Keep quiet, Ami. Want to hear what's going on
out here.'

On edge and tense, wet with sudden sweat in spite of the
biting cold, the three young grenadiers advanced cautiously
across the snow, scuffed by the feet of the first wave of the Iron
Division, stained here and there, too, by the bloody faeces of
those beaten men. Now all was silence, save for the howl of the

wind and the crunch of their heavily nailed boots on the snow. Behind them the others had disappeared into the gloom. They were suddenly the last men left alive in this miserable white world.

Suddenly the pain-racked sound came again. This time it was no longer high-pitched and eerie, but soft and tremulous, almost a moan. They stopped dead, nerves racing. Karl felt a cold bead of sweat trickle unpleasantly down the small of his back. 'Over there,' Polack whispered, jerking his big head to the right. 'It came from over there.'

Karl nodded. With his free hand he indicated the other two should spread out. They started moving again. Now Karl, slightly in front and in the centre, could smell familiar scents: male sweat and the coarse black *mahorka* tobacco they smoked. *The Popovs were out there somewhere!* He couldn't be mistaken.

Abruptly Polack froze. The other two stopped at once.

'What is it?' Karl found himself whispering.

Wordlessly Polack pointed at the snow a few metres away. Karl gulped. There lay a heap of horse turds, still steaming. The frightened grenadier had been right. The Cossack cavalry, half-wild savages from the remote border provinces of the Red Empire, were out there *already*. It meant that the bulk of the Red Army was hard on the heels of the beaten Iron Division. Karl swallowed hard. If the Fourth Grenadiers didn't get out of this godforsaken dump soon, the Popovs would slaughter them just as they had done with the Iron Division. Christ, they really were up to their hooters in shit . . .

The same dire thought was now occurring to Captain von Schorr, adjutant of the Fourth Grenadiers, known behind his back as 'Creeping Jesus', as he listened to the CO, Colonel von Heinersdorff. Sitting astride the horse saddle that was his favourite seat, swinging the broken sabre he had carried at the Battle of Bzura, the white-headed old fool seemed, in von Schorr's opinion, completely oblivious to the urgency of the situation outside.

Instead he greeted each officer with a flourish of his sword as they crouched to enter the *isba* and tried to find a place in the crowded peasant hut, devoid of all furniture save a green-tiled oven which reached to the ceiling and a low bench which ran around the whitewashed walls, making his usual inane pleasantries. 'Bit of rough weather, what, Major? Good for the troops, eh? Harden them. . . . Splendid turnout by your First Company yesterday, Captain, in spite of the conditions. Excellent, excellent . . . got to keep up the traditions of the Fourth Grenadiers, even in these trying times, what.'

Finally they had all crowded in, faces suddenly flushed in the tremendous heat coming from the stove, the company officers already beginning to scratch as the lice, with which they were all infested, started to wake up in the abrupt warmth.

Colonel von Heinersdorff sat bolt upright on his saddle and whacked his sabre against the side of his boot. 'Well, gentlemen, let us say the situation is decidedly, er, *shitty*' – he beamed at his officers – 'but not impossible, what.'

Creeping Jesus could have groaned aloud. What had he done in this life to be cursed with such a cretin? Any officer in his right mind – even the most junior subaltern – knew that the only thing to do now was to pick up his hind legs and make a run for it before it was too late. But here was this senile old shit playing games, as if this were a damned pre-war exercise in the tactical control of troops. Didn't the old fart realize that the Popovs were at the door? It was virtually every man for himself!

But the CO seemed to feel no sense of urgency. As the wind howled outside, the snow slashing at the dirty window panes of the *isba*, he said, 'Well, let us have a little look at the tactical situation, gentlemen, shall we? He turned to the big map

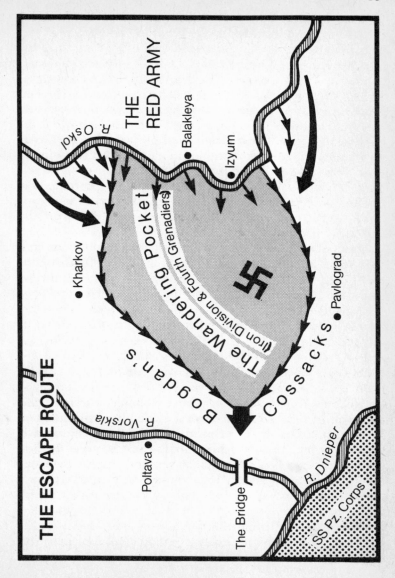

pinned up on the dirty wall behind him, sweeping it with his broken sabre. '*The enemy!* To our left flank, there is their Fourth Guards Army. To the right, their Sixth Siberian. That much we know. To our rear?' He shrugged easily. 'What's out there is anyone's guess. Intelligence is completely in the dark, I'm afraid. Could be loose Ivan recce parties, partisans, even whole armies. At present, all we know is the route we shall take to the west – here.'

Creeping Jesus's heart leapt at the words. It meant that something was going to be done after all. They were going to withdraw. New hope welled up inside him.

'This route is *supposedly* held by several German rear echelon formations, with the first real German positions, those of Dietrich's SS Panzer Corps, here on the Dnieper.'

Major Hardt, who commanded the regiment's 1st Battalion, whistled softly and said, 'But sir, that's over 500 kilometres away!'

'I know, I know,' the CO replied brightly as if it were every day that the Fourth Grenadiers were cut off 500 kilometres from the main German front in the depth of the Russian winter.

Watching him Creeping Jesus could only contain his mounting anger with difficulty. But there was worse to come.

'Now, as you all know,' the Colonel continued, 'the remnants of General Sobel's Iron Division have commenced passing through our lines this morning. Sobel's chaps have been badly hit, very badly hit indeed. There is very little they can do for themselves. Most of their motor transport has gone, their losses have been very high and they are burdened with some 1,500 wounded men, who simply cannot be abandoned to the enemy.'

There was a murmur of agreement at this.

The Colonel nodded as if it were the kind of response he expected from the officers of the Fourth, which could trace its

history to the days of 'Old Fritz'* himself. 'Now it is proposed
that we bring out what is left of the Iron Division till we reach
the SS –'

'But sir,' Creeping Jesus protested fervently, unable to hold
himself back any longer, appalled at the old fart's acceptance
of a totally impossible situation, 'what kind of progress can we
make if we are burdened, not only by the Iron Division, but
also by the Division's wounded – and no real transport? Let us
say that we could cover two or three kilometres a day, it
would take us' – he made a quick calculation – 'perhaps a
third of a year to reach our own lines!'

There was a murmur of agreement from some of the others,
especially the younger officers who had joined the Regiment
more recently, to make up the great gaps in its ranks.

Creeping Jesus pressed home what he thought was his
advantage. 'Surely, sir, we must be prepared to sacrifice the
minority – the wounded – for the benefit of the majority, those
who are still capable of moving and fight –'

'Is that so, *Herr Hauptmann*.' A familiar throaty voice cut
into his words, as the door of the *isba* was rudely flung open to
admit a flurry of snowflakes and a blast of icy air.

They all turned, startled.

It was the 'Pill', Staff-Major Heinz, the Regiment's senior
medical officer, bareheaded, old, and very angry, his craggy,
lined face crimson with the wind – and rage. Behind him,
suddenly awkward in the presence of so many officers, stood
Grenadier Carstens and the big one they called 'the Polack'
carrying something hidden beneath a greatcoat on a door
serving as a stretcher.

'Well, Pill,' the CO began in his hearty bumbling manner,
as Creeping Jesus prepared to ask the reason for this
unwarranted intrusion, 'tell me, old chap, where's the fire –'

'Here's the damned fire!' the MO cut him short in his brisk
Saxon manner. At the best of times the Pill was no respecter of

* Frederick the Great, the eighteenth-century Prussian king.

persons, for he had been a member of the Fourth Grenadiers longer then anyone. Indeed he had served in the Regiment as a young ensign back in the days when it had been still known as the 'Crown Prince's Own' in the old Imperial Army. Now he was beside himself with anger. 'Grenadier Carstens – remove the damned greatcoat!'

Reluctantly Karl did so, trying to avert his gaze from the 'thing' they had cut down from the telegraph pole half an hour before. Behind them, laden with three rifles, Ami retched and grew paler than ever.

Someone gasped. Creeping Jesus's elegantly manicured hand flew to his mouth. Even the CO was shaken enough to murmur, '*Ach, du lieber Himmel!*'

On the wooden stretcher lay the naked form of a German soldier, identifiable on account of his 'dice-beakers'.* His arms were stretched in a savage, sadistic parody of Jesus on the Cross. But this was not the Christ of the sad, composed face, gaze mild and saintly. This unknown German soldier had been cruelly tortured, his throat cut from ear to ear in a great ragged wound about which the blood had already clotted in an ugly black scab.

'Lower with the greatcoat, Grenadier,' Pill ordered ruthlessly, his burning eyes not moving from the shocked faces of his fellow officers, no sound now disturbing the heavy tense silence save the howl of the wind outside.

Karl bit his bottom lip to prevent himself from vomiting and tried hard not to look as he removed the greatcoat from the dead man's bottom half and lowered it gently to the dirt floor.

'God in Heaven!' Colonel von Heinersdorff exclaimed, the broken sabre falling from suddenly nerveless fingers. 'They've cut . . . cut his . . . *thing* off!'

'Yes, Colonel.' The Pill's voice was harsh, grating, brutal. 'The murdering sadistic swine ripped off his penis while the

---

* Soldiers' nickname for jackboots.

poor wretch was still alive. I will not sicken you any further by telling you what they did with it then.'

Outside Ami, who knew what the torturers had done with that severed organ, could contain himself so longer. He leaned against the outer wall and began to vomit, his skinny shoulders heaving violently.

The Pill did not seem to notice. His whole being was concentrated on imposing his will on his fellow officers. As Karl hastily drew the greatcoat over the naked tortured body of this unknown soldier from the Iron Division, the Pill cut into the tense heavy silence. 'That poor fellow – God rest his soul – was a straggler from the Iron Division. The Cossacks caught him and had their little fun with him – their usual *jokes*!' The Pill's face contorted in angry disgust. 'All of you have heard of the sort of thing that they can sink to – they're nothing better than savages! Now we all have seen it with our own eyes.' He turned his attention on a suddenly ashen-faced Creeping Jesus. '*Herr Hauptmann*,' he snapped, 'are you *now* prepared to sacrifice the minority – the wounded – for the benefit of the majority, knowing that this might well happen to any man of the Iron Division unfortunate to be left behind? Could you live with your conscience, if you made a decision of that kind, Captain?'

'But a retreat burdened with the wounded would take weeks . . . months,' the hapless adjutant stuttered. 'We might never make –'

'Can you still seriously propose we abandon the wounded?' the Pill repeated, eyes blazing.

Creeping Jesus gave in. He bowed his shoulders and looked at his boots.

Hurriedly Colonel von Heinersdorff picked up his sabre and said, 'Of course not, Pill. The honour of the Fourth Grenadiers would not allow the Regiment to take such a despicable course. We shall ensure – cost what it may – that the *whole* of the Iron Division . . .'

But the old doctor, who had seen too much misery and too

much suffering in his seven years in the front line over two wars, was no longer listening. Wordlessly he nodded to Karl and Polack and they carried their burden outside into the howling wind, leaving the assembled officers staring at their backs in numb, shocked silence.

Hastily Ami closed the door as the Pill leaned against the wall of the hut, all energy abruptly spent, looking old, very old.

After a while he became aware of the three young soldiers staring at him and he forced a weary smile. 'All right, lads,' he said, voice normal once more, all anger spent, 'Cover him up with a bit of snow and you, Carstens, put your coat on again. This wind will freeze up anybody's outside plumbing. And when you're finished, go over to the medical quartermaster. Tell him I sent you. Each of you has to be given a measure of brandy – for strictly medicinal reasons, *klar*!'

'*Klar, Herr Stabsarzt*,' they echoed as one, stumbling awkwardly to attention.

Airily, the Pill shook his hand in a mixture of a salute and a wave and then he was gone, shoulders hunched, stumping heavily through the ankle-deep snow.

'Brandy!' Ami exclaimed happily.

'Perhaps it'll stop my wet farts,' Polack said.

But Karl remained obstinately silent. Even the prospect of the medical spirits, his first drink in months, could not lighten his gloom. He knew he could overcome that first terrible sight of that naked man, nailed to the telegraph post, with his own penis dangling from his contorted, bloody lips, but he couldn't forget that arsehole of an adjutant's words so easily. What had he said? '*A retreat burdened with the wounded would take weeks . . . months. We might never make it.*'

CHAPTER 2

On the last day of February 1942, 'the Wandering Pocket', as it later became known in the history of the *Wehrmacht* in Russia in World War Two, set off westwards on its long odyssey. In the centre, covering an area of some fifty square kilometres moved the battered remnants of the Iron Division. To the rear and on both flanks, the Fourth Grenadier Regiment, split up into three battalions, provided the necessary cover. To the immense relief of Creeping Jesus, who now lived in constant fear that he might be taken by marauding Cossacks and suffer the same terrible fate as that unknown soldier on the door, the Fourth was not asked to provide troops for the van. That would have meant that the Goulash Cannon Company, which he now regarded as his personal bodyguard and which was the Regiment's only reserve, would have been given the task.

The 'honour' of leading the Pocket, as Colonel von Heinersdorff called it, was given to the Iron Division's sole remaining infantry battalion that was in decent enough shape to do any fighting. As General Sobel, a big hearty man with a black patch over the socket of his left eye, remarked to von Heinersdorff, 'Damned glad to have you with us, Colonel. Always knew one could rely on the Fourth in a sticky situation. But it wouldn't look good if I allowed some other chap to take my division out. For the record, you understand?'

'Understand perfectly, Herr General,' von Heinersdorff had answered in the same clipped jovial manner. 'Honour of the Division and all that. I would have done the same. My chaps'll be disappointed all the same. Only too eager to be at the sharp end, the Fourth Grenadiers. Always have been.'

Sobel had beamed at the other officer. 'Just like the Fighting Fourth, always wanting to be in the thick of it.'

Creeping Jesus could have groaned out loud. What thick-headed idiots the two of them were! Instead, he had said, 'Hear, hear, sir! The Fighting Fourth is exceedingly jealous of its combat reputation!'

'*The frigging Fighting Fourth!*' King Bull had sneered when Creeping Jesus had repeated the conversation to the massive head cook. 'Oh, my aching ass! That shower of shit that's masquerading as soldiers'd rather fuck than fight!'

'My sentiments exactly, *Oberfeld*,' Creeping Jesus had agreed without any rancour at the NCO for having talked so obscenely in the presence of a senior officer. The two of them knew each other well enough by now. Ever since 1939 they had been stealing the men's rations and selling them on the black market in half a dozen countries. King Bull knew, too, just what a craven coward the elegant, superior, supercilious adjutant was. He'd do anything and everything to save his precious hide.

'This means that we can withdraw your company to HQ, *Oberfeld*,' Creeping Jesus had continued. 'It's the company's rightful place, providing the Grenadiers with whatever food it can *under these terrible circumstances*.' He lowered his voice significantly. His meaning was clear. Even in retreat there were pickings for those who knew how to 'organize' things correctly.

King Bull had nodded his understanding with his great brutish head, small pig-like eyes thoughtful. Unlike the adjutant, King Bull was not a coward. But he was extremely proud and possessive of his little empire in the kitchens, which so far had provided him with those things he valued most in life – prestige, power, and pussy. Constantly he lived in dread that he might be wounded or otherwise incapacitated so that the control of 'his' kitchens might, in his absence, pass on into less worthy hands.

Thus it was that Goulash Cannon Company was withdrawn from the line – to the great relief of King Bull and the adjutant, each for his own reasons – and joined the long HQ convoy, which was placed relatively safely to the rear of the left flankguard.

Life became the same old freezing, back-breaking routine once more, with the weather more of a problem than the enemy; for since that first terrible day no more marauding Cossacks had been sighted and the constant snowstorms made it difficult for the pursuing Red Army – wherever *it* was – to locate and attack the Pocket from the air. Hour after hour, day after day, huddled in any extra clothing they could find, the frozen drivers in the open cabs of their carts urged on the skinny exhausted horses that pulled the goulash cannon. Their soup kettles boiled all the time, smoke pouring from the chimney attached to each mobile oven, for King Bull had threatened a terrible punishment on any one of his 'command' (as he called it proudly) who let the stove go out whatever the circumstances. '*Any creeping, crap-assed cripple* who does that,' he had thundered, raising his massive fists upwards to the leaden heavens, as if invoking the gods themselves, 'is gonna have his nuts sawn off personally by me – *with a blunt razor blade!*'

But time and time again the harassed drivers of the Goulash Cannon Company's column barely escaped that terrible fate. For the going across that endless steppe was horrific. Over and over again, the back wheel of one of the carts would slip into some deep shell crater concealed by the snow. The wheel would crack and perhaps break, the shafts rising in the air, carrying with them a panicked, kicking snorting mule or pony.

In an instant all would be panic, confusion, noise: NCOs bellowing orders, officers shrilling their whistles, those in trucks hooting their horns, while the mud-splattered drivers laid into their shivering unruly animals with their whips and frantic pearl-divers, down on their knees in the snow, attempted desperately to keep the goulash-cannon doors from opening and discharging its contents. More than once, cooks, tears of pain streaming down their agonized faces, would burn and scald their hands forcing back the burning logs and boiling soup before it escaped, as somewhere to their rear in the snowstorm an enraged King Bull would shrill his whistle in anger and roar terrible threats of what would happen if the oven went out.

It was a killing pace for the animals. Those bringing up the rear of the long, slow, weary column would find the progress of those before them marked with abandoned gear – stools, ikons looted from some church, munition boxes, gas-masks – and horses. Every few hundred metres there'd be a dead nag with a swollen belly, with the crows, which appeared from nowhere once an animal died, already feasting on the glazed eyeballs.

But on the fourth day of the great trek westwards, the misery of the retreat and King Bull's awesome threats began to be forgotten as on the horizon individual signal flares started to sail into the leaden sky at regular intervals. Now and again there were short bursts of machine-gun fire, which died almost instantly. The first walking wounded from the flank-guard, a kilometre or two to the south of the HQ column, commenced their painful progress towards the Pill's dressing station, holding their wounded arms or hobbling along with the aid of an inverted rifle, eyes glazed and unseeing, their only desire the blessed oblivion of morphine and sleep.

The drivers and the others of the King Bull column commenced casting anxious glances at the south. They knew instinctively that the wildly cheering Cossack hordes were already hidden out there in the snowdrifts just waiting for the right opportunity to charge and seize captives, who would be tortured to death in the same cruel manner as the man they had found on that first day.

It was about this time that Polack lapsed into one of the blue moods which seemed part of his Slavic temperament. More than once Karl and Ami tried to rouse him from his moody reverie as he slumped on the hard wooden seat next to them, rifle resting like a child's toy on his big knees. But they

could get little out of him save, 'I'm thinking, comrades.
Leave me in peace. I'm thinking.'

Ludwik Zimanski, nicknamed 'Polack' in the Fourth Grenadiers, had thought for over two years that he would get away
with it. Who would have suspected that a Pole wanted for
murder would join – of all things – the German Army? Of
course, he had never thought of his crime as outright murder.
It had been more of a spontaneous reaction; the way that any
man, Pole or otherwise, would act when his pride and honour
as a man had been insulted . . .

The thin pig of an SS man had locked them in the
schoolroom, all the able-bodied men of the village, declaring,
'No one is leaving this room before he has signed up for the
SS. You Polack pigs, here we are handing you the opportunity
on a silver platter to become real Germans and not Slavic
shit-shovellers and you turn it down. Heaven, arse and
cloudburst, either you join here and now, or damn well go to
the camps –'*

It had been then that his nerve had snapped. He had swung
the sickle, which he had brought with him straight from the
September harvest field. It had caught the thin SS man
directly in the centre of his forehead. He had reeled back, the
carved farm instrument sticking grotesquely from his head, to
slam against the classroom wall. For a moment he had simply
hung there stupidly, dying on his feet, then he had started to
trail down the wall, leaving a bright scarlet smear behind
him.

Then he had made a run for it, diving through the window
in a spectacular clatter and tinkle of broken glass. Next
moment he had been running all out down the village street,
scattering startled German infantrymen to left and right.
Twenty-four hours later he had gone underground, enlisting

* See *Rebel One – Cannon Fodder* for further details.

in the Fourth Grenadier Regiment as his only way to escape the vengeance of the SS.

But in the end it hadn't worked, at least not for his parents and his young brother Jan. They had left the village the same day, heading for the anonymity of the big city, Warsaw. Now in this winter of 1942 someone had betrayed them to the Gestapo – the capital was riddled with informers: Jews, Poles, Germans, all betraying their fellow countrymen to save their own skins or to gain a loaf of bread or a half kilo of ersatz coffee. That was about what a life was worth in German-occupied Poland.

As the closest relatives of the missing murderer 'Zimanski, Ludwik, born Altstadt, West Prussia, 1919' they had not had a chance. Probably, Polack had told himself when he had heard of their deaths months after they had taken place, they had not even protested. What other fate but death could they expect? Weren't they subhuman Poles whose accursed offspring had had the temerity to murder one of the master race?

But now as they plodded ever westwards through the nightmarish steppe, with the Russians again beginning to test for soft spots in the defences, Polack brooded as only a Slav can brood. His bitterness and resentment grew by the hour. '*Half-breed, water-polack, booty German,** *border scum,*' that's what they called him behind his back, even those comrades of the Fourth Grenadiers who depended upon him for their lives. Why should he sacrifice himself for them? There had to be a way out for him – and naturally Karl and Ami too – some escape from the Popov trap slowly closing in on them? '*Boshe moi,*' he cursed to himself, heavy unshaven face set and grim, 'why should we go down with the shitty sinking ship? *There's got to be a way out before it's too shitty late?*'

*

* A contemptuous name given by the Germans for 'ethnic Germans', officially classed as members of the 'master race'.

The Rata spotted them on the fourth day of the trek. '*Sewing machine, sewing machine!*' the cry of alarm went down the length of the column, being passed from vehicle to vehicle as the putt-putt of the little unarmed reconnaissance plane grew ever louder. On any other occasion the appearance of the biplane, which the troops nicknamed the 'sewing machine' on account of the noise it made, would not have alarmed the front-line veterans. The plane was unarmed, vulnerable, and carried no bombs. But this day was different. The biplane was coming in low beneath the clouds, taking in the long columns spread out below, as if on a silver platter.

Karl put the others' thoughts into words. 'Christ, once that Popov pisser has worked out who we are, he'll be off back home to his base to report what he's seen like a frigging fiddler's elbow going all out. *Ponemayu?*'

'*Ponemayu!* I frigging well *ponemayu* all right,' Ami snorted angrily. Like all the rest of the front swine who had been in Russia ever since 1941, he mixed Russian words into his German. Without waiting for orders, he unslung his rifle and took aim as the little Russian came closer and closer.

Now Creeping Jesus, beside himself with fear, was screaming further down the column, 'Open fire, you boneheads! Knock him out of the sky! *Schnell!*'

But Ami did not hear the scattered ragged firing which now opened up, as the cooks blasted away at the Rata. He concentrated his whole being on the biplane approaching over his sights. Now he could see the pale blob of the pilot's face behind the whirling propeller of the radial engine. He tried to control his excited breathing. Carefully, very carefully he eased his finger around the trigger. The plane was almost above them now. He took first pressure. In a moment he would fire. *The Rata had to be knocked out of the sky!*

The noise of its engine was deafening. He could see the greasy oily patches where fluid had leaked below its undercarriage. Below the snow was whipped into white dancing flurries by the Rata's prop wash. It was now or never. He took second pressure, aiming directly at the gleam of the perspex which protected the pilot's cockpit. The rifle smacked back against his shoulder. A crack. A whiff of cordite. Then he was firing all out, ejecting the spent cartridges, ramming home the bolt again, pressing the trigger.

Suddenly, startlingly, the Rata faltered in mid-air. A whiff of smoke spurted from its radial engine. It missed a beat or two. For a fleeting second the little biplane seemed to be about to stall. White glycol jetted up against the cockpit.

'You've got him!' Karl yelled exuberantly. 'You've got him, you little garden dwarf!'

'Well done, Grenadier Doepgen!' a suddenly relieved Creeping Jesus shrieked an instant later, 'there'll be a piece of tin* in this one for you!'

Everywhere along the abruptly stalled column there was a spontaneous outburst of cheering as the biplane came lower and lower, its engine spluttering alarmingly, seemingly about to cut out altogether at any moment, the pilot fighting desperately with the controls. They were saved! These Russian reconnaissance planes had no radio, and this one was certainly not returning to base to report what he had just discovered in the middle of nowhere.

Even Polack seemed to come out of his reverie, as he shielded his dark eyes and followed the progress of the Rata, which was now skimming just above the surface of the steppe, whipping up a wild wake of whirling snow behind it. For the first time in hours his broad-cheeked Slavic face showed some kind of animation. Next to him on the cab an excited Karl cried, 'It's gonna hit the deck. He's gonna –'

Suddenly the words died on his lips. In the very nick of time, when it seemed the pilot *must* strike the ground and wreck his stricken plane in a ball of fire, the engine perked up.

---

* Slang for a medal.

The hectic spluttering vanished. It was replaced by a sweet solid sound. The engine was functioning again. The little Rata began to climb once more.

An enraged King Bull's voice cut sharply into the sudden dead silence. '*The frigging flyboy's getting away!*' He ripped up his machine pistol and fired a full burst at the Rata. To no avail! Already it was climbing steeply, the angry slugs cutting the air purposelessly far below it. Moments later it was a dot on the horizon. Then it was gone altogether.

Below the abruptly sombre Grenadiers stared at each other in numb silence, while the mules and ponies fidgeted in their traces, as if impatient to be off, as if they already knew what was to come and they wanted to move on before it was too late . . .

One moment the grey sky was completely empty – not even a bird flew – the next they were hovering over the column like sinister metal hawks seeking prey.

Creeping Jesus, hands shaking, praying fervently that they were their own Stukas, but knowing instinctively they weren't, flung up his glasses. Hurriedly he adjusted them. The three planes, apparently motionless in the leaden sky, sprung into focus, clearly outlined in the gleaming circles of calibrated glass. He gasped. There was no mistaking that sinister blood red star on their fuselage. They were Soviet dive-bombers.

'*Stormoviks!*' someone yelled.

'Hit the frigging dirt,' another cried.

The men needed no urging. As Creeping Jesus lowered his glasses and flung himself from the cab in a shallow dive, landing with a gasp in the deep snow, the men of the Goulash Cannon Company abandoned their carts everywhere, running heavily across the steppe, burying themselves frantically in the snow like panicked rabbits, furiously trying to seek some cover in the naked plain.

Up above the leader waggled the wings of his plane. It was the signal. Below the cowering soldiers tensed. '*Here they come –*' someone began to scream, as with an ear-splitting shriek, the leading Stormovik fell from the sky, its engine howling frighteningly.

Hands clasped about his ears to blot out the tremendous noise, Karl watched from the snow as the Russian plane came hurtling down at a tremendous speed, almost vertically. Surely nothing could stop it smashing into the ground below? It appeared to fill the whole sky: a metal monster intent on self-destruction.

Suddenly it happened! The pilot jerked back the stick. The Stormovik levelled out. A myriad ugly black little eggs started to tumble from its ugly blue belly. Karl tensed every muscle. Next to him Polack was rattling off his prayers in Polish, while Ami attempted to burrow even deeper into the frozen snow. Like the angel of death, the Stormovik swung over them, dragging its evil black shadow behind it. Then all hell was let loose, as the bombs began to land.

The very earth shook and trembled. Fist-sized shards of gleaming metal zipped lethally through the sky. Everywhere great cherry-red spurts of flame and flying earth erupted. From all sides came the piteous screams of agony and alarm of those who had been hit. In an instant only destruction and sudden death reigned. A horrified Karl, his eardrums threatening to burst at any moment, watched as a cook was hit. His body was flayed alive. The shrapnel ripped it apart, leaving a pile of steaming red meat, a tangle of severed limbs, on the melting snow like a pile of offal outside a butcher's back door. He choked back the vomit.

One of the goulash cannon was hit. The stove went sailing through the air, leisurely jetting bright green pea-soup onto the snow. The piteously whinnying, absolutely panicked horse slammed into a skeletal tree and hung dead in the black branches like some piece of monstrous fruit.

Then the dive-bombers were gone, sailing high into the

grey sky, executing wild ecstatic victory rolls, leaving behind them dead and dying men and animals, while over on the horizon red flares started to sail into the air, indicating a forthcoming ground attack.

CHAPTER 3

'I told you I'd been thinking,' Polack said with unusual speed and urgency for him, as to the flank, the Grenadiers started to dig in, hacking away at the frozen earth beneath the mantle of snow. 'I've been thinking for quite a bit o' time.' He wiped a dewdrop neatly from the end of his long red nose and flung it down on the charred snow next to the body of a dead horse already beginning to freeze rigid, its guts splayed out in a pink flurry on the snow.

'Well, think,' Ami said, as flares continued to sail into the grey sky on the flank. 'All right,' he relented, 'piss or get off'n the pot, Polack.'

On the cab Polack turned slowly to face his two comrades and Karl could almost feel and hear the ponderous workings of the big man's mind.

'I've been thinking a lot,' he repeated. 'A lot. We owe them nothing. Your father's in a camp' – he indicated Karl – 'and mine's dead. My mother as well – and those swine did it.'

Karl nodded. He knew just how much Polack had suffered since he had heard of the death of his father and mother. His own father, silly sod of an unreformed socialist that he was, was at least still alive in Neuengamme Concentration Camp, just outside Hamburg.

Suddenly Ami looked at his boots, abruptly despondent. The other two Rebels had at least *known* their fathers. He never had. His unknown soldier-father with the American Army of Occupation in the Rhineland after World War One had come, fucked, sired him and disappeared for good, leaving him to be taunted all his young life – before they had put him into the orphanage – that he had a '*Fraulein*' for a mother and an '*Ami*'* for a father. 'Not the kind of racially impure, tainted individual we need in our beloved New Order,' as the brown-clad officialdom had preached at him until he was heartily sick of them – and their frigging 'beloved New Order'.

'Well?' Karl prompted when Polack didn't speak for a moment.

'Well, all three of us know that we're for the chop here this time. The Popovs have got us surrounded. Look at them flares over there. You both know what they mean. Sooner or later they're gonna pull the drawers off'n us.'

He stopped as if suddenly exhausted by so much talk. A worried Karl and Ami stared at the flares. They'd seen the kind before. It was the Popov's signal for attack. Soon they'd either come racing across the steppe on their wiry, half-wild ponies, waving their sabres above their heads, or marching stolidly in packed ranks, shoulder to shoulder, bayonets at the ready, hundreds, perhaps thousands of them, yelling that throaty, bass, terrifying '*Urrah*' of theirs. The machine-guns would mow them down rank after rank. But Mother Russia had plenty of cannon-fodder. There'd always be more of them.

Polack spoke again. 'I speak some Russian. I've been listening to their peasants here and there. It's not too different from Polish. I could make them understand.'

'For chrissake, Polack,' Ami snorted, '*speak clear text*! What the frig are you spouting about?'

'How to surrender to them without getting shot.'

'To surrender – *to who*?' Ami yelled in exasperation at the Polack's thick-headed slowness.

'The Popovs.'

'*The Popovs!*' Karl and Ami cried in horror.

He nodded his big shaven head solemnly. Over on the flank, there was a sudden grating noise, like a diamond running the length of a glass pane.

* German slang for American.

'Why should we die out here for Adolf Hitler?' Polack said hurriedly and tapped his breast pocket with a forefinger like a thick pork sausage. He winked significantly. 'Karl, I've got 'em here. Three of them. One for each of us.' He lowered his voice. 'Popov safe conduct passes. The ones they fired into our lines and we were ordered to destroy last month.'

Ami looked at his comrade as if he were seeing him for the very first time. 'Why, you cunning old wanker,' he said, half in admiration, half in wonder. 'Didn't know you had it in yer.'

Polack beamed. 'I'm not that much of a fool.'

'Of course you're not, Polack,' Karl agreed hastily, lowering his voice too. One couldn't be too careful. They risked being sent to Torgau* or even the death penalty just for even talking about such things. 'But, you know, Polack, it's one hell of a risk. It's got to be planned very very carefully. You see, we run a risk both ways. A' – he ticked it off on his fingers – 'we stand a good chance of being shot by our own people if they catch us doing a bunk, or even raising our hands in surrender to the Popovs. B, we get shot by the Popovs if we don't do it the right way.'

'*Klar*, Karl,' Polack agreed. 'I've been thinking about that as well, you know.'

To their left six tremendous fingers of smoke were poking their way up through the grey heavy snow clouds at a tremendous rate, that terrible banshee-like wail getting louder and more frightening by the instant.

'I've come to the conclusion,' Polack went on as Ami sniffed and said, 'Ain't we posh – come to the conclusion have we –'

Polack glared at the little Rhinelander and he shut up hastily.

'. . . that we can't do it at night. Too risky. The Popovs have too itchy trigger-fingers. It's got to be done in daylight,

---

* A notorious German Army prison.

but it's got to be done when the others can't see us, but the Popovs can – with our hands plainly raised in surrender and our weapons gone.'

'Better *red* than *dead*,' Karl began as the first tremendous salvo of mortar bombs descended upon the HQ column and out at the flank the Cossack cavalry came thundering across the steppe, crying their savage war cries, their sabres gleaming; as the whistles shrilled and the machine-guns started the old old song of death; and as Creeping Jesus shrieked frantically, '*ALARM. ALARM. THEY'RE ATTACKING. A-T-T-A-C-K-I-N-G.*'

'*Stalin Organs!*' they yelled, as the shells from the tremendous multiple mortars thundered down, tearing the earth apart, ripping great steaming brown holes in the steppe like the work of gigantic moles, obscuring the cavalry racing towards the Goulash Cannon Company.

'*Fuck Stalin!*' King Bull cried above the racket, the machine pistol in his enormous fists looking like a child's toy. 'Keep yer frigging turnips up everywhere! They're just trying to make us get our heads down! Prepare to fire, your mother fucks niggers. . . . Come on, you bunch of perverted banana suckers, get them heads and rifles up!'

Reluctantly the cooks, the pearl-divers, the pan scrubbers and all the rest of the greasy hash-slingers brought up their weapons from behind the line of wagons where they crouched like settlers in a Wild West wagon train waiting for the 'pesky redskins' to attack the 'prairie schooners'.

Here and there the cavalry had broken through the line of the grenadier infantry protecting the flank of the Iron Division – there were simply far too many of them for one single battalion of infantry to stop. Now they were surging in under the cover of a tremendous mortar barrage intended to keep the defenders glued to the ground, aiming at getting to the weakened Iron Division units within the centre of the

'Wandering Pocket'. If they did, there would be a tremendous slaughter. With the Division's infantry exhausted and nearly 1,500 wounded burdening it, there would be little it could do to stop the rampaging Cossacks.

Crouched behind their goulash cannon, the pony jerking up and down in the traces nervously every time another salvo slammed into the ground, Karl squinted down the length of his rifle barrel. Funny, he told himself, ten minutes ago they had been talking of the best method of surrendering to the Popovs; now they were intent on killing them. It was a crazy world, here in Russia.

The Cossacks were coming in ragged bunches, obviously split up into groups by the initial fire of the grenadiers on the flank. Going all out they crouched low over the streaming manes of their fine horses, their gleaming silver sabres held forward and down, the little round-barrelled tommy-guns bouncing up and down on their backs. Scared as he was, Karl could not but admire the great mass of horse and rider, charging so boldly across the steppe to battle. It was like a scene out of a history book.

With startling suddenness, the tremendous mortar barrage ceased. The banshee howl, the awesome crump and bursts of flying metal of the bombs vanished and there was only the thunder of the horses' hooves.

King Bull reacted immediately. While Creeping Jesus, next to him, still cowered fearfully behind the cart, he raised himself to his full height boldly. Spitting scornfully in the snow at his feet, as if it were every day that his motley crew of cooks were attacked by the finest cavalry in the world, he blew three shrills on his whistle. 'Stand fast!' he yelled and spreading his big legs he planted his boots firmly in the snow and clasped the machine pistol to his hip. 'Them penknives can't hurt yer! We're gonna see the shits off.' Without aiming he pressed the trigger of his machine pistol. White tracer sliced the grey air. Up in the front rank of the galloping Cossacks an officer threw up his arms in absolute agony, the reins falling from suddenly nerveless fingers. Next moment he was swept from the saddle, his body falling beneath the thundering hooves of the riders coming after him.

That first savage burst acted as a signal. Everywhere a ragged, uncertain volley erupted the length of the Goulash Cannon Company's lines. In an instant their front was transformed. The front rank of the attackers fought their mounts desperately, as the German fire began tearing cruel gaps in their ranks. Cossacks and horses went down everywhere. Within seconds a mess of dying men and piteously whinnying, dying animals started to pile up. Man after man went down. Riderless horses bolted. Carried away by a totally unreasoning fear, rearing and plunging, snorting through crazy, distorted nostrils, they fought their way back, away from the murderous fire, flailing the wounded with their sharp hooves.

A Cossack reared up directly in front of Karl. High above his fur-capped head was the silver gleam of a sabre. Ami screamed, suddenly unable to move. Polack tugged furiously at his long rifle trying to bring it round. In a moment the brutal-faced Russian would bring his fearsome sword down and cleave Karl's skull in two.

Karl reacted instinctively. His rifle barked. The Cossack's crazed blur of a face exploded in a scarlet welter of gore. He flew from the saddle, as if propelled by an invisible fist, and crashed into the snow to disappear beneath the flying hooves of the horses. Karl gasped with fear and relief, feeling the hot urine spurting down his leg.

But there was no time to let up. More and more Cossacks were milling and swirling around the cooks' positions, as they fired all-out. The cooks were broken up into little pockets, every man for himself now, the air loud with screams, curses, cries of agony, calls for mercy from God on High. But God on High was looking the other way this terrible day. There was no mercy forthcoming.

Expertly a Cossack vaulted from his dying horse as it went

down on its knees, a great gaping scarlet wound on its flank. He ran lightly towards Karl's position, flinging his sabre from hand to hand as if it were a toy, as if he were attempting to confuse the defenders. Polack raised his rifle. In a frenzy of fear he pressed the trigger. *Nothing!* It had jammed. The Cossack yelled an obscenity, a crazy light of victory in his dark eyes. Easily he sprang over the cart and landed lightly on his feet in a savage crouch in front of Polack. He was about to kill.

Ami reacted first. He swung his rifle like a club. The cruel, brass-shod butt caught the Cossack in the lower face. Bones shattered. A great gob of bright red blood shot from his broken nose and splattered into the scuffed snow. The sword dropped from his hand and he went flying backwards, poleaxed, dead before he hit the ground.

Then they were gone, tugging at their reins, cursing, whirling their mounts around, seemingly undecided how they should overcome the monstrous mound of dead men and dying animals behind them, the cooks pouring a horrific volley into their undefended backs, suddenly aware they had defeated the Cossack attack – for the moment.

Gasping as if they had run a great race, eyes wild and bulging, gaze fixed hypnotically on the Cossacks retreating into the grey gloom, the cooks simply squatted seemingly unable to move. But the Three Rebels, who had experienced more than enough infantry action in these last three years, knew they hadn't much time to sit and stare. The Cossacks wouldn't give up so quickly. There were still plenty of them left. They'd be back all right.

Hurriedly they began to feed in fresh clips of ammunition, while King Bull shrilled his whistle desperately, trying to raise his men from their strange post-combat lethargy. This time, too, Karl prepared for close quarter action. He drew the stick grenades from his boots and placed them handily on the cart before him, trying to ignore the moans coming from the dying Cossacks piled up like so many logs of wood to their front. 'Anybody got something to drink?' he croaked, suddenly realizing just how parched he was.

'*Voda*,' Ami suggested, again using the Russian word, this time meaning 'water'.

Karl shook his head indignantly. 'Yer can keep that. *Voda* gives yer belly-lice. Besides, fishes fuck in *voda*.'

Reluctantly Polack pulled his flatman from his hip pocket. 'Fair shares now, mind you,' he warned. He pulled out the cork with his broken teeth before handing the precious flask to a suddenly grinning Karl.

'Firewater!' the latter said gleefully. 'Now yer talking, comrade.' He eyed the bottle professionally, before taking a hearty swig and passing the flatman on to Ami, who did the same, under Polack's suspicious gaze.

King Bull had finally got through to his dazed men. They listened as he cupped his hands around his mouth and shouted against the racket of the new barrage. 'Don't let the Popov pant-shitters get so close this time. We barely held them.' He flashed a look at the sky, which was growing more leaden and threatening by the instant. 'It looks as if God is gonna piss or snow on us agen. So watch it. They'll try to sneak up on us if it –'

Creeping Jesus's voice, sick with fear, cut into the big cook's order, '*Oberfeld*, take complete charge here. I'll hurry to the rear. We desperately need more ammo.' Before King Bull could say anything, he was doubling frantically across the snow like a frightened hare to where the HQ vehicles had formed up into a protective circle.

King Bull spat contemptuously. '*Mehr angst als Vaterlandsliebe*,'* he commented scornfully and then forgot the terrified adjutant. 'All right, you bunch o' piss pansies. Digits outa the orifice, it won't be frigging long now . . .'

They came from both flanks, spread out in an open fork, avoiding the grenadiers to their front, this time coming in

---

* A German saying, 'More fear than love of the Fatherland.'

directly behind the mortar bombardment from the 'Stalin organs'. Above, the sky grew darker and more threatening by the instant. A wind had arisen and was whipping up the 'steppe devils', little wisps of powder snow. Through them, grim and intent, the Cossack cavalry came at the walk, like grey silent avenging spectres through smoke, the sound of the massed hooves muffled. There was something completely unnerving and eerie about the whole spectacle and Karl, his eyes glued to his front, shivered. Next to him Ami must have felt the same for he bit his bottom lip until the blood came. Only Polack seemed unmoved, stolidly staring to his front along the length of his rifle, chewing on a piece of stale black bread he had found in his 'bread sack'.

Steadily, purposefully, the Cossacks advanced on the waiting Germans. Every now and again a yellow smoke shell exploded to the front of the moving horsemen, a signal for the mortar barrage to creep up more quickly. The pace of the riders quickened. It changed from the 'walk' to the 'trot'. Now they were only a couple of hundred metres away. Soon they would break into the 'gallop'.

'*Stand fast!*' King Bull urged and clasped his machine pistol more tightly to his hip. '*Stand fast the Goulash Cannon Company!*'

The cooks swallowed, abruptly dry-mouthed. Others shook their heads, as if casting blinding sweat from their foreheads. Others just waited numbly.

The mortar barrage was almost upon the German line now. Great shards of silver metal hissed lethally through the air. Here and there they howled off the steel sides of the ovens, gouging out glistening scars. A pony went down on its forelegs, whinnying miserably, its rear legs severed, jetting scarlet blood onto the snow. Above the grey sky grew ever darker.

'*Slava Krasnaya Armya!*' The great cry echoed from a thousand throats. To the front of the Cossacks, barely visible in the gloom now, an officer raised himself in his stirrups and waved his sabre around his head. It was the signal. The barrage stopped – and they charged.

In an instant the air was heavy with the thunder of hooves. The steppe seemed to tremble. Snow spurted upwards in a myriad white wakes. Men and horses became one, as the fur-hatted Cossacks lay across the flying manes of their mounts, sabres outstretched, trying to make the smallest possible target.

King Bull fired. Immediately the defenders did the same. Bolts worked furiously. Steaming bright-yellow cartridge cases tumbled to the snow. The gloom was split apart by the fury of their fire. All of them knew there was no escape if they didn't stop the Cossacks. The Russians would slaughter them mercilessly if they got through.

The wave of fire and fury drenched the horsemen with savage violence, ripping the front rank apart. Horses and men went down everywhere in crazy confused heaps. But the rest came on, the second wave springing over the dead and dying bodies of their comrades to face the wall of lethal steel.

A sweating, hectic Karl could see that the Cossacks were slipping from their mounts, springing with the agility of trained acrobats from the trembling, sweat-lathered horses, and advancing on foot, no longer such obvious targets. 'Look out, everybody,' he yelled urgently above the snap and crackle of the violent small-arms battle, 'they're infiltrating!'

But he doubted anyone was listening to his warning. Each man was wrapped in the cocoon of his own unreasoning fear, concentrating solely on saving his own miserable life, unaware that the safety of the whole depended upon the steadfastness of the individual. But then, he told himself, as he fumbled frantically to insert a new clip, 'These shit-shovellers are not soldiers – *they're frigging cooks*!'

Five minutes later, the dismounted Cossacks were every-where. Some had knives clasped between their teeth as they came forward out of the gloom seeking the terrified cooks. Others rushed forward boldly, shrieking wildly, high on drugs and vodka, swinging their sabres from left to right like butchers' cleavers. Now the battle developed into a series of murderous individual hand-to-hand encounters, with men transformed into savage animals, hacking, slicing, cutting, gouging at each other, gasping as if in the throes of sexual ecstasy, giving no quarter, animated by a primeval bloodlust which knew only – *kill or be killed*.

A giant of a Cossack came blundering out of the horrendous gloom, cap gone, blood streaming down the side of his pock-marked face, laughing like a crazy man. Polack spotted him first. He cried out something in Russian. The Russian laughed out loud, showing a mouthful of stainless steel false teeth. Next moment he kicked Polack in the groin. The Rebel reeled back, vomiting crazily, grabbing for his genitals. Ami lurched forward in the same instant that the Cossack raised his sabre to finish the other man off. He fired from the hip. The slug stopped the Russian in mid-stride. He clawed the air, gasping frantically for breath, blood gushing from a hole in his stomach from which the intestines were beginning to burst forth like a string of pink, uncooked sausages. Then he pitched face-forward in the snow, choking in his own blood.

A dwarf-like Cossack sprang from nowhere onto Karl's back. Red and silver stars exploded in front of his eyes. A mist threatened to engulf him, as the Cossack, chuckling with crazy delight, exerted full pressure on his throat. Frantically Karl swung his body from left to right, trying to rid himself of the killer. To no avail. He felt blood gush from his ears as his eardrums popped and the mist of impending unconsciousness grew ever thicker. He was being rapidly strangled to death!

His legs began to give way. He couldn't hold out much longer. Suddenly the pressure slackened, relaxed, gave way altogether. Karl sank to his knees, the stars still exploding electrically in front of his eyes. The grip on his neck had vanished, but the dead weight still hung on his back. He didn't care. For one long beautiful moment, all he was concerned about was the fact that he could *breathe*. Greedily he sucked in great gulps of the icy air, flooding his oxygen-starved lungs with its benison. Then, and only then, he shook himself like a wet dog just coming out of the water. The dwarf-like Cossack flopped to the snow. Ami's kitchen knife protruded – blooded to the hilt – from between his skinny shoulders.

'I had to, Karl,' Ami gasped, his skinny face blanched, tears streaming down his pinched cheeks. 'I had to –'

'Thanks, Ami,' Karl broke in brutally. Ami was on the verge of a breakdown; his hands were trembling uncontrollably. They all were. 'Pick up your rifle,' he commanded. 'There are still more of the bastards, you know. They won't let up so easily.'

But now nature itself took a hand in this deadly, savage action. As if sick of the whole murderous business, the skies opened at last. Snowflakes as big as a man's fist started to hurtle down in an unrelenting stream. In a flash there was a white-out. Within seconds, falling snow had blotted out the landscape of violence and sudden death. The column disappeared. So did the attacking Cossacks. The shrieks, the cries, the clash of arms were deadened immediately. Abruptly the three exhausted, sweating comrades appeared to be all alone in the thick, white, all-encompassing downpour.

CHAPTER 4

Nothing could shake Colonel von Heinersdorff. His ancestors had been commanding men in desperate situations for two centuries. He and they were used to saying the usual encouraging, inane things to young men virtually at the end of their tether. Perhaps it was because the von Heinersdorffs and their kind in the military castes throughout Europe lacked imagination. Perhaps they had no real concept of what death meant. Perhaps they were simply brave.

But now, as the Pill made his desperate plea and the snow pelted down in a flat white impenetrable sheet outside the little hut in which he had set up his command post, Colonel von Heinersdorff remained adamant, but encouraging. 'My dear Pill,' he said soothingly, as the craggy-faced, white-haired surgeon, who had been with him in the trenches as a young man in the Old War, glared at him urgently, 'let *me* recommend some medicine for a change.' He indicated the half-empty bottle on the rickety wooden-plank table. 'Absolute rot-gut, I admit, but it is drink.'

The Pill shook his head firmly. 'No thank you, Horst.' When they were alone like this, he always used the CO's first name. 'There is no time left for classy chats about the cosmos over cognac.'

There was no mistaking the bitterness in his rasping Saxon voice. Even von Heinersdorff, unimaginative as he was, noted it. 'Steady on, old house. It's not as bad as all that, you know, Pill.' He indicated the whirling snowflakes outside. 'This snowstorm is going to be the saving of us.'

'Is it?' the Pill asked pointedly, eyes blazing. He glared out of the little window at the mounds everywhere outside. They marked the bodies of the recent dead, who had been fated to perish here in this trackless steppe, not even knowing the place's name. Soon their flesh would rot away, their bones

would disappear into the earth and they would be gone,
leaving no trace. He renewed his plea with fresh energy.
'Listen, Horst, my dressing station is full of fresh wounded.
Our casualties are mounting all the time. And I don't have to
point out to you the terrible situation in which the Iron
Division finds itself.'

'So?' the Colonel said, swinging his broken sabre carefully,
face abruptly sombre, for he half-guessed what was coming.

The Pill didn't react immediately. Instead he said, 'You
know as well as I do what a terrible mess we are in. I think even
that wooden-headed General Sobel does, too. We know we
have been sacrificed. We were sacrificed in the first place by
being sent here and now we are being sacrificed to the bitter
end.'

'What do you mean?'

'The *others*.' He emphasized the word and von Heinersdorff
nodded. Like the first name it was a word they used between
themselves when they were alone. The 'others' were the Party
and everything that went with it. 'They sent us here to this
goddamned place, ill-prepared for what was to come. Sure
they had their easy victories. Last year's. Now this year they
are facing defeat. Will they admit it? Of course they won't!'

'But you said something about being sacrificed to the bitter
end, Pill?' the CO said quite calmly, though he hated this talk
of the Party. He wished the National Socialists had never
made their appearance. They *did* interfere with the business
of soldiering.

'Yes, I did – and you know it. They cannot have a whole
German infantry division surrendering to the Ivans. So Sobel
has been ordered to make this tragic, nonsensical retreat. But
there can be no hope of success. The Ivans are all around us,
to our rear, to our front. What hope can we have of ever
getting through to our own lines? *None* – and you know it!'

'Oh, I say, Pill,' the CO began to bluster, but the surgeon
cut him short brutally.

'Listen, Horst, the others – goddamn it, the High

Command and the Party, if you wish!' he blurted out fiercely, 'have abandoned us. If we do happen to get through, they will hail it as a great victory. If we fail, which is more than likely, they will also hail it as proof of the tremendous fighting spirit of the German soldier, who would rather fight to the death than surrender to the Red subhumans!' He thrust his hands forward, fingers extended, as if he might well start shaking his old comrade into some realization of the terrible fix they found themselves in. 'Don't you see, Horst? There is only one way left to save what is left of this unholy mess!'

Stubbornly Colonel von Heinersdorff refused to swallow the bait. Numbly he waited for his old comrade to put into words the dread thoughts he hardly dared think.

The Pill glared at him. Then he said it. 'Surrender! It is the only way to save the lives of those poor suffering creatures who are still alive.'

'*Surrender!*' von Heinersdorff echoed aghast. 'Pill, that is absolutely, totally unthinkable! Besides' – he raised his hand, wrinkled and covered with liver spots, to stop the surgeon from interrupting – 'it is also a physical impossibility.'

'What do you mean?'

Colonel von Heinersdorff had not reasoned the matter out as well as Polack had, but he did understand the physical difficulties of surrendering to the trigger-happy Red Army. 'They wouldn't even give us a chance to step out into the open and raise our hands in surrender,' he said dogmatically. 'You know what they're like. They'd shoot us down like dogs.'

The Pill nodded impatiently. Outside the wind howled and the snow came hurtling down in bright white sheets. Visibility was down to zero. God, how the poor stubble-hoppers of the old Fourth must be suffering out there, he told himself, and the thought lent urgency to his pleas. 'I know, I know,' he said. 'But there are more ways to surrender than just walking out of your trench with your hands up. It can be done formally from a distance, without either side being within firing distance of one another.'

Von Heinersdorff frowned. 'Pill, I don't understand.'

'A formal surrender offer, transmitted by radio to the local Red Army commander. One officer offering his sword to the other. They're professionals too, you know, Horst,' he added urgently, 'they speak the same language we do.'

'That would mean General Sobel?'

'Naturally, what do you think? Sobel would have to speak to his Russian equivalent.'

Von Heinersdorff shook his head slowly. 'He wouldn't do it, Pill,' he said with an air of finality. He patted the surgeon's knee. 'Nor would I. In two centuries a von Heinersdorff has never surrendered to the enemy, you know. We have learned how to die for Germany.'

'In three devils' name, Horst,' the surgeon cried in exasperation. 'Can't we begin to learn how to *live* for Germany? What purpose does it serve to die for the others, I ask you, Horst?'

But Horst von Heinersdorff had no answer for that overwhelming question . . .

'What now, Karl?' Ami hissed, posing yet another over-whelming question. They crouched in the howling storm, hanging onto the goulash cannon for all they were worth, as the wind ripped and tugged at it. The skinny horse which had pulled it had long vanished, perhaps wrenched from the traces by the wind – they didn't know or care which. At this moment they were solely concerned with saving their own skins. They'd face King Bull's wrath for the loss of the nag later.

Karl brought his mouth close to Ami's ear, as the three of them huddled together, white with snow, the wind buffeting their pinched frozen faces cruelly. 'Stick tight,' he cried, the wind snatching the words from his mouth. 'We've got enough fodder.' He slapped the still warm side of the oven, filled with lukewarm pea-soup. 'There's enough fart-water in there to last us for days. Besides they're still out there, I know it.'

Polack nodded his agreement. He had stuck a contraceptive at the end of his rifle muzzle to keep the wet outside. 'What do you wanna do,' Ami had queried cynically, as he had done it, '*fuck 'em to death*?' 'With a bit o' luck,' he growled, cupping his hands around his big mouth, 'it might clear up so that we can see them and they can see us.'

'You mean?' Karl commenced.

'Why not?' Polack cut in. 'There's no time like the present. If we're gonna surrender, let's do it as soon as we can. I don't like them frigging penknives those Cossacks carry. They could do serious damage to a man's health, especially his outside plumbing.'

Ami shuddered dramatically.

'So I say, hang on and see what comes, comrades.'

What came was the muted clip-clop of horses' hooves five minutes later and suddenly, frighteningly, a giant Cossack, he and his horse caked in snow, appeared out of the whirling white gloom. A moment later another came into view – and yet another.

'Down!' Karl hissed urgently.

The three of them pressed themselves against the goulash cannon, which, unlike everything else around, had not been covered in snow because of the warm, soup-filled oven. Fervently Karl prayed that, without the nag in the traces, the Popovs would take it for a piece of abandoned equipment.

Another couple of Cossacks had appeared, bent low over their saddles, cracking their long black knouts, and calling in gruff, muted voices, '*Davai! Davai*!'

Karl, as white with snow as the background, chanced a cautious look from their hiding place. He frowned. The Cossacks were herding half a dozen dejected, absolutely exhausted grenadiers inside a circle of horses, two of them bleeding badly still from their wounds. They were obviously at the end of their tether. They wouldn't last another five minutes. Even a fleeting glance showed that. The Cossacks seemed to know it too. The taller one, wielding his cruel knout purposelessly on the prisoners, rose in his saddle and cried something to the rest.

'*Da, da, Tovarisch Sotnik*,' the others replied.

'*Sotnik*, that's their commander,' Polack whispered into Karl's ear as the group stopped moving and the exhausted German prisoners immediately slumped to the ground, all save one man.

Karl peered through the whirling snow. He recognized the man who had remained standing, and caught his shocked gasp of surprise just in time. It was Major Hardt who commanded the 1st Battalion.

'Now yer know why they're still in the land of the living,' Ami whispered.

'Yes, Hardt's too big a fish to be slaughtered out of hand,' Karl whispered back. 'That lot o' poor sods must be his headquarters' clerks, something like that –' He stopped speaking suddenly.

The *Sotnik* had tossed what looked like a sharp knife to one of the Cossacks who had dismounted next to the prisoners, grouped, fearful and exhausted, around the standing major. The man caught it expertly. Next moment he plunged the sharp blade directly into the eye of one of the sitting Germans.

The man screamed and thrashed crazily as the Cossack ground the knife round in the eyeball before withdrawing it, its blade covered in bright blood. Next moment the prisoner keeled forward, head first, obviously dead from shock.

Karl stared at Polack and Ami aghast. '*What did he do that for?*' They could read the unspoken question on his suddenly bloodless lips.

The next moment they had the answer to the question. The *Sotnik* cracked his knout fiercely, the black lash curling across Hardt's face. He reeled back, a sudden purple weal running the length of his ashen face. The *Sotnik* yelled something at him in broken German.

'He wants to know where the General is,' Polack, who as a

countryman had the most acute hearing of the three of them, said. 'His bosses want to know where General Sobel's HQ is located.'

Hardt, shaken and hurting, remained silent. He looked up at the *Sotnik* defiantly, his lips compressed to a tight thin line. He was refusing to give the required information.

The *Sotnik*, his snow-covered hat set at the usual bold Cossack angle, shrugged easily. He nodded to the Cossack with the thin, razor-sharp knife. The man didn't hesitate. He strode over to the next prisoner and slashed it across one of the man's eyes. There was a scream of absolute agony which brought the small hairs erect at the back of Karl's head. Karl groaned.

Next to him Polack groaned too. 'It's no use,' he hissed through gritted teeth. 'No use!' He raised his rifle.

Karl and Ami did the same. They couldn't surrender to savages like these. They could not allow their comrades to be tortured like this either.

Polack took aim. There was a single muffled crack. The butt of the rifle slammed against Polack's big shoulder. The *Sotnik* flung up his arms, knout falling from suddenly nerveless fingers. Dead, he slumped over the mane of his rearing, terrified mount. The three comrades worked their bolts back and forth, feverishly pumping lead into the surprised Cossacks. There was no other way – for the present. They were still trapped by man's inhumanity to man; the cruelty of their fellow human beings in a world gone stark raving mad.

That night the Pill stared at the stars casting their spectral light on the snowbound steppe below, through a hole in the roof of the abandoned *isba*, that was the aid station's billet for the night.

Everywhere in radius of ten square kilometres the exhausted survivors of today's bitter attack slept. He couldn't. His mind

was too full of the horrors and the uncertainties to come. Not
that he worried about his own fate. He was old. He had had
his fill of life. His children had already left home, though
fortunately they were not eligible for military service yet. He
could die knowing he had missed little.

No, his concern was the thousands of young German men
out there in the steppe, destined for an early death, or at the
best for years of cruel remorseless captivity in the hands of a
savage unrelenting foe. The thought filled him with infinite
sadness. For it would be the bravest of them who would be
betrayed most cruelly. They were the ones who had believed
in the righteousness of the National Socialist cause; not the
Party hangers-on and those who had marched into Russia
like tame sheep because they had been ordered to back in
June 1941. The rattle of the kettle-drums, the bombastic
blare of brass, all the fine words and phrases were past. This
was the final reality. This was the moment of truth.

The Pill's mind wandered. He remembered the accounts of
the retreat of Napoleon's *Grand Armée* from Moscow when the
Russians had burned down the capital right under their very
noses back in 1812. Out of 350,000 soldiers who had
commenced that winter retreat, only 50,000 had managed to
reach the French positions in Poland.

For over a thousand kilometres, the hard-pressed French
had fought the Cossacks, the winter weather, partisans,
wolves, even themselves. For there had been cases of soldiers
killing each other for a hunk of bread or a scrap of firewood.
There had been cannibalism, too. It had been the worst
retreat in recorded history, more bestial, cruel and savage
than anything that ever had gone before.

Now the Fourth Grenadiers and the Iron Division were
facing something similar, without the genius of Napoleon to
guide them out of the trap. He knew now that neither
General Sobel nor von Heinersdorff would surrender. They
were too foolish or too brave – it depended on the way one
looked at it – to do so. They would die courageously at the

head of their troops, he had no doubt of that. They would not flee the sinking ship like Napoleon did in the end, abandoning his troops to their awful fate.

In short, there was absolutely no hope of convincing them to change their minds. They would go on until the inevitable overtook them. But he could, he thought, suddenly wide awake in spite of his own initial exhaustion, make them see that the wounded could be rescued, not by surrendering them to the Russians but by detaching them from the fighting formations and sending them west to the rear independently.

He sat up suddenly, full of enthusiasm for his new scheme, the adrenalin pumping new energy into his weary old frame. A mobile column of wounded in the van of the 'Wandering Pocket', guided and guarded by a mere handful of soldiers – Sobel and von Heinersdorff could grant him a company at least, surely? – might just make it before the Russians attacked in full force. How could the two commanders object to his plan? The wounded were a hindrance anyway. Get rid of them as soon as possible and the 'Wandering Pocket' would be able to fight more efficiently. That's the way they would reason.

Hurriedly he grabbed for his boots which served him as pillow, in the very same instant that the harsh voice of Metzger, his station sergeant, bellowed, 'All right, you bone-menders, hands off'n yer cocks and on with yer frigging socks! There's casualties coming in.'

CHAPTER 5

'Thanks, Anton,' the Pill said gratefully as the orderly fed him another sip of 'nigger sweat'. Then he took a puff at his cigarette which he smoked by means of a surgical clip. He was in between operations on the wounded of the night and his fine, clever hands were still clothed in surgical rubber gloves. He didn't want to destroy his antiseptic state.

The Three Rebels, enjoying the fine coffee ('Real bean coffee,' the medical orderly had stated proudly, 'none of yer ersatz muck.') smiled at the picture despite the biting dawn cold: the old surgeon easing his back against the wall of the operating tent being fed coffee and bread by Anton, who hovered over him like a fussy mother. It was an hour now since they had brought in the casualties of the Hardt group. Now they wondered where they should go next. Should they report back to King Bull, somewhere out there in that fresh sparkling white waste? Or should they hang on here in the dressing station, which, in spite of the stink of ether and the moans of the wounded, seemed at least human, remote from the general slaughter all around?

For a while the Pill humoured them. He knew his hairy-assed stubble-hoppers, though these three were supposedly 'pearl-divers'. Any excuse and they'd try to find a nice warm corner, complete with 'lung torpedoes' and 'nigger sweat', as they called it. Besides these three young men had seen action enough; their chests bore the Iron Cross and the black Wound Medal. They had shed their blood for Folk, Fatherland and Führer. 'A man is wounded, Grenadiers,' he declared. 'One moment he is an active, eager young man, part of something. The next he is out of it, useless to the Army and his comrades, concerned solely with his own pain and hurt. They stick a needle in him and some time later he wakes up in a circle of bright white light on an operating table, where, God willing, he ceases to be a lump of suffering animal matter and becomes a patient. How is this done, Grenadiers?'

They shook their heads, half-amusing, half-admiring.

'This tiny miracle is achieved with a piece of finely honed steel, weighing a couple of hundred grams. A scalpel. You call it the "knife", I know. Behind that piece of metal is me, naturally.' He grinned at them with his yellowed, worn teeth and they grinned back. 'Plus a couple of hundred years of research and experimentation. We surgeons bury our mistakes, of course.' His grin deepened, and then it vanished abruptly as he remembered what he had been planning before the call to attend the fresh casualties had come. 'Now we've got fifteen hundred of those poor unfortunate lumps of suffering animal matter, plus our own men who have been hit since we set off. But my lone knife and that of the surgeons of the Iron Division cannot transform them all into patients, in other words into human beings with needs and hopes again. There isn't the time, we have so few facilities, and we are constantly on the move.' He paused, as if he expected the three younger men to say something. Karl put down his steaming hot canteen and ventured, 'What do you think can be done, *Herr Stabsarzt?*'

The Pill told them while they listened intently. Inside the tent the other man who had been blinded by the Cossack's cruelty moaned softly, as if he might be coming out of the drugs, and muttered, 'Why can't I see? What have I got this bandage on for? Say, comrades, what's this bandage for?'

The Pill frowned.

Hurriedly Karl said, as if to take the doctor's mind off what was going on in the tent, 'But where would you get the troops from that you'd need to guard the wounded, sir? As far as I know, sir, resources are stretched to the limit.'

'They are, Grenadier Carstens,' an authoritative voice snapped, 'to the very limit.'

It was Major Hardt, his arm now dressed and supported by a sling, his face pale and shocked.

The three soldiers made as if to click to attention, but he waved at them to remain where they were. 'No time for that kind of barrack square nonsense now,' he barked. 'And by the way, once again, you three, thank you for saving the hides of my poor chaps, and naturally mine, too.' He flashed them a hard-faced smile.

'But there must be some men available,' the Pill protested. 'Pen-pushers, military policemen, clerks . . .' The words died away on his lips as Hardt shook his cropped head slowly.

It was then that Karl spoke. 'With your permission, gentlemen, there is the Goulash Cannon Company.'

'*The what?*' the two officers exclaimed in unison.

Hurriedly, a little embarrassed at being the focus of attention of two senior officers, Karl explained how Creeping Jesus had armed King Bull's kitchen personnel and thrown them back in the line before they had contacted the Iron Division; and how the cooks had now been stood down and returned to the HQ of the Fourth Grenadiers.

The Pill laughed and Hardt snapped, 'Cooks, hash-slingers and pearl-divers as infantry! Heaven, arse, and cloudburst, what next?'

'Well,' said Pill, 'perhaps *Oberfeld* Bulle' – he meant King Bull – 'can do a better job fighting the Popovs than some of his so-called cooks can *slaughtering* our rations, what?'

Hardt gave them and Pill his tight-lipped smile. Then he said, 'Hm, perhaps you're right. Anyway, if you can convince the regimental adjutant you might find your guides – there.' He stretched out his good hand to indicate the Three Rebels. 'Goulash Cannon Company, indeed!'

With a sniff he went on his way into the icy, bright-blue dawn, as the Pill released the clip of the surgical fixture and let his cigarette end drop into the snow. Hastily Anton pulled back the blanket which covered the entrance to the operating tent so that the doctor did not have to touch it with his gloved hands. Then he was gone, leaving the three comrades staring at each other, wondering just what was going to happen next to the 'Goulash Cannon Company' . . .

They had come for Karl's father one Friday afternoon when he had returned home to the workers' settlement just outside Hamburg, his slater's tools and the odd bits and pieces he always bought on pay-day strapped to the rack at the back of his bike. The silly old fart had been distributing leaflets for the illegal SPD* Party outside Hamburg's *Dammtor* Station during his midday break from the building site – some crap about how butter prices had gone up under the Nazis, as if the German working class had ever eaten butter, even before the brownshirts had appeared on the scene!

There had been four of them in their ankle-length green leather coats which creaked whenever they moved, middle-aged, slow-moving men who smoked cheap cigars and wore felt hats pulled down low over their faces like cops in the movies. They had poked around in the house while his mother had cried, throwing her white apron in her face in panic, and his father had glowered, cracking the knuckles of his hands – 'stone-crushers', the neighbours called them – as if he would have liked to have strangled the Gestapo men one by one – *slowly*.

Of course, they had found some more of the socialist crap. His father had always been a fool. How many times in the past had his cronies advised him over a '*luett un' leutt*',† drunk outside in the privacy of his allotment, to get rid of any papers 'from the past'. But had he listened? Had he hell!

Outside they had begun to beat him up a little, as they pulled him to their waiting car. In a stolid, routine sort of a way. Without any malice. They always treated 'political'

* German Socialist Party.
† 'Little and Little' – north German workers' drink of a small beer and a small gin.

prisoners like that. A few years before, when Hamburg had been socialist, they had probably beaten up Nazi suspects in the very same manner.

Before they had arrested the old fart, he had never interested himself in his father's affairs, with his frigging Bebel, the 'Bloody Sunday in Altona', and that heap of socialist shit. After all, he had been in the Hitler Youth himself until he had started his apprenticeship and had enjoyed it, hadn't he? When they had taken the old man away, his main concern had been filling his belly and cocking his leg over any willing factory girl ready to spread them. What did it matter to a randy sixteen-year-old who ran the country, who had so much ink in his fountain-pen that he didn't know who to write to first?

That had changed after he had visited the old man at Neuengamme, the new concentration camp they had set up for German communists and socialists – 'the red pack', as the Nazis called them – just outside Hamburg.

The barking police dogs, the shouts, the barked commands, the strutting guards, who strode around proudly, slapping their clubs against the sides of their highly polished jackboots, had not moved him one way or other – fear or hate. As long as he could remember, Germans had always shouted and strutted around in uniform, even the 'Red Pack'. *'Grosse Schnauze – nix dahinter,'** his mother had always maintained and he had agreed with her.

The old man had looked a lot thinner when they'd brought him. Even his 'stone-crushers' had not looked so powerful as they had taken the cuffs off him. Of course, the old woman had begun to cry again, twisting the little brown paper parcel they had allowed her to bring for him round and round in her hard hands. His teeth had all gone. That was to be expected after over a month under 'investigated arrest', as they called it, and one of his ears was permanently swollen to twice its

* 'Big trap – nothing behind it.'

normal size. But the beatings and the torture seemed to have made his father tougher, more resolute than ever.

He had ignored his wailing wife and had concentrated exclusively on his son, as he squatted in the centre of the bare visiting room under the watchful eye of the fat guard. 'Listen Karl,' his father had said urgently, 'never serve them. *Never!* Promise me, my son.' He had seized Karl's hand in one heavy 'stone-crusher' and had pressed it fervently, despite the guard's frown of warning.

Karl knew who 'they' were. The fat-bellied, big-mouthed, middle-class grocers strutting around in their brown boots and uniforms, showing off the medals they had won in the old war, shoving other people off the pavement, getting drunk and wrecking Jewish shops. Yes, he knew *them* all right!

At that moment he had been seized by a fierce love for the old fart, one that he had not experienced since he had been a little kid – 'three cheeses high', as the saying went. He had returned the heavy grip and whispered with equal fervour. 'Don't worry, Papa . . . don't worry . . . *I'll never serve them* . . . !'

That had been over four years ago now and he was still serving 'them'. Try as he may, he had been unable to escape from those vulgar, jackbooted masters, who had wrecked his parents' lives and those of many another ordinary working-class boy like himself. How often had he and the other two Rebels schemed and planned in these last three years not to have to carry out *their* orders, and expand and maintain that Nazi reign of terror; and how often had they failed!

Now Polack had come up with a plan that might bring it all to an end, however risky that plan was. Yet, as the handsome young man, with the broad open worker's face, sipped the last of his 'nigger sweat' that beautiful winter dawn, he wondered. Could the three of them go – just like that – and say 'fuck you' to the rest, sorely injured youngsters – hundreds, thousands of them – who like themselves had not been asked to come here to Russia to die for the Führer? *Could they*?

*

King Bull's big beefy face cracked into a slow smile when he heard the exciting news that Creeping Jesus had just brought from HQ. The two of them were crouched round the tiled stove of the *isba* where King Bull had slept in solitary state the previous night. 'Rank hath its frigging privileges,' he had warned his corporals when they had grumbled, 'and don't you frigging well forget it!' He had guffawed spitefully and said, 'Don't forget it – there's plenty of vacancies in the frigging infantry, yer know.'

'It will mean,' Creeping Jesus gushed, beside himself with relief, 'that the Goulash Cannon Company will be right up front, an independent command. That old fart of a CO will be no longer breathing down our necks. And,' he beamed at the big NCO, 'we will be the first to reach our own lines, perhaps days, even *weeks*, before the rest of the Pocket.'

King Bull nodded his understanding, his mind on other things. 'What's the wounded's ration scale gonna be?' he asked, cutting into the excited flow of words.

For an instant Creeping Jesus considered whether he should snap, 'And put a "sir" on that, *Oberfeld*!' But he decided not to. He would need Bulle in the days and weeks to come, out there in the van in an independent command. 'Scale One, *Oberfeld*,' he answered instead. 'Why do you ask?'

King Bull didn't answer directly. He said, 'A lot of them wounded are gonna turn into stiffs before the march out is completed, I'll be bound. There'll be a lot of rations wasted, unless . . .'

Creeping Jesus took his point. 'Unless *we* take care of them, Bulle.'

King Bull winked sagely and tapped the side of his big nose in a knowing manner. 'Exactly, *Herr Hauptmann*. It'd be a damned crying shame if all that good fodder doesn't find some taker, if you follow my meaning? Scale One means white bread and chicken. . . . A lot of people'd give good hard money for grub like that.'

'I follow you exactly,' Creeping Jesus said enthusiastically, as the blood-red sun started to rise, a glowing ball on the horizon, flushing the white gleaming new snow a deep, rich hue. 'What do you think then?'

'What do I think, *Herr Hauptmann*?' King Bull echoed. 'I think we should go down on our bended knees and thank the Pill for what he's done for us. I don't know about the rest of this shower of shit' – with a wave of his arm he indicated the ragged columns of horses and battered trucks forming up everywhere on the steppe, waiting for the signal to move off – 'but I know he's saved our hides, *Herr Hauptmann*. Very definitely. We're getting out from under, while the going is still good. Yessir, that old pill-pusher over there deserves a prayer!'

Creeping Jesus beamed. 'Good, then that's settled. I've got you some additional horses to make up for the ones you lost yesterday.'

King Bull nodded his approval, his mind already racing, working out what all that fine white bread and chicken, intended for the wounded, would bring on the black market to the rear.

'Now then, Bulle,' Creeping Jesus continued jovially, feeling well pleased with himself this fine sunny winter dawn, 'your first task today is to proceed with an advance party to the village of Granitska. Here, I'll show it to you on the map.' He produced a map from the deep cuff of his officer's greatcoat and held it up for the NCO to see.

King Bull took in the details. There were few villages on the steppe and it wouldn't be too difficult to find, especially if the weather held.

'There is a forward field hospital there,' Creeping Jesus said, 'being run currently by grey mice,* who the General has

---

* Grey mice, a nickname for the female auxiliaries of the German Army.

ordered evacuated in case the Popovs get their filthy paws on them. He doesn't want our German women sullied by those Red swine.'

King Bull grinned nastily. 'I wouldn't mind sullying a couple of 'em myself, *Herr Hauptmann.*' He gripped the front of his trousers dramatically. 'God, it's been an age!'

Creeping Jesus pretended not to have heard. It was all these damned common soldiers thought about – their bellies and cheap, willing women. 'General Sobel has ordered that all the Division's wounded will be concentrated there before we move off. Provision will be made, God knows how, that there will be transport for all of them. I shall remain here to ensure that is done. By tomorrow at the latest. Once that is completed, I shall come up to Granitska, and we set off. Your job, Bulle, will be to ensure that everything goes smoothly there. Better take a few reliable men with you. There could be partisans or marauders on the way to the village. They'll be on the look-out for small parties like yours.'

'Never fear, *Herr Hauptmann,*' King Bull said heartily, his mind now dwelling on other and more delightful things than Popov partisans, 'I'll take care of everything.'

To Creeping Jesus's great surprise, the massive NCO snapped to attention and swung him a tremendous old Regular Army salute, barking the standard formula, 'Permission to dismiss, *sir?*'

'Why . . . why, yes, Bulle,' Creeping Jesus stuttered, unused to such courtesy on the part of his fellow conspirator. 'Please, dismiss.'

'Thank you, sir,' King Bull replied, an unholy grin on his big face. He turned and marched off smartly, happily whistling the soldiers' dirty ditty about the 'maiden who was never satisfied' until her worried father built her 'the prick of steel'.

'I'm satisfied, the maiden cried,' a happy King Bull sang softly, as he disappeared among his goulash cannon, 'I'm satisfied, but the prick of steel . . .'

Creeping Jesus frowned, and told himself it was a hard life trying to be an adjutant. Then he too turned and headed for the warmth of the CO's *isba*.

CHAPTER 6

The night was pitch black. In spite of having the Volkswagen jeep's heater going full blast, the cold penetrated to their very bones. Not a word was spoken as they bounced up and down over the hard frozen snow. The only sound was the roar of the engine and the steady tick-tack of the windscreen wipers trying to keep the frost from settling on the windscreen and blinding Ami, who was driving. King Bull was sitting next to him clutching his Schmeisser a little apprehensively.

They had been going most of the day in the vehicle borrowed from the Iron Division. As usual, the pre-war staff maps of Russia, based on the old Imperial Army surveys done of that godforsaken country back in 1917, were hopelessly inaccurate. They should have reached Granitska hours ago. Yet the steppe village still was not in sight. They might well have been the last men alive in the whole world, as they rattled and bumped across the seemingly limitless plain.

But the four of them crouched in the fetid atmosphere of the jeep, which stank of unwashed feet, rancid male sweat – and fear – knew that wasn't the case. Twice white flares had sailed effortlessly into the velvet, star-studded sky to their right and had flickered for a while until they had zoomed to the ground like falling angels. Once a machine-gun had rapped out a short burst and had been followed by isolated rifle shots. They might have been German, for this was nominally German-held territory. But the four worried young men packed in the jeep, each one of them occupied with his own gloomy thoughts, knew it could be the Russians, too. The area teemed with partisans.

Time passed. Now and then King Bull risked turning on the spotlight (for they were driving blacked-out), searching the area for a hurried, frightened moment for any sign of their destination. To no avail. It seemed to have disappeared from the map.

The flares commenced once more. A dull thud and the flare would hiss into the night sky, hovering for an instant at the dead point before falling slowly, shimmering with intense light. Momentarily the whole of the steppe to their front would be flooded with its glowing luminosity. The uncertain shadows would suggest to the frightened men a world of ghosts. Again and again they thought they saw something stirring, caught sight of a shadowy outline. Always, however, it turned out to be no more than a large boulder protruding above the snowfield or a bush. All the shapes were so unreal, Karl couldn't help thinking, that it all might well be just a fantastic dream.

An unhealthy one, though. For the crisp night air was heavy with tension. There was no mistaking the brooding mood of the lonely steppe. There was something out there and Karl told himself it boded no good for the four men isolated in the little, canvas-roofed vehicle.

More time passed. In the east the sky was already beginning to flush with the ugly white light of the false dawn. Worn out by staring out into the darkness for so long, Karl felt his attention beginning to wane, his senses dulled. In an hour it would be really light, he told himself, and then the partisans, if they were really out there, would vanish. They were creatures of the night. To attack by daylight was too dangerous for them. His head started to fall onto his chest. Next to him Polack was already snoring softly.

'Halt. *Wer da?*' The harsh abrupt challenge cut startlingly into Karl's dream. He jerked his head up as Ami changed down noisily and the little vehicle started to slow down.

Karl blinked several times and craned his head over King Bull's shoulder. To their front, poorly outlined in the dim light, someone had set up a rough-and-ready roadblock of bushes and what looked like timber dragged from some country cottage. Next to it there was a bunch of soldiers, muffled up to the eyes in greatcoats and scarves, though the helmets they wore were unmistakably German.

'We must have hit our own lines,' King Bull said thickly, rubbing the sleep from his eyes. 'Thank God, my ass feels as stiff as a plank.'

Ami slowed down even more. To his immediate front a big fellow, with the silver plate of a military policeman around his neck, was raising both hands for them to stop.

'Chain-dogs!' King Bull commented. 'Didn't think those frigging hell-hounds would be this far forward –'

He never finished his comment about the hated MPs, whom the soldiers called 'chain-dogs', for suddenly Polack lunged forward, grabbed the wheel from Ami's surprised grasp and flung it to the left. The jeep careened from the track, bumped its way up and down a ditch and jolted into the snowfield beyond. 'Hit the tube, Ami!' he cried fervently. 'Them's Popovs! I can smell the stink of *mahorka* even in here . . .'

Even as Ami reacted, King Bull cursed mightily and as the jeep gathered speed again, the men at the barrier opened fire. Tracer zipped lethally through the air. Karl ducked hurriedly as the canvas above his head was suddenly stitched with a line of smoking holes and there was the abrupt cloying stench of escaping petrol. A grenade sailed towards them. Ami swerved madly. The jeep seemed to hang on two wheels. 'Stay put, you frigging son-of-a-bitch!' Ami shrieked, as the Volkswagen appeared about to turn over. *'Come on . . . come on!'* Another grenade exploded close by. The blast caught the jeep at the other side and blew it back on course in the same instant that King Bull ripped up the little perspex window at his side and loosed a wild burst at the partisans.

The big 'chain-dog' screamed shrilly, as scarlet buttonholes were suddenly stitched across his head. He flew backwards and slammed against the barricade, dead before he hit it. That unsettled the partisans. They dropped to the snow on all sides. For a moment their fire slackened.

Ami didn't need a second chance. He pressed his foot down to the floor, head ducked between his skinny shoulders. The jeep shot forward, bouncing clean off the ground every time its wheels hit an obstruction. The others held on for their lives, praying as they had never prayed before that the Popovs would not commence aimed fire again. And all the while the stench of escaping petrol grew stronger and stronger . . .

It was the smell of wood smoke carried far on the still dawn air that first alerted them to the presence of a human habitation, as the Volkswagen engine spluttered and coughed in its last throes. Over on the horizon the smell was followed by the straight plumes of ascending grey smoke.

King Bull bit his bottom lip with worry, as Ami fought the dying engine, the snow behind revealing a trail of lost petrol. 'What do you think, Carstens?' he asked, knowing that the blond young man was the leader of the Three Rebels.

'Don't think we've got much choice, have we, *Oberfeld*?' Karl answered. 'This old crate won't last much longer.'

'You're right there, Karl,' a frustrated sweating Ami at the wheel agreed with a grunt. 'The gas tank's about empty. All the juice has gone and the reserve can was holed back there.'

'Shit, shit, shit!' King Bull cursed, slamming his clenched fist against the dashboard. 'Just when I thought I'd got it tied up – gash, chicken and white bread!'

Polack pricked up his ears as he always did when it came to the subject of food. 'What was that about chicken?'

'Shut up!' King Bull commanded. 'All right, get ready for trouble.' He clicked back the bolt of his Schmeisser.

The others did the same and with his free hand Ami readied an egg grenade which lay on a shelf underneath the dash. 'Mother-fuckers are not taking me alive,' he declared angrily.

Karl allowed himself a fleeting smile. Only a little while back, they had been discussing the possibility of surrender to the Popovs. Now here was Ami stating he'd rather die than be captured by them. A crazy world, a crazy frigging world indeed!

Now they could see the snow-heavy roofs of the huddle of cabins from which the dawn smoke was ascending: a Russian hamlet like all the others they had ever seen in the year they had spent in this miserable, godforsaken country. Poverty-stricken huts where the peasants didn't even have a pot to piss in. The benefits of the workers' revolution. Karl grinned again. What was it someone posh had once said about Russia? 'I've seen the paradise – *and it don't work*!'

Abruptly the engine cut out altogether. In the sudden silence, the four of them looked at each other and then at the hamlet. Nothing stirred as the Volkswagen jeep finally rolled to a stop, the only sound the wind in the skeletal trees and the drip-drip of escaping petrol on the snow.

King Bull swallowed hard and made up his mind. 'All right,' he snorted, grabbing his Schmeisser and heaving his cruelly muscled shoulder against the little door, 'don't keep on sitting there like wet farts waiting to hit the side of the thunderbox. Bale out.'

'What are we gonna do?' Karl asked a moment later, as they stood staring uncertainly at the hamlet, shivering in the dawn cold.

'What can we frigging well do?' King Bull grunted. 'Have a look-see at the frigging place. It's that or have our nuts frozen up out here. Come on, let's go.'

Reluctantly, ankle-deep in the fine powder snow, breath steaming about their pinched faces, they set off in a tight V with a suspicious King Bull in the lead, all of them tense, fingers wet with warm sweat where they gripped weapons.

'The place looks dead,' Polack opined after a while.

King Bull didn't look round; his eyes were fixed to his front. But he sneered: 'God, what a dumb potato Polack you are!

The place looks dead! So who lit the frigging fires, eh. Snow White and the frigging Seven Dwarfs?'

Polack lowered his head and muttered something under his breath. At any other time, Karl would have sniggered at his old comrade's discomfiture. But not now; the situation was too uncertain.

Ami heard the strange straining noise first, like a gate with rusty hinges blowing back and forth in a light wind. He told them and said, 'It's coming from over there. Next to that barn, or whatever it is.'

Without orders from King Bull, they changed direction and began plodding through the snow, unmarked by human or animal footmarks, in the direction of the sound. They skirted a grove of snow-heavy trees and stopped as one.

'Boshe moi!' Polack breathed and crossed himself hastily in the elaborate Slavic manner.

Ami swallowed hard and spat into the snow for luck, while Karl could do nothing at all; he was too transfixed by the sight. To their immediate front there were the charred timbers of what had once been a cottage, little patches of smoke still coming from them, as if the fire had not been so long ago. Besides the ruin there was the stark-black skeleton of an old oak tree. On that tree like monstrous fruits out of season were three bodies – all stark naked, frozen stiff.

'Gott im Himmel!' Even King Bull was shocked by the gruesome sight, as they twisted in the wind, tongues hanging out like purple leather, the chins dug into unnaturally long necks. 'One of them is . . . a woman!'

There was no denying it, as the wind draped long flaxen hair over the heavy breasts. They gaped at the triangular blonde thatch over feet that had turned blue and purple with the cold.

Karl said angrily, 'All right, we're not a bloody lot of battlefield tourists. We've seen stiffs before, haven't we?'

'But a woman,' King Bull breathed. 'Why hang a dame?'

*

But there was no rhyme or reason to what was taking place in the nameless hamlet that day, as the handful of SS men, drunken for the most part, hearts filled with hate and that senseless racial superiority which had been drilled relentlessly into them, went about their work of death and destruction.

Bottles of vodka and cheap gin in their fists, eyes red-rimmed and glazed, they staggered through the place, cracking their whips, whacking left and right as they chased the few remaining villagers out of their huts, crying, 'Not a stick left standing . . . Burn the lot . . . *Scorched earth!*'

A few had dogs, great black evil-looking creatures, ears held back along their sloping skulls and quivering with tense expectant excitement as they watched what was going on. Now and again, when the SS thought the terrified Russians, mostly boys, old men and women, were not fast enough in getting out with their pathetic bundles, they would slip the leashes. The hounds would be off like a shot, ripping and tearing at the Russians, setting them off shrieking and screaming while the SS laughed uproariously, thinking the sight the finest joke in the world.

The Three Rebels glowered, faces set and angry, holding their weapons with hands that were now tense with repressed anger. But King Bull saw only the SS men's drunkenness and the fact that no one seemed to pay any attention to them as they wandered forlornly through the hamlet, which obviously was soon to be set to the torch.

'What in three devils' name is frigging wrong with you, comrade?' he kept asking angrily as SS men brushed past him, his questions unanswered. 'Can't yer frigging well speak good German or something? How we're gonna get to Granitska?' But the men in black were concerned solely with their own drunken, self-imposed tasks.

They passed a larger place than the rest of the hamlet – it was the usual 'House of Culture', which every Soviet village, however small, possessed. But there was little cultural about what was going on in the place this morning. From outside they could plainly hear the regular squeaking of rusty bedsprings and the hectic gasping of someone obviously in the throes of sexual passion. They stopped. Polack, the biggest of them – bigger even than King Bull – raised himself on his toes and peered through the dirty window.

A blonde girl, pale and naked – she couldn't have been more than twelve – was lying pinned down and half-smothered under the bulk of an SS *Scharführer*. He wore his helmet and black jacket, with his muddy jackboots, stick grenade thrust down the side of the left one, straddling her bare feet. Only his breeches were down, as he humped frantically, his fat, fleshy, yellow buttocks lathered in sweat.

As the girl whimpered in pain or outrage, Polack didn't know which, for he could not bear to look any more, King Bull cried, 'Come on, leave the bugger to his mattress polka. There's an officer over there.' Polack swallowed hard and told himself he had to get away, *he had to*! The Popovs couldn't be any worse than this. He dropped down to the soles of his big feet again, his whole big body trembling with absolute rage.

Hastily Karl squeezed his arm. 'Polack,' he commanded harshly, 'steady. Steady, do you hear!'

He saw the lethal red glow in Polack's dark eyes and repeated the command, squeezing even harder, as they followed to where the SS officer was standing: a portly, large man, black whip hanging from his wrist as he posed, hands on fleshy hips, looking every inch the Teutonic conqueror.

King Bull gave him a grudging salute and after barking out the usual formula, 'One NCO and three men – Fourth Grenadier Regiment – reporting for duty, *sir*!' he asked urgently, '*Sir*, any chance of some transport to the village of Granitska? Our CO has ordered us to get there immediately. We were attacked by partisans and had our vehicle wrecked, *sir*!'

The fat SS officer raised his whip in languid salute and gazed at King Bull's frightened red face as if he were having difficulty in focusing properly.

Karl could see that he was drunk like the rest of them. These weren't the regular SS, he realized suddenly, fighting soldiers, however brutal, fanatical and cruel. These were the men of the 'General SS', the same swine who were now guarding his father in far-off Neuengamme. These were the carrion who had swept in after the fighting troops back in the summer of the previous year when all had been victory. They had exterminated the 'sub-human' Slavs, raped and pillaged, filled their pockets, sending back whole trainloads of loot to the Reich. Now they were on the run. But before they left, they were leaving something for 'the natives' to remember that the SS had once passed this way.

'It's all fucked up,' the SS officer said apropos of nothing, his voice slurred and without resentment. 'All fucked up, you know, of course.'

King Bull didn't know or care. All he wanted was a vehicle to get him out of this doomed awful place as soon as possible. 'Granitska, sir?' he prodded hopefully.

The SS man did not seem to hear. Instead he took a silver flask from his hip pocket, unscrewed it and took a delicate sip. 'How did the swine do it?' he asked. 'That's what I want to know. How did the Red swine manage to beat – *us. HOW?*' Suddenly two great tears began to roll slowly down his fat face.

CHAPTER 7

Morosely Karl wandered through the crazy village. King Bull had given up on the tearful, drunken SS officer. Knowing that time was running out rapidly (already the flares were sailing up into the sky to the east, heralding all kinds of new dangers), he had snapped, 'All right, you bunch, spread out. See if you can find something with wheels – anything that can move. But quick. These piss-pots of asphalt-pounders* are gonna find themselves with their asses in a sling soon – if they don't move it. *Los!*'

All four of them had gone off in different directions, trudging through the mud and snow, looking for transport, while the SS continued their orgy of death and destruction, some of them so drunk now that they no longer seemed aware of the imminent danger. Karl, too, could not seem to sense the urgency of the moment. The place and its sights had affected him. He had become sombre and sad, overcome by a strange sort of black depression. What kind of life was this? he asked himself. Why were human beings like this, worse than the savage animals in the wild? Was it the war? Or was it something deeper, more basic? At that particular moment Karl almost felt he could unsling his rifle and blast a bullet through his brains, putting an end to it once and for all.

Idly he kicked an empty can down the muddy gutter, past what was left of a dead dog, parts of its haunch skewered on a stick and still smouldering on a dying fire. The burnt flesh stank terribly. But Karl did not seem even to notice. Nor did he question who had attempted to roast a stray dog in this godforsaken place. His mood was too depressed.

He went on, still kicking his can. Before him the usual cage

* Name given by the *Wehrmacht* to the SS on account of their fondness for parading and 'pounding the asphalt'.

that was present in every Russian village loomed up. Even the *Wehrmacht* had them; they had been a feature of all the places the Army had conquered. Into it went the priest, the village schoolteacher, all able-bodied males and female members of the Stalin Youth – anybody, indeed, that the authorities judged might be capable of rallying these Slavic sub-humans into resistance against their new masters. They had become so commonplace that Karl and the rest did not see them any more. They appeared as much part and parcel of the normal Russian village as the onion-towered church and the only other stone building in the place, the Soviet House of Culture, together with the obligatory statue of Lenin outside it in full flow to the 'workers and peasants'.

He paused at the wire gate hanging open and sagging from its hinges. It was unguarded, as were the two stork-legged towers which flanked it, though the machine-guns were still in place up there. Karl puffed out his cheeks and told himself, as he eyed the usual collection of drab-brown wooden huts grouped round the square over which the crooked cross flag of the oppressors hung limply, the guards had done a bunk. Or perhaps they had gone on the rampage, together with the rest of the SS. One last orgy of wanton brutality before Fate caught up with them.

Idly he kicked the can off into the far distance and tugging up his rifle sling to a more comfortable position on his right shoulder, he wandered into the place, which still stank of Russians and human misery. What terror this place must have seen in these last months, he told himself, as he walked in the mud between the huts, their windows smashed, bits and pieces of personal possessions hanging from them, as if they had been looted hastily.

'Guardsman of the Gate, I was –' The hoarse croak in the strange German of the Slavic countries startled him. He turned swiftly, grabbing for his rifle.

But he relaxed the very next moment when he saw who had spoken to him: a toothless old boy with scraggy white hair, dressed in the striped pyjamas of a camp inmate, cap held in his gnarled hands in an ingratiating manner. 'Who the hell are you?' he asked, as the little man with the great hook of a nose above a toothless mouth beamed up at him, twisting his cap, the perfect picture of willing humility.

'Yakob, sir,' the little man replied with a bow. 'I was their Selector First Class as well as being Guardian of the Gate.'

Karl reasoned the 'their' referred to the SS who had fled. 'And what was that when it was at home?' he asked, a little bewildered, snapping out of his black mood for some reason he couldn't quite explain. Perhaps it was the strange little man's obvious high spirits and optimism.

'The gentlemen used to say that I had the finest Yid-sniffing hooter in the whole of Russia, sir.' He saw the bewilderment written all over Karl's handsome face and added hastily. 'You know what people are, sir, dishonest the whole lot of them! Coming in here with their dyed blond hair and the curls snipped off, washed all over in cologne, pretending they were Ukranians or White Russians or something like that, saying that's why their Russian sounded accented.' He touched his huge beak of a nose. 'But they couldn't fool the old hooter, sir. No way! I can smell a Jewish Yid fifty metres away . . . maybe a hundred.' He smiled up at Karl proudly with his toothless gums. 'Once I told the gents that they were denying they was Yids and it was down with the britches. That was the final test, sir – a dangling dick with the foreskin docked off by the rabbi!'

Karl gawped at the man. 'But you're a Yi – a Jew yourself,' he stuttered.

He smiled winningly again. 'Of course, sir, naturally, sir.' He rubbed his skinny claws together. 'By religion and heritage, but not in my heart – here.' He tapped his skinny chest proudly. 'In there I am one hundred per cent genuine Aryan German – just like yourself. The gents often said that if I'd have been ten years younger, they would have had me in the SS.'

Karl had had enough. 'The Guardian of the Gate' with his Jew-sniffing hooter was as crazy as the rest of them were in this place. The little Jew hadn't got all his cups in his cupboard. 'Listen,' he said, trying not to see the mad look in his eyes, 'I need wheels. You know, transport. *Dalli, Dalli!*'

'Wheels . . . transport . . . *dalli dalli,*' the little man repeated the words obediently. 'You'll have to see the *Lagerführer, Hauptsturm* Kroeger. Oh yes, he'd be your man, sir.' He laughed and the saliva trickled down the side of his mouth from toothless gums.

'Where do I find him?' Karl snapped. He wanted to get away from this doomed place before he went crazy, too.

'Up there . . . beyond the huts. He's doing some sorting out, sir.' Suddenly the Guardian cackled with mad laughter, the saliva swinging from left to right as he swung his head back and forth. 'Yes, *sorting out*, that's what he's doing, sir . . .'

Hurriedly Karl went on his way, followed by the demented laughter. It had started to snow again, the snowflakes coming down in sad slowness. Above him the hard blue was changing to a leaden dullness. Soon it would be snowing heavily. It was time to be on their way again. Conditions on the steppe were bad enough as they were.

He came across the *Lagerführer* as he turned a corner in the camp. There was no mistaking him. The silver braid on the black overcoat draped around his fat shoulders like a cloak and on the cap thrust to the back of his glistening bald pate indicated his rank. Casually, without taking aim, he was firing single shots from his pistol, like a boy shooting at rats on a rubbish dump, into a trench to his front from which were coming groans, cries, moans, followed by a soft slithering noise as if a body was falling with difficulty.

Slowly the *Lagerführer* became aware of the young soldier below, staring up at him in the slowly falling snow. He turned and grinned drunkenly, showing a mouthful of gold teeth. He might well have been one of the well-fed burghers back home one saw every evening at some small-town *stammtisch*, welcoming an old friend for another round of beer, cards, and political chat. 'You look as if you can use a drink, soldier boy,' he said thickly. With his free hand, he reached into the crate on the snow next to him and tossed a bottle to Karl. 'Be my guest. Not leaving any of this good stuff to the Russkies, eh, soldier boy?'

Karl caught the bottle and glanced at the label. It was the finest French champagne.

The SS officer raised his pistol, fired and at the same time laughed. 'You're thinking we rear-echelon stallions are living it up, aren't you, soldier boy? While you front-line swine are dragging your arses in the shit, eh? Go on – say it. But I'll tell you this. It's not all roses back here, believe you me.' He beckoned to Karl with his smoking pistol. 'Come on up here and I'll show you.'

Still clutching his bottle, Karl stumbled up the little slope to where the fat officer squatted. He gasped when he saw what the pit at the officer's feet contained – a packed mass of men, women and children, gazing up at him with huge bulging eyes from skull-like faces, crouched among those already dead, their shaven skulls cracked like eggshell with the impact of the officer's bullets at such close range. He shook and almost dropped his bottle.

'Someone's got to do it, you know, soldier boy,' the officer said easily, reading his mind. 'They don't mind, I don't think. Shitty life they led. There's not much to lose, is there?' He aimed casually and the skull of a woman to the right shattered easily, great wads of scarlet gore splattered her neighbours. They hardly flinched. They accepted it – and their fate – stoically like dumb animals waiting to be slaughtered.

'Though a man's got to have a strong stomach for this business. After a while it gets to you. I suppose they are human beings after all.' The officer mused. As an afterthought he reached in the crate, took out a bottle, cracked off the top with a tap from the butt of his pistol and drank the foaming hissing liquid straight from the neck, spitting broken glass as he did so.

Karl stared at him in horrified disbelief. 'But who – who are they?' he stuttered. 'What – what have – what have they done?'

The fat SS officer pulled a face, as if the question was too much for him. *'Da bin ich uberfragt,'** he admitted. 'The others round 'em up and bring 'em in. We count 'em, of course. There's no place for sloppy records in our organization. Berlin wouldn't like it –' Suddenly he broke off and frowned. 'Of course, we've had it now, haven't we, soldier boy?' He guffawed, loud, cynical and raucous. 'Clock in the piss-pot and all that – as you hairy-arsed soldier boys say.' Abruptly for no apparent reason he ripped the War Service Cross, First Class, from the front of his black tunic and flung it into the trench of trapped prisoners and those who had already been slaughtered. 'We can frigging well get rid of the laurels now, can't we, soldier boy?' he cried, his lips twisted in a scornful grimace. 'The good frigging days are over!'

'Where's transport?' Karl said through gritted teeth, vomit and revulsion welling up in his throat.

'Transport?'

'Yes, fucking *transport?*' Hardly aware that he was doing it, Karl unslung his rifle and clicked off the safety.

'Over there behind the shed. There's my duty Mercedes – Why do you ask, sold –'

Karl fired from the hip without consciously taking aim. He pulled the trigger and felt the weapon slap against his thigh. The range was so short, he simply couldn't miss. The slug exploded right in the front of the SS officer's chest. The rib cage disintegrated and broken bone suddenly gleamed like polished ivory in the mass of oozing red that instantly appeared. Slowly, very slowly, the SS officer, a look of

---

* Roughly, 'There I have been over-questioned,' i.e. 'You're asking too much.'

absolute complete surprise on his fat face slipped backwards into the pit, still clutching his bottle of champagne.

Karl trudged away in the steadily falling snow, trying not to hear the cries of the prisoners in the pit. Whether they were cries of joy or despair that they were now left to be masters of their own fate, he didn't know. He told himself with a kind of weary sadness that they were trapped. There was no escape for him, Ami and Polack. There was no way out. Both systems – German and Russian – were equally brutal, cruel and totally corrupt. There was nothing else for them but to soldier on. Whatever their fate was going to be in this crazy white world of the steppe, they would have to accept it. No escape.

Bent like a very old man, collar tugged up around his ears against the storm, he trudged sadly through the falling snow. *There was no escape . . .*

BOOK TWO

The Cauldron

CHAPTER 1

It was nearly dawn.

Beyond the village of Granitska, to the east, the sky was beginning to flush the ugly white of the false dawn. In the skeletal trees, those of the birds which hadn't been shot for food were beginning to caw. Somewhere one of the 'grey mice's' roosters crowed. In thirty minutes it would be first light.

'*Crack!*' Across in the Russian positions yet another flare hissed spluttering into the sky. It exploded in a shower of incandescent sparks and remained suspended for what seemed an age, illuminating the men waiting below in its eerie, white-glowing light. Finally it sank to the earth like a fallen angel.

'The Popovs're nervous,' Polack commented slowly, swallowing the last of his breakfast ration of bread.

'They're not the only frigging ones,' Ami grunted surlily. 'I'm pissing down my left leg already.'

Karl smiled softly, but kept quiet. He was going to need all his energy for what was to come this dawn.

'The Popovs are not in the line in strength,' Creeping Jesus had lectured them the night before. 'In fact, Intelligence thinks there're only a handful of regulars of the Red Army, supported by a bunch of old men and boys from the partisans. Just rabble, playing soldiers.'

'Don't care what kind of Popov pricks they are,' Ami had grumbled as they had gone outside and the convoys had started to form up, dozens, scores, hundreds of vehicles laden with wounded, filling the village and extending to all sides right out into the steppe. 'They can still hold a rifle and blow off my frigging turnip!'

'Hold yer fart-cannon, will yer,' Karl had commenced, but

in the same instant a deep bass voice had chided, 'I will not have that kind of disgusting language in my presence. Indeed, I won't!'

They had swung round as one to be confronted by an enormous woman in Red Cross uniform, who was at least a head taller than Polack, her grey hair cropped as short as any recruit's, with a definite suspicion of a black moustache beneath a great beak of a nose, from which at that particular moment, a large dewdrop hung. For the first time they had met the redoubtable *Schwester* Klara, in charge of all the grey mice in Granitska. She had been a frightening prospect; they had fled hurriedly.

But now this morning, both Creeping Jesus and *Schwester* Klara were forgotten, as the Three Rebels and the rest of the Goulash Cannon Company eyed their front anxiously, waiting for the order to attack. The moment of truth was about on them. There were ten minutes to go.

Fifty metres away, crouched low in a shell crater half-filled with snow, Creeping Jesus trembled with both fear and cold. Every five minutes or so for the last two hours, he had risen to urinate. Now he fought back the burning desire to do so again. It was growing too light. He didn't want any Popov sniper taking a pot-shot at him now.

King Bull next to him was unmoved. He ignored the adjutant trembling like a leaf next to him. His mind was set on *Schwester* Klara. He told himself she was a fine body of a woman, something for a man to get a grip on – all juicy arse and tits. By the Great Whore of Buxtehude, he'd dearly love to dance the mattress polka with her! Besides, she had power. With her on his side, they could forge all kinds of ration returns. Together they could make a fortune. But first she had to be properly broken in. Instinctively he grabbed his bulging crotch to reassure himself that it was still there, and told himself that all she needed was a good length of prime

German salami and she'd be eating out of his hand. He guffawed softly to himself. 'And eating something else, I'll be bound, too,' he thought.

'Have you ever noticed, sir,' King Bull said conversationally, 'that when you're about to go into action, your tool seems to get smaller, nestling in low between the eggs? Funny that.'

'Mine has probably disappeared altogether,' Creeping Jesus moaned. 'Why did I ever volunteer for this? I thought it was going to be plain sailing in the van.' He groaned. 'Do you mind awfully, *Oberfeld*, if I urinate here in the hole next to you? I'd rather not stand up – now that it's getting light.'

'As you wish, sir,' King Bull agreed readily, his mind full of tits, white bread and chicken mixed together in pleasurable anticipation. 'Pee away!'

There were five minutes to go now.

Karl flung a hasty glance at his wristwatch. He felt the adrenalin pump new energy into his bloodstream. Sixty seconds to go. Over on the Russian side, the flares were hissing into the sky with increased frequency, as if the Popovs suspected something. Next to him Polack fixed his bayonet wordlessly. He, too, was resigned like the rest. There was nothing they could do but to accept their fate, whatever it might be. '*Thirty . . . twenty-five . . . twenty . . .*' Creeping Jesus started to count off the seconds in a thin quavering voice, '. . . *fifteen . . .*'

Ami crossed himself rapidly and muttered rapidly, 'God, kill every fucking Russian. God, kill every fucking Russian. God . . .'

'. . . *Ten . . .*'

Karl gripped his rifle in sweaty hands.

There was a sudden rushing noise. A frightening, gurgling, sucking, hissing noise. The men of the Goulash Cannon Company looked upwards, startled. Behind them on the horizon the sky quaked and shivered. Huge spurts of scarlet flame shot into the air. At some unseen signal a series of giant blast-furnaces had suddenly burst into full furious life.

'*ZERO!*' Creeping Jesus yelled, excitement even in his voice now as he was carried away by the sheer, unreasoning atavistic craziness of war.

King Bull shrilled his whistle and sprang to his feet. 'All right, you Christmas tree soldiers. *Up!* The captain's got a hole in his arse . . . follow him!'

'*The Captain's got a hole in his arse!*' they echoed fervently and jumped out of their holes . . .

To the Three Rebels' right a heavy Russian machine-gun started to chatter ponderously like an irate woodpecker attacking a very hard tree. Tracer, at first slowly, then gathering speed, began to hiss their way. They ducked and ran on, the slugs cutting purposelessly over their heads to strike the snow in an angry hissing, searing sound. Almost casually Polack pulled a grenade out of his boot top, ripped off the china pin, and lobbed it in the direction of the machine-gun, running with the others all the time.

A flash of scarlet. A muffled crump. A shrill scream of absolute agonized pain. Suddenly the gun was silent and a severed head, complete with helmet, rolled a little way across the steppe and came to a stop like an abandoned football. They ran on.

Rough shadowy figures loomed up out of the smoke. Someone ran at Polack crying shrilly. He was waving an ancient sword. Polack parried the partisan's thrust easily. There was the clash of metal striking metal. For a moment bayonet and sword locked. Polack laughed out loud. It was too easy. He slipped the bayonet from under and out of the sword's reach. He lunged forward, his inexperienced opponent still with his sword raised. The man screamed hysterically as the bayonet went deep into his stomach and then was dragged out with a wet, squelching sound. The man hung there clutching his stomach. Polack kicked him and he reeled back.

One of the partisans tossed one of the little spluttering bombs the Russians used. *'Hit the dirt!'* Karl cried fervently. They struck the ground as one. Even as the steppe to their front erupted in a ball of vivid red flame and snow and earth pattered down onto their prone bodies, Ami's head was up and he was pumping a full magazine into the partisans. They went down in a crazy heap like ninepins. It was all too easy.

Now they were pelting through the first abandoned Russian positions, firing to left and right, whooping like Red Indians crazy on firewater, shooting up the town. The shelling had smashed them hopelessly, the timbers shattered, the bunkers still smoking, dead bodies littering the places like bundles of abandoned rags.

To Karl's front there was a sudden burst of angry fire. He hit the dirt again, as what looked like part of a sheep came flying in his direction. 'Christ almighty,' he gasped to Polack, 'they're flinging fucking sheep at us –'

'Mines!' King Bull's bellow cut into his words urgently. 'They've planted mines to our front!'

'What about the mutton roast?' Polack began as Karl gave him a hefty shove in the shoulder and he stumbled to his knees in the snow and cut off his complaint.

'Thank God those poor ba-lambs got in the way or we would have walked right into that frigging minefield,' Karl gasped, as he dropped to his knees next to Polack and Ami to peer into the smoke at their front, trying not to hear the shrilling scream of some poor sod who hadn't heard King Bull's warning in time. 'What's the drill now, I wonder?'

'We try to outflank it,' Creeping Jesus, his face ashen, dark circles under his eyes, commenced.

'He means *we* try to frigging well outflank it,' Ami whispered under his breath, as they crouched there in the snow, listening to the obviously frightened adjutant giving his orders. The breakout of the wounded had been stopped dead by the surprise minefield, covered by a handful of partisans and Red Army men armed with hand-fire weapons. Back in Granitska the convoys waited fearfully for the order to move, the wounded panicking at the sound of gunfire, agonizing at the thought they might well yet be left behind to the mercies of the partisans. For they all knew the partisans took no prisoners. But before they dispatched the hated 'Fritzes', as they called the Germans, they toyed with them in their own brutalized, savage manner.

Creeping Jesus nodded to a silent, pensive Karl. 'You will take the left flank with those two rogues of friends of yours. You, *Oberfeld* Bulle, will come in from the right flank.'

'And you?' King Bull asked pointedly, deliberately omitting the 'sir'.

Creeping Jesus's ashen face flushed, but he did not react to the insult. Instead he said, 'For your information *Oberfeldwebel* Bulle, I shall remain in charge here, supervising the whole operation, directing the machine-guns which will cover you.'

King Bull snickered. It wasn't a pleasant sound; it expressed what he felt about the craven adjutant at that moment.

Creeping Jesus looked at the snow.

With a sigh King Bull got to his feet and slung his machine pistol. 'All right, girls,' he simpered in what he took to be a good imitation of a female voice, 'put on your party dresses. Mother's gonna take yer to the frigging ball!'

'Fuck mother!' Ami husked sotto voce.

King Bull looked at him threateningly. 'Did you open yer fart-tube, Grenadier?' he demanded.

Ami smiled up at his tough, unshaven face sweetly. 'Yes, Sergeant,' he said, 'I said, "Good luck, mother."' He smiled winningly.

King Bull frowned at him suspiciously. Then he waved a
hand like a small steam shovel in dismissal. 'All right then,
let's not frig around. *Move it!*'

They moved it . . .

The partisans hidden in the group of skeletal trees spotted the
two little assault groups immediately. Machine-guns started
to spit scarlet fire. The glowing white tracer bullets curved to
left and right, gathering speed all the time. The attackers
started to run heavily. They zig-zagged around the smoking
shell craters. Now and then they skidded and slipped on the
snow. Almost immediately they were up again and pounding
forward through the lunar landscape of abandoned equipment
and still, shattered corpses, already freezing in the awesome
cold. For they knew that to stop without cover meant instant
violent death.

Karl and his two comrades dashed forward in a straight
line. By now they were veterans, unlike the rest of the Goulash
Cannon Company. They knew the machine-gunners would
have to pause and reload at given intervals. So they flung
themselves behind any bit of cover as soon as the machine-
gunners zeroed in on them and hurtled forward once the firing
momentarily ceased again. Bit by bit they got closer to the
grove of shattered trees.

Karl, eyes blinded by drops of sweat, chest heaving
painfully, with his heart seemingly threatening to burst out of
his rib cage at any moment with the effort, knew instinctively
that King Bull's group was closing in on the grove too. He could
hear the cries of rage in German and the sudden screams of
'*Sanitater* . . . *Sanitater*, come and get me, *please* . . .' as yet
another poor unfortunate 'pearl-diver' was hit.

Whatever else he was, Karl knew the big head cook was no
coward; he'd press home the attack to the best of his ability.
He would not let the Three Rebels down.

Now they were some fifty metres away from the grove of

trees. As one they hit the ground as one of the two machine-guns located there turned its fire on them, the slugs hissing across the surface of the snow like a flight of angry red hornets. For a while they lay gratefully, gasping painfully, as Karl studied the gunpit: the usual box of logs, covered with sod and earth. Primitive, indeed, he told himself, but quite capable of standing up to a direct hit by one of the stick grenades they all carried.

After a few moments, Polack turned over the dead body of one of the partisans who lay huddled where they crouched. The customary peaked cap they all wore flopped off into the snow, to be followed by a mass of blonde curly hair. Polack whistled through his teeth, while Karl shook his head at the sight – a woman, quite pretty in a heavy sort of a way, save for the hole neatly bored through the centre of her forehead by a bullet.

Ami was his usual cynical self. 'What a waste of good female gash,' he panted. 'And look at the pair of lungs on her. You could get between them and not hear a thing for a month o' Sundays.'

'Have you no shitting respect?' Polack snorted indignantly. 'You'll be fucking dead next, pig!'

'What else is there for a hairy-arsed stubble-hopper like –'

'Shut up, the two of you!' Karl cried hotly. 'I can't damn well hear myself think.'

'Yes, *Herr Offizier*,' Ami started, but Karl held a clenched fist under his nose and hissed, 'I'll polish your frigging visage with my knuckles in a minute. Now – *shut up*!' That stopped him and Ami relapsed into a sulky silence while Karl considered the problem confronting them.

The Popovs knew they were there. What did their gunners think the Fritzes would do next? Desperately, his brain racing crazily, Karl tried to outthink the Russians. Of course, they'd think that if the Fritzes were to attack at all, they'd run to the left or right flank and try to work their way round behind the position. They'd be waiting for the Three Rebels to break cover that way, wouldn't they? Karl said a swift prayer that he had guessed right. Then he dismissed his doubts. Time was running out. Soon Granitska itself would be under attack! The wounded would panic. There'd be an awful slaughter if the partisans ever broke through there. Even that frightening *Schwester* Klara wouldn't be able to stop that.

'All right,' he said, swallowing hard at his own temerity, 'this is what we're gonna do.'

CHAPTER 2

Slowly the Pill drove into Granitska past the abandoned equipment, strewn everywhere like the aftermath of a terrible flood. Everywhere there were broken-down vehicles, dead horses with swollen bellies, legs sticking stiffly upwards so that they looked like tethered barrage balloons, corpses; and as usual on a battlefield the crows and other carrion were having a field day. As soon as his vehicle approached they rose from the corpses with a heavy sullen flapping of wings. Immediately he was past, they were down again, picking at the eyes, noses, ears and the other soft tender bits, bickering and squabbling with each other when one found some particularly attractive piece of human flesh.

Now he was rolling by the waiting convoys. It looked as if the barns, the garages, the farms of all of Central Russia had opened their doors to disgorge this mass of vehicles. There were clumsy, bullock-drawn farm carts; many of the usual *panje* carts, drawn by skinny ponies, ancient aristocratic carriages, heavy with dust; wood-burning rickety cars, dragging puffing boilers behind them; long wickerwork baskets on wheels used for transporting paralysed persons, which he remembered from his early days as a medical student; even wheel-barrows – anything with wheels. But all of these disparate vehicles had one thing in common. They were all laden with sorely wounded, terribly frightened men.

Pill frowned. There was going to be one hell of a massacre if the Russians caught the wounded like this. There was only a handful of armed fit men about and they, he knew, were cooks and general bottle-washers, who would be little use once the shooting started. He tapped his driver's shoulder as he saw the only stone building in the place loom up to his right. 'It'll be over there,' he ordered. 'Park outside, Anton – and don't forget to keep the engine running.'

Anton, his Austrian orderly, flung him a quick grin over his shoulder. 'Never fear, *Herr Stabsarzt*,' he said in his thick Upper Austrian accent, 'we Austrians are not all like our well-known fellow countrymen.' He meant Hitler. 'In fact, myself included, we can be considered devout cowards. *Sicher!* You can bet your life on it, sir, I'll keep the engine running – and then some!'

Anton changed down to second, weaving in and out of the convoys which blocked the road, their drivers and guards ankle-deep in the freezing mud, impatiently waiting the order to move out, and came to a stop outside the building, which was adorned with large red crosses.

The Pill shook his head sadly. 'The invisible flag,' he had once called that Red Cross flag, 'the flag of humanity' under which he had been proud to serve in the knowledge that on the other side of the line, whatever their uniform and their political beliefs, there were other doctors who were equally proud of it and believed that humanity was more important than any war. Now he knew different after a year of combat in Russia. Now that 'invisible flag' fluttered limply over a lost and defeated cause.

Hurriedly he stalked down the packed corridors of what had once obviously been a Soviet school. High up where the soldiers could not reach them there were the yellowing pictures of Soviet worthies – Engels, Marx, Lenin and the rest of those nineteenth-century purveyors of that monstrous political creed. Lower still were crude, fantastic pictures in crayon and water-colour, obviously painted by children now fled into the woods, hate for the Germans bred into their very bones, or long dead.

Now the place stank of hospital: that old, old mixture, a compound of ether, shit, and suffering. Somewhere, too, his trained ear could hear the steady grating of a bone saw. Someone was amputating yet another limb, turning a young fit virile man into a morose cripple for life.

'Excuse me, sir.'

He turned startled. A bespectacled orderly in a white coat, flecked with rusty bloodstains was attempting to pass, cradling a huge pile of chamber-pots in his arms, full of dark brown urine, flushed here and there with blood. 'Gut-shot!' he told himself automatically. Aloud he said, 'They're pissing well, at least.' It was often the case that when a man was hit in the guts, he started to retain his urine due to shock. It was quite a problem to get them to commence urinating again.

The orderly, an old hare, grinned back. '*Jawohl, Herr Stabsarzt*. But are you surprised with *Schwester* Klara?' She'd make even a mummy piss a bucketful!'

'Ah yes, the redoubtable *Schwester* Klara,' Pill agreed. She had fought right throughout the campaign, as far as the gates of Moscow itself. The big sister was known throughout the Army. They didn't come tougher than Klara. He moved to one side and let the old hare – a 'bedpan jockey' as they called themselves – get on with his balancing act, trying to get the chamber-pots safely to the sluice. Then he continued his progress down the loud echoing corridor, now aware of the angry snap-and-crackle of a fire-fight to the west. He frowned. The Popovs were obviously still holding up the big break-out.

'*Achtung . . . achtung . . . platzmachen bitte . . . Schnell! Schnell!*'

Old hare that he was himself, he reacted swiftly for his advanced years, pressing himself up against the wall as the stretcher-bearer team, lathered in mud and gasping for breath like fish just pulled out of the sea, came doubling up bearing their bloody burden.

On the stretcher lay what was left of a man, both hands gone, and with one leg hanging on barely to the stump by a few strips of blood-red flesh, the whole thing dripping blood onto the floor as the hectic stretcher-bearers hurried forward.

The Pill held up his hand. 'Doctor!' he snapped.

'It's the Pill,' one of them, an older man with an unshaven chin and no teeth, hissed.

'Yes, the Pill,' he agreed, knowing what the stubble-hoppers called him behind his back. But unlike so many of his colleagues he wasn't merely a 'pill-pusher', hence the name. He had not become blasé about the grievously wounded men he had to deal with. They were still human beings to him; not just 'lung', 'leg', 'gut' and all the other names that harassed surgeons gave to their cases. 'What was it?' Even as he asked the question, he was peering down at the grievously wounded man, automatically noting the pallor, the white-pinched end to the nose, the hectic breathing.

'Mines, *Herr Oberstabsarzt*,' the old stretcher-bearer hissed, promoting him a couple of ranks or so.

He wished he could have smiled at the old soldier. But he couldn't. The boy on the stretcher was obviously soon to die unless God took a hand. 'Got a meat wagon?'

The old one shook his head. 'No. And there's nowhere to go with it, sir, even if we had.'

The Pill didn't hesitate. 'All right, put him down – quick!'

With a sigh of relief the four of them did so and began massaging their burning hands, while the Pill tugged his emergency kit from his big pocket plus a silver flatman.

He pulled out a scalpel, ripped the top off the flask with his teeth and said, 'I know it's a waste of good French cognac' – the old hare's red-rimmed eyes sparkled at the word 'cognac' – 'but pour some over the scalpel, my hands, the wounded leg – and the rest is yours.'

The old hare needed no urging. Hurriedly he carried out the task, while the young soldier on the blood-soaked stretcher remained motionless, out to this world. Pill prayed he would remain so, as he eyed the tremendous wound, virtually a traumatic amputation.

Under these circumstances he knew his primary objective was to save the young man's life. The preservation of his physical capabilities were of secondary importance. Perhaps the young man would live to thank him – or to curse him. He would never run again, nor would he ever be able to caress a woman's breasts, *but he would be alive*! Already the Pill knew that he really should amputate above the knee, just to make quite sure, just in case gas gangrene set in. Gingerly he touched the torn flesh. If the infection had already been present, he would have experienced a crisp, crackling feeling. But there was none, though that wasn't to say that it might not come later. But the kid had been hurt badly enough as it was; he didn't want to make him more of a cripple.

His decision made, he set to work. Swiftly, he severed each of the surviving tendons and hunks of flesh until with a nauseating thunk, the foot fell to the canvas of the stretcher. Now the Pill began cleaning up the stumps of the hands the best he could, while the old hare (without orders) started to still the flow of blood at the stump. 'Where is the minefield?' he asked, while he worked, oblivious to the passing traffic down the corridor.

They told him and the old hare added, 'It's a bitch, *Herr Oberstabsarzt*, a real bitch. Them perverted Popov banana-suckers've got it covered with machine-guns. Them frigging pansies of hash-slingers – everybody knows all cooks are queer – ain't got a hope in hell of finding a way through it.'

The Pill continued to cut away, but his mind was racing as he absorbed the information about the minefield.

'ALL RIGHT!' Karl bellowed above the bark and rattle of the massed machine-guns firing on King Bull and his group, as they too tried and failed to rush the Russian positions. 'Get this. I'm gonna have a go!'

'But it ain't right, Karl –' Polack began but Karl cut him short with a bitter snarl. 'Write to the fucking Führer and fucking well complain,' he cried. 'Now here I go!' Before they could stop him, he was up and running all out, straight for the machine-guns, head tucked in deep between his shoulders, arms working like pistons.

The nearest machine-gunner spotted him a fraction of a second too late. Uselessly the sudden stream of vicious tracer cut the air just to his right. Karl slammed against the side of the log bunker and collapsed there, chest heaving frantically, vision blurred and wavering. He had done it. He was in position.

From the cover he had just left, Ami said to Popov, 'All right, you arse-with-ears, now play it safe. That Ivan with his popgun will be expecting you.'

'I know, I know, but we can't let Karl do it all by himself. Got to give him –'

'Fuck it, no speeches, Polack. I know, I know. Zig-zag to the left. Just when he thinks you're gonna try to go over there, go all-out straight for the dugout. Like a currant-crapping quartermaster with the wind up his baggy knickers. Clear?'

'Clear!'

Ami clapped him on his big shoulder. *'GO!'* he shrieked.

Polack burst from cover. He darted forward with amazing speed for such a big man. The gunner spotted him at once. He hit his trigger. The machine-gun burst into hectic frenetic activity. Tracer stitched the air all around the running man. Lead kicked up furious little spurts of snow at his feet. Suddenly Polack stumbled.

Ami gasped. To his front Karl, looking over his shoulder, groaned out loud. Had their old comrade been hit at last?

Next moment, however, Polack was up again and running all out. Furious at being cheated, the machine-gunner opened fire once more. Karl could see the little spurts of snow and earth, tinged with an angry red, beating a pattern behind his flying heels. In one moment more, the gunner would have Polack directly in his sights. This time there would be no mistake; he couldn't miss!

Suddenly Polack changed direction. Now he ran all out, knowing he was racing against time. Head held high like a marathon runner, sucking in great gulps of air, arms flailing, he belted towards a frantic Karl. The change in direction put the Russian gunner off for a moment. By the time he had recovered and swung his Maxim round, Polack had slammed into the trees next to Karl and collapsed on the snow, gasping crazily like a dying fish, mouth gaping.

Karl gave him a moment and then signalled to Ami – three rapid knocks on the top of his helmet. Ami got it immediately. It was the signal for vigorous activity. He raised his rifle and started firing rapidly at the bunker, blazing off a whole magazine in seconds, the wood splinters raining down at the two crouching soldiers tensely waiting for the gunners to turn their attention on Ami.

They did. Karl waited no longer. He ripped the stick grenade from his boot, pulled the pin, flung it overarm and rushed forward. The grenade burst right on top of the bunker. A log flew in the air in a burst of angry yellow flame. Someone screamed shrilly. Another voice cried out in agony. Yelling terrible obscenities, carried away by the unreasoning bloodlust of the battlefield, he stumbled through the smoking earth ploughed up by his grenade, while just to his rear, Polack stood bolt upright, snapping shot after shot into the bunker.

A Russian burst out of the trees, a stocky, pock-marked runt with a yellow wolfish face. Without halting he threw the egg grenade he carried in his right hand. Karl ducked instinctively. The grenade sailed over his head and exploded harmlessly metres away. But the runt didn't hesitate. He dived forward in a low tackle. Karl was caught off guard. He was slammed to the churned-up earth, winded, helpless for a moment, his nostrils were assailed by the stink from his attacker.

But there was no time to think about the smell. The runt had ripped a wicked-looking knife from his pocket. For a crazy moment or two they rolled back and forth while the Russian sought desperately for an opportunity to use his knife. Twice he slashed down and twice Karl managed to avoid the killing blow.

Desperate and crazed with fear now, Karl acted instinctively. One hand shot up and grabbed the wrist bearing the wicked knife like a vice and the other sought and found the Russian's skinny throat. With all his strength he squeezed, as the Russian tried to break his grip, his yellow face contorting crazily.

The Russian's eyes bulged from a face that was turning crimson. His tongue hung out of his gaping mouth like a piece of wet leather. He began making strange whimpering noises like a trapped animal. Karl increased the pressure, carried away by the mad desire to kill. The sweat poured down his face in rivulets.

The Russian's eyes started to roll upwards. Abruptly the knife fell from nerveless fingers. Karl didn't relent. He kept up the murderous pressure. The Russian went limp. Now Karl was merely supporting a dying body. But he was taking no chances. Freeing one hand, he sought and found the blade the Russian had dropped. With all his strength he brought it up and plunged it deep into the Russian's back. It grated against a bone and then sank in with a horrible, wet, sucking sound.

The Russian's spine arched like a taut bow. For one long instant his eyes opened again, wide, staring, wild, glaring down at his murderer with a look of naked shocked accusation. Then the life vanished from them for good. They glazed over. He fell across Karl – *dead*.

Karl screamed. As Polack and Ami finished off the surviving gunners, he thrust the dead Russian from him, the saliva dribbling from his slack lips, mumbling meaningless sounds, as he lay there next to the man he had killed. A moment later he started to sob like a broken-hearted child.

'Thank God,' Creeping Jesus said fervently, as a sudden silence settled on the battlefield. 'Those damned machine-guns have stopped. *Oberfeld* Bulle or the others have done it – knocked the damned things out.' He licked his cracked parched lips.

The Pill, who had crawled the last hundred metres to where the adjutant crouched in the snow, nodded. 'Good, but what are you going to do about the minefield?'

'What?'

The Pill repeated his question, adding, 'The situation is impossible back there at Granitska. The wounded are panicking badly. If we don't get the convoys started soon, those who can are going to make an attempt to run for it. They are beyond all reason. They know it won't be long before the Russians attack in strength. They are sitting ducks back there – and they know it.'

'But we have no engineers, Pill,' Creeping Jesus protested. 'And so far we don't know just how safe the flanks are for the convoys –'

'Since when has infantry needed engineers to get them through a minefield?' the aged doctor cut him off scornfully. 'What has a stubble-hopper got his bayonet for?'

'But my men are cooks, Pill. They wouldn't know a mine from a pan of pea-soup. I can't just sent them into a minefield to prod for the damned things –'

'But you're not a cook!' the Pill interrupted brutally once again. 'You are a trained infantry officer. *You* know how to detect mines!'

Creeping Jesus blanched. Instinctively the Pill noticed how his hands had begun to tremble. God, he told himself, what a craven coward he is! Angrily he heard himself say, 'Well, if you won't do it, *Herr Hauptmann*, then someone else must, eh?' He turned to the gawping cook just behind him. 'You, give me your sidearm, please,' he commanded.

A hundred metres away, crouching next to the Volkswagen jeep, Anton caught his breath and cried, *'Herr Doktor – nein! Sie sind viel zu alt . . .'* The protest died on his lips as the old doctor stood bolt upright, lifting a bayonet like a man in the early morning testing the air. Still crouched in the snow, Creeping Jesus pretended nothing was going on.

'Right,' the Pill declared, as he had done often enough just before an operation. But this time the operation might well have a lethal outcome, not for the patient, but for him. 'You, cook, mark well the way I go.' His laughter was a little forced. 'Gretel dropped corn in the magic forest when she went to find the peppercake house. My footprints in the snow will have to suffice.'

'Yes, sir,' the cook replied dutifully enough, though he was bewildered by the reference to Gretel and the 'peppercake house'. Had she been some kind of cook? For his part, Creeping Jesus continued to pretend nothing was happening.

'Here we go then,' Pill said with an air of finality. Crouching stiffly he advanced into the minefield, prodding the earth with his borrowed bayonet as he went . . .

It was thus that the Three Rebels saw him, crawling across the field of snow on his hands and knees, moving with the stiff painful gestures of an old man, his bayonet flashing in the thin light of the winter sun as he prodded systematically to left, right and then the centre.

'It's the Pill!' Polack said, as they stood among the dead Soviet gunners.

'He's looking for mines,' Ami said tonelessly, realizing at once the old doctor was carrying out this task himself, risking death for the sake of others, because no one else in the Goulash Cannon Company dared take the risk.

Karl bit his bottom lip and remained silent. *Why?* he asked himself. Why had it to be the Pill of all people? He was old; he had done enough already. Why should he have to take this risk after all the others he had taken since the Fourth Grenadiers had first marched into this accursed land? He could have remained home, pushing a cushy number in some base hospital in the Reich, going home at night to his pipe and slippers and a fat comfortable wife. Instead he was on his hands and knees in the middle of nowhere, chancing having his limbs blown off – or worse – at any moment. *Why?*

Ami watched and wondered too, though his thoughts were different. Here was the greatest army the world had ever seen, he thought, which had conquered Europe from the Channel to the Urals. Now down there at the point of that whole massive army retreating westwards – at the head of millions of men, equipped like no other army in the world – was one creaking over-age medical officer, prodding the earth with a bit of steel. How pathetic!

For his part Polack stood in tense silence, tears coursing unheeded down his broad Slavic face.

Pill was almost to the other side of the minefield, identifiable at the far end by a line of rusting barbed wire (the Soviets never identified their minefields save to protect themselves). In five minutes or so the aged bent medical officer would have done it and the convoys could roll. Already Creeping Jesus was poised with his signal pistol, ready to fire the flare which would tell those waiting impatiently at Granitska that they could make the break-out.

Hardly daring to breathe, Karl bit his bottom lip until it bled, willing the Pill to make it. The distant figure prodded, prodded and prodded again before creaking on in his self-imposed death-defying task. There was only a score of metres left before he reached that rusting wire. Surely God could not be so cruel as to harm the old man *now*?

With horrific, startling suddenness it happened. A muffled crump, a patch of black on the snow, a puff of brown smoke and the Pill was hurtled forward, bright red blood jetting in an arc from the stump of his right leg and staining the snow. They heard his groans even at this distance in the shocked silence which had followed the explosion.

Slowly, very slowly, he began to stir, probably still shocked and dozy from the explosion, not really aware of what he was doing.

'*Nein!*' Karl shrieked, suddenly all too aware of the new danger. 'Don't move, Pill!'

'*DON'T MOVE, PILL! PLEASE!*' the others joined in frantically. '*DON'T MOVE –*'

Their words were drowned by another explosion, as Pill's arm touched off a mine to his right. The explosion raised him off the ground, arms flailing wildly, as the series of explosions continued right to the wire. When they ceased, the poor old man hit the ground once more and lay still in the shattered smoking earth like a bloody bundle of abandoned rags.

Polack groaned out loud. Ami snorted, 'Why in three devils' name did he do it?'

Karl knew. He had sacrificed himself for the rest. But he did not tell the others that. What use would it be?

Slowly the three of them began to thread their way down to the rest of the Goulash Cannon Company. The signal flare hissed into the sky and from the village a great excited roar rose followed moments later by the rusty squeak of wheels and the throaty grind of reluctant motors starting up on a frosty morning. The great trek could commence.

One hour later, after they had all passed, the Pill's body was crushed like a cardboard figure deep, deep into the mud and snow, his sacrifice forgotten already . . .

CHAPTER 3

'By God, Corporal Teitze,' King Bull breathed as he eyed the
massive red flannel knickers hanging from the improvised
line between the two carts, frozen stiff and extended at the
gusset so that they looked like a suspended red giant, 'only a
man like me with something in his britches could satisfy what
fits into them bacon-bags!' He straightened his shoulders
proudly. 'There isn't a man in the whole of the Fourth
Grenadiers who could match that collar size, I'll be bound.'

'And what concern are my kni – my underthings of yours,
Sergeant?' *Schwester* Klara's deep resonant voice demanded.
'Pray, speak.'

King Bull flushed and fell back, as if he feared some kind of
physical attack, instinctively catching hold of the Corporal's
arm, gasping, 'Nothing at all, *Schwester*. I was just passing by,
sort of.' He fell back another pace, as the gigantic matron
stomped through the mud wearing a pair of soldier's dice-
beakers.

'Passing by!' she sniffed, staring at him with her gimlet eyes.
'A likely tale. After the skirts that's what you are, Sergeant,'
she declared. She thrust her arms to cover her magnificent
bosom, puffing it out even more so that it reminded Karl of
one of the barrage balloons which hung over his native
Hamburg. 'I know what you men are like. That's all you ever
think about.'

King Bull retreated yet another pace, as if he feared he
might be impaled on the massive bust. 'I am not like that at
all, comrade,' he stuttered, growing red. 'I made a genuine
mistake. I didn't realize that them draw – er, female
undergarments belonged to such . . . well, someone like you.'
His red-rimmed eyes, usually so angry, were suddenly full of
longing and dog-like devotion.

'Oh fuck me, for I'm to be the fucking Queen of the May!' Karl hissed in amazement to a grinning Ami. 'I do believe the big bastard's actually gone and fallen in frigging love! Will wonders ever cease?'

'All he ever fell in love with was a bit o' hairy gash,' Ami opined cynically, 'and hissen of course. Nobody bloody well loves King Bull as much as he loves himself.'

Karl wasn't listening. His whole attention was concentrated on these two star-crossed lovers, as they faced up to each other, each waiting for the other one to relent and declare their love.

King Bull's conciliatory remark had its effect. Her stern look relaxed a little. The harshness, too, had gone from her voice when she spoke again. 'Everyone can make an honest mistake, comrade,' she said. 'We have all been sorely tried these last weeks, haven't we?'

King Bull nodded eagerly.

'Especially we weak women.' She lowered her head coyly and blinked her eyelashes several times.

'Oh, my aching arse!' Ami exclaimed. 'We frigging *weak* women! I, for one, wouldn't like to meet that particular *weak* woman on a dark night, I can tell yer that, mates.' He grunted and added obscurely. 'With that one, yer need yer name engraved on the soles of yer dice-beakers, so that they can identify yer afterwards. Otherwise yer'd disappear for good.'

But King Bull obviously had no such fears. He was all sweetness and light as he advanced a little towards *Schwester* Klara, though he was careful enough not to get too close to those formidable breastworks. 'Perhaps, comrade,' he said softly, 'after duty hours you might do me the honour of coming over to my poor provisional kitchen. Perhaps we might partake of a bowl of good fart-soup' – he corrected himself hastily – '*pea-soup* together?'

'I would be honoured, Sergeant Bulle,' she simpered like a sylph-like teenager, 'though I hope you will not attempt to take advantage of me? We weak women are no match for you great hairy men with all your cunning ways.' She beamed at him modestly.

'*Never,*' King Bull declared stoutly. 'Never in this world. I know a decent, clean-loving young woman when I see one. Your honour is safe in my hands, *Schwester* Klara. Why, my kitchen is as good as a monastery as far as you are concerned' – he lowered his voice and gave a hasty look to left and right to see if he were being observed – '*Liebling*!'

Schwester Klara blushed a deep red and gave King Bull what she thought was a playful push nearly knocking him off his feet.

Karl groaned. Polack looked the other way. Ami farted derisively . . .

For three weeks now the slow convoys had been moving westwards, grinding kilometre after kilometre over the limitless steppe, covering perhaps five or six kilometres a day, the biting cold and the snow more of a danger than the enemy. Ever since the Pill had sacrificed his life to enable them to make the break-out from Granitska, they had been untroubled by the enemy. Admittedly, more than once they had caught glimpses of riders on the far horizon, stark black, stationary and vaguely threatening. But always they had been swallowed up by yet another furious snow squall.

'They're trailing us all right,' Karl opined morosely afterwards, as they sat over their pathetic little fires in the evening before blackout, trying to keep warm and failing badly. 'But for some reason they're not attacking, although we're such easy meat.'

'Perhaps they're too busy with those poor sods to the rear?' was Polack's comment.

Generally it was thought that that was the case. For far to the rear, especially at night, they could see the silent flickering pink shadows of gunfire and hear now and again the drone of many aircraft. But what was going on back there was unknown to them. Creeping Jesus's radioman had failed to contact the Iron Division, or even their own unit, the

Fourth Grenadiers, for over a week now; and it was generally assumed that the Popovs and their partisan helpers were concentrating their attacks on the main bulk of the 'Wandering Pocket'.

Although Creeping Jesus publicly bewailed the fact that they had no contact with the rest, privately he was glad and made sure that his hard-pressed, frustrated radioman didn't remain on the air too long; he didn't want their position to be given away unnecessarily. Like the coward he was, he thought that by sticking his head in the sand, the problem would go away.

But on this bright morning, as the great convoy rested, the adjutant knew he had to do something about a problem that would not go away. According to his map, in one day's march they would strike one of the tributaries of the River Dnieper, which flowed in a north–south-westerly direction and effectively barred their progress unless they were prepared to make a detour of several score kilometres; and that Creeping Jesus was *not* prepared to do. Every day counted. He wanted to reach the SS lines before the inevitable happened. He knew that once the Russians had dealt with the main body of the 'Wandering Pocket' it would be the turn of the van.

Just after King Bull's first declaration of love to *Schwester Klara*, therefore, he sent for the big NCO and over canteens of real bean coffee, generously laced with cognac, the two of them discussed what was to be done next in the glowing warmth of the adjutant's personal motorized caravan.

'As you know, Bulle,' the adjutant explained, 'these Popov rivers can be perfect bitches. They are all fast flowing and mostly without fords – at least there are few fords marked on these damned useless maps Berlin sends us.' He knocked his knuckles on the map spread out between them on the little table.

'In this kind of weather,' King Bull opined slowly, half his mind still on Klara's opulent fleshy charms, 'I should think the bitch is frozen over.'

'Possibly, possibly,' Creeping Jesus agreed. 'But how long would the ice stand up to the pressure of so many damned vehicles crossing it hour after hour? What we need is a bridge!'

'What you need,' a cynical contemptous voice at the back of King Bull's head snarled, 'is a new pair of britches. 'Cos yer shitting the present ones agen!'

And King Bull's inner voice was right. For the adjutant had reverted to his usual jelly-like state of overwhelming fear this morning as he realized the dangers before them. For a while he had considered going ahead in his caravan 'on a recce' and crossing the river straight off. But on second thoughts he knew that was out of the question. There could be partisans out there; and even if he did get through, what would headquarters say if he turned up alone and without his charges? It would mean disgrace or even worse. These days Berlin was having officers who abandoned their commands executed without trial by the public hangman. He knew he had to stay with this pathetic bunch of cripples and cooks to the bitter end.

'Any sign of a bridge on the map?' King Bull asked, sipping the coffee which came from his own secret private stock.

'Several,' Creeping Jesus answered a little wearily like a man who was sorely tried. 'But can we be sure that the official who supposedly did the survey – God knows when – actually did so? Besides, have the bridges been blown by the partisans in the meantime, supposing they actually exist?'

'There's only one way to find out, isn't there?' King Bull said easily, draining the last of his coffee.

'You mean send out a patrol to check the river bank?'

'Genau.' King Bull craned his big shaven head over the map and Creeping Jesus wrinkled his nose in distaste at the NCO's raunchy smell. How he wished the rank and file would wash more often. They smelled, most of them, as if they had just emerged from the sewers. Didn't they even possess any eau-de-cologne?

'There.' Creeping Jesus pointed along the blue line of the river. 'There's the first supposed bridge. As far as I can make out from the few details it is a road and rail bridge capable of bearing the kind of traffic we would put across it.'

'How far?'

Again Creeping Jesus noted the absence of the 'sir', but he knew he could not say anything about it – not just yet. For the time being he was completely in the power of the big ox sitting opposite him. He behaved as if he were a damned equal, when all he was was a trumped-up cook! 'From here to Nikolaev where the bridge is located is about ten kilo-metres.'

King Bull did a quick calculation. 'Under these conditions,' he announced after a few moments, 'a day's march for fit young men.'

Creeping Jesus nodded his agreement and waited.

For his part King Bull ran his mind over his men – 'a bunch of frigging Christmas tree soldiers, the lot of 'em' – until he came to the Three Rebels. For years now he had been trying to break their spirit, without success. But he knew that they were the best men he had, though they were only to be trusted when they were ordered to do things they wanted to do. A little angrily he told himself the Army was going to pot. Like Creeping Jesus, he promised himself he'd 'make a sow' out of the three of them once they reached safety. Aloud he said, 'The best of a bad bunch are Grenadiers Carstens, Zimanski and Stevens. I'll send them.'

'An excellent choice, though I regard the three as very insubordinate.'

King Bull ignored the comment. He said, 'My guess is that they'll be back to report by tomorrow. In the meantime I think we should close up as tightly as possible and be prepared to move off immediately.'

Creeping Jesus shivered at the thought of a surprise Popov attack and said, 'A louse must have run over my liver.'

'Yer,' King Bull said to himself contemptuously at such

obvious cowardice, 'wearing a pair of frigging hobnail boots at that!'

'And will you command the reconnaissance, *Oberfeld* Bulle?'

King Bull looked at the officer as if he had suddenly gone mad. '*Me?*' He jerked a thumb like a hairy pork sausage at his big chest. 'Do I look as if I've got green in my eyes?' he demanded insultingly. 'That *meschugge* I am not! No, I'll leave that to Corporal Teitze. Naturally I'm needed more urgently here.' A sudden vision of *Schwester* Klara, totally naked, exhibiting all her ample charms flashed before his eyes and he swayed, suddenly dizzy with lust.

'Of course, you are, *Oberfeld*,' Creeping Jesus agreed hastily. 'What would we do without you, what indeed?'

'Creep,' Bull said to himself, and with a flourish drained the rest of his *Kaffee-Kognak*. 'So that's the way we gonna do it, then?' he said.

'Yes, that's the way we, er, are gonna do it,' Creeping Jesus echoed. 'Let these young bloods risk their necks for a change. We old hares have done enough, don't you think?'

King Bull said nothing; his mind was too full of *Schwester* Klara. For his part Creeping Jesus reasoned that if those insubordinate young swine failed to find a bridge, he could still attempt his 'recce' and never come back. He had tried, hadn't he, he would tell anyone who might query his miraculous escape from the débâcle that would take place if they didn't manage to find some way of crossing the river.

Thus it was that the fates of the Three Rebels were decided by a craven officer and a randy senior sergeant. As always in war it would be the young men who would pay the butcher's bill – with their own blood . . .

CHAPTER 4

'We had a Corporal Teitze once,' Ami said as they trudged through the deep snow along the river bank, the ice on the water gleaming a dull silver in the thin winter sun. 'Same name and rank as you. Snuffed it back in '39, or was it '40? A lot of corporals have snuffed it since the war started, come to think of it.'*

'That wasn't *Teitze*,' Polack corrected, 'that was *Tietze*. "Titty"† they used to call him in the cookhouse. Nice feller for a cook – and a corporal,' he added with a wink for Karl, who was staring at the snow geese flying in a low V across the water. They and the birds seemed to be the only things alive in this white waste. 'Pity the Frogs croaked him. Frogs have no respect for corporals, don't yer think?'

Teitze, a tall, skinny man with a tea-strainer moustache, who looked as if he were in his late thirties, said, 'I shouldn't be here in the first place anyhow. Reserved occupation I had in Berlin. Window cleaner to the Reich Chancellor's office. Many a time the Führer has looked out while I was polishing his windows and given me a smile. Whenever I think of that old cow with her one leg who lost me my job, I could shit bricks, the bitch!'

'What happened, Corp?' Ami asked, humouring him and trying to break up the monotony of the slog through the snow. 'I mean, how did the old cow with one leg get yer posted to the stubble-hoppers?'

The skinny corporal whipped the dewdrop off the end of his pointed nose and said miserably, ''Cos I've got a good

---

* See *Cannon Fodder* for further details.
† The word can mean 'teats' in certain parts of Germany.

frigging heart, that's how come. Cleaning the windows at the Reich Chancellory, I was, when I heard this voice. "Can you help me, *Herr Fensterputzer*?* Please can you help me?" Of course, being the kind of nice bloke I am, I step in and start looking for the speaker. Nowhere to be found, and still the old cow went rabbiting on until I figured out where the cunt's voice was coming from – beneath the bed!'

'Beneath the bed!' they exclaimed, scenting some sort of exotic sexual hanky-panky. Everyone knew that was what went on all the time in the Party bosses' houses. They were at it all the time, like fiddlers' elbows.

'Yer,' he said indignantly, 'and if I'd have frigging well known what was gonna happen, she'd be frigging well there in the same place even now.'

'Go on, Corp,' they urged. 'Get to the filthy part.'

'There were no filthy part. But anyway, in the end I found her underneath the bed – and stark naked!'

They whistled happily and expectantly.

'Natch I looked the other way. I didn't want to see the old bag's bits and pieces and I said to her, "I'll feel under the bed for yer legs and pull yer out, like." So I got one leg and started to tug and then I thought, where's the other one? I sez, "Hey I can't find yer other leg, *Frau General*." She was the wife of some bigshot general, you see. She sez, "I'm not surprised, 'cos it's in the Charité."† "The *what*?" I sez. "Yes," she sez, "last week the chief surgeon Professor Sauerbruch, whipped it off."' The corporal paused and whipped another dewdrop off the end of his nose. 'I should have thought . . . I should have thought,' he moaned. 'What a horned ox I was, but I didn't –'

'Go on, Corp,' they chortled, intrigued by his tale. 'What frigging well happened then?'

'What happened? I put my frigging big foot in it. I sez,

* Mr Window Cleaner.
† A famous pre-war Berlin hospital.

"Well, *Frau General*, I've never met a woman before who could spread her legs that bleeding wide!" '

Karl chortled mightily, as did Ami. Even Polack, who tended to be somewhat prudish due to his strict Polish Catholic upbringing, ventured a smirk.

'I say,' Ami exclaimed, 'that's a frigging good one! *Never met a woman who could spread her legs that bleeding wide!*' He wiped the tears from his eyes. 'All the way from the Reich Chancellory to the Charité, eh?'

The corporal sniffed. 'It wasn't so shitting funny for me, I can tell you that! How did I know she was a damn friend of Frau Goebbels? The fuss, the frigging hysterics, the cries. I thought the old bitch was going to have an organ concert there and then! They pitched me down the stairs, punching me all the time, and threw my frigging bucket after me. Said I'd never work again in Berlin. Said I was a sexual pervert, saying things like that to well-born ladies. Said all I could think about was women spreading their frigging pearly gates! Said it came from too much looking through frigging bedroom windows. Said I was lucky not to have the end of my dick docked off – the way they do to them frigging mental effectives, or whatever yer frigging well call them frigging idjuts!' Angrily he tossed his head to one side, gasping for breath at talking so much. Karl ducked hastily as yet another dewdrop went whizzing by dangerously close.

'So, that's how you came to join the glorious Grenadiers, Corp?' Ami said, grinning maliciously, with a wink to the other two. 'But come to think of it you did make rank, Corp. I mean you are somebody *now*!'

Corporal Teitze gave him a lowering glance, as if he realized his skinny shank was being pulled. 'Give me being a window cleaner any frigging day,' he said sombrely. 'What man in his right senses would be in this arsehole of the world –'

The single rifle shot, like a dry twig being snapped underfoot in a hot summer, cut into his words startlingly.

They dropped as one, weapons raised instantly, as the solitary slug went whistling harmlessly over their heads, their gaze tight and concentrated as their eyes swept the opposite bank, peering the length of the snow-heavy bushes.

But nothing moved. Whoever had fired at them had gone to ground completely.

Slowly the corporal rose to his feet, face shocked, his misadventure as window cleaner to the Reich Chancellor's Office completely forgotten now. 'What . . . what did you make of that?' he asked in a voice that trembled slightly. 'You lot call yersens old hares, come on, out with it – what was that in aid of?'

The Three Rebels looked at each other and then back at the opposite bank. Karl, his face thoughtful, said slowly, 'I don't make anything out of it, Corp. If that had been a regular Popov sniper, one of us'd be looking at the taties from below by now. They don't miss. Besides they'd have pumped off a whole mag before they went to ground.' He shook his head as if very puzzled, while the others nodded their silent agreement.

'What do we do then?' Corporal Teitze asked, still staring at the opposite bank fearfully. 'Should we go on?'

'Yes,' Karl replied. 'If we don't, King Bull'll have our goolies off. Yer know what he's like. Besides,' he added firmly, thinking suddenly of the Pill's sacrifice, 'we can't let those poor sods on the stretchers snuff it because we get a case o' the shits. We've got to have a try to find that bridge at least.'

'Yer,' Ami and Polack agreed heartily, 'we can't let them down, Corp, can we?'

'Suppose yer right,' Corporal Teitze said a little reluctantly, as if he would rather face King Bull's wrath than the unknown. He slung his rifle and said, 'Come on, let's get on with it. In another couple of hours it'll be dark.'

One hour later they started to make their way cautiously through the hamlet of Nikolaev. Old hares that the three of them were they hugged the walls of the little whitewashed *isbas*, strung out in single file with ten metres between each of them, pelting all out across gaps, with Teitze, his rifle unslung and the safety off bringing up the rear as their 'tail-end Charlie'. But fortunately their caution was not needed. The little village was completely deserted and when finally Karl kicked in the door of the hovel at the far end of the place and peered inside, he could see the dust lying on the green-tiled stove was millimetres thick. The place hadn't been lived in for weeks, perhaps months. Karl relaxed and waited till Corporal Teitze caught up with him.

'Well?' Teitze demanded.

'Empty, Corp,' Karl answered. 'Often like this in Popovland. Don't know how they do it, but the peasants often seem to get wind of an offensive or a battle to come long before the brass does – and they take off.' He shrugged. 'Into the hills, the forests, anywhere. They just disappear into thin air.'

'Does that mean there's gonna be trouble here?' Teitze asked apprehensively.

'It could,' Karl said thoughtfully. 'All things mean trouble in this accursed country. But again it might mean that the trouble's been and passed. Now, Corp, what we gonna do? Are you in favour of staying here for the night or pushing on and trying to find if that bridge – if it really exists – is still standing and then coming back here?' He looked at the darkening sky. 'Once it gets dark, it's gonna be colder than a witch's tit out in the open. We've got to get under cover soon.'

Teitze carefully excised a dewdrop from the end of his nose and considered, while Ami stamped his feet with the cold and Polack poked around in the empty *isba*, appearing finally with a dusty flitch of bacon to announce proudly, 'The Popovs must have done a bunk in a hurry. Not like them chow-hounds to leave no meat behind like this.' He blew off the dust, then taking out his bayonet, cut off a slice. 'Not bad,' was his verdict a moment later. 'Not bad at all, though it could have been smoked a bit longer.'

'Here, you greedy sod,' Ami protested, as Polack chewed

hard, the juice and saliva running down his unshaven chin, 'don't scoff the frigging lot. Think of your mates.'

'What mates –?'

'*Schnauze!*' the NCO cut in decisively. 'Hold yer piss. Let's go on. I don't like this place.' He shivered dramatically and stared apprehensively as the dark shadows began to run down the tiny village street. 'Anything could creep on yer here. Perhaps if there is a bridge we can find one of them bridge guard huts for the night.'

Karl nodded his agreement. He knew the places, a little concrete pillbox type of structure usually occupied by an armed guard to protect the bridge and also to check the identity documents of anyone crossing it. In the 'Workers and Peasants' Paradise' you couldn't even move from one village to another without a permit. Despite all the rules and regulations, Fascist Germany was liberty hall in comparison. 'You're right, Corp,' he said. 'One of those railway guard huts would be better . . . easier to defend, in case.'

'In case, what?' Teitze snapped, his face suddenly pale and apprehensive.

Karl shrugged. 'In case *nothing*. Shall we get on with it? The light's going fast.'

Half an hour later they broke out of the snow-heavy firs and there it was: a large double span steel-and-concrete construction, bearing both a road and at a higher level a railway line – completely deserted. As they crouched, peering through the grey gloom, they could see that even the guard shack was deserted and to judge from the absence of footprints on the snow-covered road, no one had been over it since the last snowfall.

'Whew!' Ami whistled softly through his front teeth as they surveyed it. 'I can't believe it. It's just like the village. Not a frigging soul – and the bridge is intact as well. Wonders will never cease.'

'Don't let's count our chickens,' Corporal Teitze said, 'let's check it out first.'

But the bridge at Nikolaev was deserted and intact. Karl clambered over the side while the others stood guard and inspected the usual detonator chamber beneath the first span. It, too, was empty of explosive and heavy with dust, as if no one had poked around in the place for years.

'Not a sausage,' Karl called as he clambered back over the balustrade. 'It looks as if the Popovs forgot they ever had the frigging place.'

But there young Karl was wrong. High above them in the range of low hills which fringed the western bank of the river, glass glistened momentarily in the last rays of the setting sun, as the watcher hastily lowered his binoculars. He had seen enough. Now it was time to leave and report his findings before the stupid Fritzes on the bridge spotted him and grew alarmed.

CHAPTER 5

'Have you ever thought, *Schwester* Klara, what you are going do after the war?' King Bull asked conversationally, as they strolled through the dusk towards his provisional cookhouse, where he had laid on what he called an 'intimate little supper' for the two of them: a mound of *sauerkraut*, well larded with two kilos of smoked *speck*,* plus another two kilos of excellent Thurginian *bockwurst*, which would be washed down with a small hogshead of good Munich beer.

'After final victory?' she mused. Tonight, as a concession to the romantic mood of the occasion, she had dispensed with her uniform cap and placed a crêpe-paper bandage red rose behind her right ear. (Usually they used the paper to tie up the mouths of the stiffs to prevent them falling open after death and looking stupid.) 'I have never given it much thought, Sergeant –'

'Call me *Egon*,' King Bull said softly and squeezed her arm in what he thought was a tender caress. In a normal woman the bone would have snapped clean through. *Schwester* Klara hardly felt it. She breathed, instead, 'How gentle you are with a weak woman – *Egon*! But why do you ask about after the war?'

King Bull drew a deep breath. 'Surely,' he commenced a little hesitantly, 'a fine German woman like you has given some thought to settling down? You know, meeting Mr Right, finding a home and then having . . .' He let his voice trail away before risking it '. . . having children?'

'Now that you ask, *Egon*, I suppose I have. One has one's duty to the Führer as a loyal German to further the future of our stock.'

* A kind of hard long-lasting bacon.

'Exactly,' Bulle agreed, though his mind was on other things than furthering the future of the stock. He calculated that being married to a woman like Klara could mean the tripling of his income after the war. Why, with someone like her running a base hospital and him in charge of the kitchens of the local barracks, the money would come rolling in. There was nothing easier than fiddling the kitchen returns of a hospital. Why should the greedy sick sods be allowed to lie in bed for days on end, feeding their guts? 'Ever since I met you, dearest Klara, the thoughts of such things have been running through my head.'

'Why, Egon,' she gave him a playful push and he slammed against the nearest wall, the breath knocked out of him, 'I know you men, you'll promise anything as long as you can get your way with us weak women.'

'No . . . no,' he gasped, 'I'm not like that, Klara.' He fought to get his breath back, telling himself the old bag had certainly broken at least half a dozen of his ribs on the right side. Wait till he got her into the hay! He'd rattle her frigging ribs.

'Well,' she said, a little appeased, 'you must remember, Egon, I'm not one of those fast women you soldiers run after. You know? All war paint, cigarettes, black silk stockings and' – she blushed and lowered her gaze demurely – 'frilly underthings.'

King Bull thought of her enormous bloomers on the washing line and shuddered at the memory. 'Christ,' he told himself, 'the things I do to get a bit ahead!' Aloud he said, 'That is exactly why I like *you*, Klara. You don't go in for that kind of silly stuff. You're solid, very solid.' *'Yer, like a brick shit-house is solid!'* A little voice at the back of his head snapped cynically. 'You know what the Führer says?' he went on. 'A German woman neither smokes nor uses make-up on herself.'

'Yes,' she agreed happily. 'I know what you mean, Egon.' She threw out her magnificent bosom. He retreated hastily, but she held onto his hand like a vice. 'We women must keep our bodies pure and healthy so that we can give our beloved Führer his next generation of soldiers.'

'My sentiments exactly, Klara,' he agreed, keeping a watchful look on her breastwork. He squeezed her big paw and hoped she wouldn't respond; she'd crush all his frigging fingers to a pulp. 'A real man doesn't want one of those fly-by-night types of women. He wants someone who has been tried by war . . . who is solid.' '*Solid!*' the little voice inside his head exclaimed, '*Christ, she's made of heavy metal all the frigging way through!*'

'Do you . . . you really mean that, Egon?' she breathed.

He nodded solemnly, deciding he'd better not say more. A bit of the old two-backed beast on the bed and a taste of his salami and that'd be it. He'd have her eating out of his hand. '*And something else, too, you filthy swine,*' the little voice hinted darkly. He smiled to himself at the thought.

'I know little of these things, Egon,' she simpered coyly, fluttering her eyelashes like miniature Indian punkahs being worked flat out by the punkah-wallah. 'Love and, er, everything. You must teach me, Egon, be patient with me. But I promise, my darling, I will honestly try.' She attempted to crush him to her massive bosom in an excess of emotion, but he dodged her grasp neatly and indicated the *isba*. 'Here we are, Klara, let's have a bit of supper first.'

He opened the door, thrust her through, aimed a kick at the cook who had prepared the steaming mound of *sauerkraut*, which, heavy with steaming meat and sausage, rose from the serving plate like a mini Mount Everest, whispering out of the side of his mouth as he did so, 'Fuck off, fart-face, and keep an eye open so that me and *Schwester* Klara are not disturbed. We're discussing business, get it.'

'Got it, *Oberfeld*.' The little runt actually dared wink as he hurried out of the hut.

But King Bull was in a good mood. He let it pass. Instead, as *Schwester* Klara settled her huge bulk on the wooden bench, which groaned and creaked under the sudden weight like a sailing ship in the midst of a typhoon, he looked out into the evening gloom and happily gave the sign of the cross. It was as if the Pope were blessing the multitude from his balcony in Rome. 'The Good Lord be with thee, my beloved children,' he intoned softly to the darkening sky. 'May He, in all His goodness, make thine loins fruitful and thine vessels overflow with goodness.'

Chortling hugely to himself, the coast clear at last, he ducked and entered the *isba*, already fumbling with his flies. Unfortunately for him, however, King Bull's 'vessels' were not fated to 'overflow with goodness' this particular night . . .

A hundred metres away, in the pleasant fug of his motorized caravan, Creeping Jesus prepared to settle down for a restful evening before enjoying a good night's sleep. His thoughts were not in the least carnal. He did not believe in such piggeries save when on leave in Berlin, where twice a year he visited a high-class officers' brothel to be 'relieved of the tension', as he phrased it, by discreet middle-aged ladies who addressed him by rank and accepted the fruits of his loins in respectful Prussian silence.

No, the adjutant was concerned more with the prospect of saving his skin. For most of the afternoon he had had listeners out to the front of the convoy listening attentively for any sound of firing from the direction in which Corporal Teitze's patrol had gone; anything that would indicate they had run into trouble. But they had reported all quiet. There had not even been the sighting of a single flare. It was almost as if the war had gone to sleep.

Now more confident than he had been for a long time, Creeping Jesus made his plans for the future. He could see there would be no chance of promotion in the Fourth Grenadiers until that old fart Colonel von Heinersdorff finally bit the dust. Besides, service in a front-line infantry regiment in Russia, even on the staff, was becoming decidedly dangerous. What he needed was a rapid promotion to the rank of major which would give him the opportunity of transferring from the adjutant's position to the staff, preferably at corps or even army where he would be well away from the firing line. If he successfully did manage to get the wounded back to their own lines, it could well mean a decoration and that promotion which was the key to everything.

Creeping Jesus adjusted the monocle he affected more firmly in his right eye and glowered at the portrait of the Führer that adorned the wall of the caravan. It was all his fault. If he hadn't declared war on this damned Russia, he and the Fourth Grenadiers would have still been in Occupied France, living in luxury. But still, he consoled himself, war meant death – as long as it wasn't his – and death meant promotion; and he would dearly love to retire as a general.

For a little while, delicately sipping the last of the French cognac he had brought with him by the crate the previous June, he basked in the thought: a retired general, married to the daughter of some wealthy landowner in his native East Prussia – naturally not too demanding in bed, but who had sufficient money to allow him to indulge in the hunting of wild pig, the shooting of grouse in season, great festive St Hubertus* hunts, and all the rest of that joyous slaughter which made up the life of a wealthy country gentleman. He sighed and drained the last of the golden-brown liquid with an air of finality.

'How curious,' he said half-aloud, addressing the Führer, who glowered back at the monocled captain, as if he had little time for such upper-class foolishness, 'that the events of the next forty-eight hours might well decide the whole course of my future life . . . until my death.'

He shuddered slightly at the mention of the word 'death'. It was not a word he liked to hear, especially in reference to himself.

---

* The patron saint of the hunters of deer.

Abruptly his rosy train of thought was disturbed by an urgent hammering on the door. 'Sir, sir,' a voice gasped. 'A signal for you.'

Hurriedly Creeping Jesus tossed the empty bottle of cognac on his bunk and covered it with a monogrammed pillow – one had to keep up standards even in Russia. 'One moment,' he called, pulling on his boots and at the same time checking that the bottle was really covered by the pillow. It didn't do to let the other ranks see that an officer drank; there was always talk.

He opened the door and peered out into the darkness. 'What is it, man?' he demanded of the flustered radioman. 'Where's the fire, pray?'

'A signal . . . just come in from Corporal Teitze –'

'Teitze?'

'Yes, sir. Very faint but I did my best. Didn't get all of it. There seemed to be some kind of jamming –'

'Give it here.' Creeping Jesus snatched it from the signaller's hand and turning towards the light let his gaze fly across the pencilled message, his heart leaping with excitement and relief as he did so. *'Bridge intact,'* he read. *'No sign of enemy . . . Am remaining here on guard with patrol . . . What are orders? . . . Urgent there are . . .'*

'Message went dead at that point, sir,' the signaller said apologetically, as he judged the adjutant had come to the end of the signal. 'Tried to raise Corporal Teitze for ten more minutes, then I judged it was time to come and bring you –'

'Yes, yes,' Creeping Jesus cut him short hastily. God, how these other ranks did waffle! Lack of education, he supposed. They could never express themselves succinctly. 'Sound the alarm,' he ordered. 'Everyone to stand to at once. The women will have to prepare the wounded for an immediate move –'

'An immediate move, sir?'

Creeping Jesus's brain raced electrically. Why risk a daylight move at this stage of the game. Get the lot of them to the bridge and over it by first light, then they were virtually home and dry. He could already see those new major's stars in his mind's eye. 'Yes, an immediate move!' he snapped. 'Now just don't stand there, man. And get *Oberfeldwebel* Bulle round here – *at the double*! Now trot off, man!'

Obediently the signaller 'trotted off' into the darkness, as to the west the first urgent flares commenced sailing into the night sky. In his haste, the adjutant, his head full of silent tunes of glory, missed them altogether. It was going to be an unfortunate oversight.

Some twenty kilometres away another officer with dreams of glory was also receiving an urgent message from the German side of the river. This time it came in morse and he slapped his knout impatiently against the side of his riding boot, Cossack cap tilted to one side of his shaven skull, as he waited for the operator to decipher the morse in the overhot, stinking *isba*.

Colonel Bogdan, the commander of the First Cossack Cavalry Division, was a huge man, who looked even bigger in his fur-trimmed Cossack coat, the cartridge cases bulging at each breast, the inevitable curved silver dagger tucked in his belt. For nearly a quarter of a century, ever since the Revolution, he had been trying to make his way in a Red Army prejudiced against the Cossacks, the *Stavka** still regarding them as the former reactionary police force of the old deposed Imperial Monarchy. How he ever made colonel was sometimes beyond him. It had taken four wounds, three decorations for bravery and the dead of many thousands of his brave fellow Cossacks before those in Moscow had finally given him his rank and his command. Now he would show them just what the Cossacks were made of.

Nervously he fingered the bag of his native earth from the banks of the River Don he wore around his neck just below

* Soviet High Command.

the massive scar that ran right from his temple. Like all Cossacks he wanted to be buried in his native soil. So, if they couldn't take his body to the Don, then at least they could throw a symbolic handful of Don earth into his grave.

He grinned at the thought, nervousness forgotten for a moment, dark eyes set in a tough face that had seen much war, many women and a great deal of 'little water.'* Damnit, why think of death, he told himself. He wasn't about to die on the morrow. Instead think of the glory to come and what it would bring with it, promotion, women and even more pepper-flavoured vodka.

At last the operator was ready. He pushed back the earphones, leaving an ugly, red mark on both sides of his head. 'They are beginning to move out, Comrade Colonel, he said urgently. 'Our man there reports activity everywhere. They are not taking the most elementary blackout precautions. There are lights blazing everywhere.'

Bogdan laughed deep down inside his huge scarred body and slapped his knout against his boot happily. 'Ah, so the Fritzes think they are going to have it easy, eh?' He spat on the floor and snapped, 'All right, signal the engineers to commence moving in. Another signal to the Air Corps. Respectfully request the Red Air Fleet provide Stormovik squadrons for low-level bombing attacks at' – he pulled the great fat old-fashioned silver watch which had been his father's, the *hetman*'s,† before the Reds had executed him – 'zero ten hundred hours. The light should be good enough for even those pansy fly-boys by then. And tell them the Fritzes don't have any flak. I don't want them wetting their knickers already.' He took out one of his long, cardboard-tipped *pappyrokis*, lit it with a flourish and stuck it in the corner of his broad, sensual mouth in true Cossack style. 'That's all. *Horoscho!*'

* i.e. vodka.
† Headman.

The operator sprang to attention as Bogdan went out into the night with a swagger. The orderly was already there, holding Sasha, his great white stallion, scarred by bullet-holes just like its master. He sprang effortlessly into the saddle and cantered to where the Division waited: rank upon rank of silent horsemen, the only sound the snort of impatient horses and the clatter of silver bits.

'Cossacks!' he cried, as the horses tossed their heads and shivered in long grey plumes of frozen breath in the icy cold. 'Cossacks, tomorrow we attack the Fritzes. They know not that we come. We will attack and wipe the Fascist scum off the face of the earth.'

His Cossacks remained silent, but one of the *Politruks* cheered at the mention of the 'Fascist scum'. Such things, Bogdan knew, pleased them. His Cossacks were interested in other matters. 'We have borne a heavy cross in the past, Cossacks. Our customs, our way of life, our loyalty to our homeland, have often been misunderstood. On the morrow we must prove ourselves.'

He looked along the silent ranks in the purple gloom and although he could not see their faces he sensed they understood well enough. Suddenly carried away by the crazy Cossack lust for battle and violent, sudden death, he unsheathed his dagger with a flourish and cried, '*Vperjodi ze osvobashdenije rodim!*'* at the top of his voice, standing high and proud in his silver stirrups.

'*Forward to the freedom of the Homeland!*' The great cry was taken up by thousands of hoarse throats, as the *Sotniks* started to bellow the order to advance.

On the other side of the river Karl stirred uneasily in his sleep in the freezing concrete hut and then fell into a troubled slumber . . .

* Forward to the freedom of the Homeland.

CHAPTER 6

'Heaven, arse and cloudburst!' King Bull moaned, as the slow column of the Goulash Cannon Company wound its way across the freezing steppe into the dawn. 'You've never seen a pair of drawers like that in yer whole frigging life before, Adolf. Worse than the frigging Siegfried Line.'

The other sergeant sitting on the cab next to him, both of them wrapped in sacks and extra blankets to keep out the freezing cold, nodded wearily, as the old nag pulling the cart plodded on stolidly.

'*Grosse Kacke am Christbaum!* Did I have to work at them before I could get them off. Buttons and bows and frigging loops and her wriggling inside of them like the bleeding virgin queen, saying all the time' – he imitated what he thought was a girlish falsetto – ' "And you will be gentle with me, Egon. You will be gentle. I've never done it before." ' He spat sourly at the nag's skinny buttocks and the spittle frizzled and spluttered in the cold. 'I was scared stiff she'd land me one. She'd have knocked me arse over bollocks if she had.'

'Did yer dip it in?' the other sergeant asked, bored and still tired from the long night's trek. 'I ain't dipped my wick for months now. But go on, she *did* spread her pearly gates, didn't she, *Oberfeld?*'

'Of course she did – well, almost,' King Bull answered in sudden irritation. 'I got the drawers off'n her, natch, and I'd just got the old salami in position for a nice hot mattress polka when that arse-with-ears, the adjutant, blew the whistle on us. Christ on a crutch, I ask you, Adolf, ain't there no justice in the world?'

Adolf tugged the end of his nose, as the column slowly started to come to a halt above the slope which ran down to the river and the bridge. 'Tough shit, really tough shit. But in a few days, with a bit of luck, we'll be behind the lines, living it up in the knocking shops. Now there you really can . . .'

But King Bull was no longer listening. Instead he was staring at the banks of the river, which meandered along like a dull-silver snake. Below, illuminated by the bonfires that the wounded and their attendants had started already in order to cook their meagre breakfasts, there were hundreds of wounded, most on foot, but others lying in their carts or on their litters towed by bent old nags, and all packed together so tightly that the steppe was no longer visible.

It was a perfect target for the Red Air Force, King Bull told himself, and one that they couldn't miss. There'd be mass slaughter if the Russians spotted the packed wounded the way they were now. And all the lazy shits seemed to think about was lying there and cooking their frigging breakfasts.

King Bull was little concerned with the fate of the wounded, but he was concerned that this perfect target might attract the Stormoviks and their bombs. Not only would the wounded go for the chop, but the bridge would as well, he knew that, and he was determined to be one of those who crossed it and enjoyed whatever goodies there were to be had once they had reached their own lines.

He gave the reins to his neighbour. 'Here, Adolf,' he snapped, very business-like now, his misfortune with Klara forgotten, 'keep the Company together and don't let them pearl-divers and hash-slingers stop. Keep 'em going right to the bridge.' With that he sprang from the cart and started to push his way through the happy mob.

'But where you going, *Oberfeld*?' Adolf cried after him.

'To see a frigging man about a frigging dog,' was all the answer he received, as King Bull disappeared into the throng, heading for where he had seen the pennant of Creeping Jesus's mobile caravan.

An angry King Bull found Creeping Jesus parked with his caravan some fifty metres from the entrance to the bridge, not far from *Schwester* Klara's convoy, which was packed tightly together, as the lightly wounded hobbled about bearing hunks of black bread and mugs of 'nigger sweat'. He was sitting calmly on the steps of the vehicle, drinking coffee too, but out of a china cup naturally, and occasionally staring down at the map spread across his knees. For all the world he looked like some country landowner enjoying the first air of the day before strolling off leisurely onto his estate to kill something.

King Bull was even more enraged when he saw him and said cheerfully, 'Oh hello, Bulle. Fancy some nigger sweat? My chap can get you a cup –'

'Stick your nigger sweat!' King Bull cried.

'I say,' Creeping Jesus began, but again King Bull cut him short. 'What in three devils' name are you fart-arsing about on this side of the river for?' he demanded, fists clenched, face brick-red, towering above the alarmed officer.

Creeping Jesus could see that this was no time to attempt to pull rank on the giant NCO, so he explained tamely, 'I thought it best to do two things before we started crossing.' He ticked off the points methodically on his grey-gloved hand. 'A, the order of the convoys to cross – slow first and fast second. B, work out the route after we have crossed the bridge so that –'

'Sit on that, you silly fart!' King Bull raised his own massive middle finger and poked it upwards threateningly. 'While you're *planning*, the piss-arsed Popovs are probably already getting ready to knock the shit outa us!'

Creeping Jesus looked alarmed. The hand holding the cup shook dramatically. 'But there are just no signs of the Reds.'

'They'll be attracted to this lot, like frigging bees to frigging honey.' King Bull yelled, besides himself with rage. 'This is no time to sit on our arses and play with ourselves!'

'What am I to do?' the officer asked miserably.

'Get this lot moving – *now*! Put the Goulash Cannon Company across, with *me* in charge,' he smote his massive chest, 'and then let's get this mess of carts and things dispersed – *and moving, too!*'

'Oh, my God!' Creeping Jesus exclaimed and upset his cup of coffee. 'Do you really think it's that bad, Bulle?'

'I'm thinking nothing,' Bulle snarled. 'I'm just guessing. And I want to be around for a long time to go on guessing. Now, do we move?'

'We move!'

'Right.' Bulle aimed a kick at the nearest fire, letting off steam. The canteen boiling on a stick above the fire went flying and a wan man, with one arm missing, cried something. As King Bull rushed by, he cried, 'Hold yer frigging water, cripple! Or I'll rip off yer other frigging flipper and stick it right up yer dirty arse!' And with that he was gone, running heavily across the snow towards the little concrete hut on the bridge.

Slowly, ponderously, the first convoy of seriously wounded men started to creak across the bridge, bearing its cargo of human misery. The drivers felt no sense of urgency. To their front the steppe was empty and it was too early. They were not really awake. They thought this sudden move was just another move in that eternal army game of 'hurry up and wait'.

To their front, King Bulle spread out the Goulash Cannon Gompany in a rough-and-ready perimeter, though he had not ordered his men to attempt to dig in. As soon as the first lot of cripples were across, he told himself, they'd be on their way. He was not going to stay near that frigging bridge a moment longer than necessary. Anxiously he stared across the white waste to the hills beyond. But all was silence. There was not the slightest movement. It seemed as if the war had gone to sleep at this remote place. Yet the nagging doubt still plagued him. *Why had the Popovs left the bridge at Nikolaev intact?*

Like noiseless white ghosts in their snow suits, the Russian engineers stole in single file along the frozen bank of the river, hugging the dawn shadows. Above them on the bridge they could hear the rusty creak of the carts and the rattle of their wheels, intermingled with muted snatches of conversation and the occasional moan as a cart struck a pothole.

The leader paused. The men behind him, each one laden with a box of explosive or detonators, stopped automatically. They needed no order to do so. They were the cream of the elite, each man an NCO and member of a Guards Engineer company. The leader flashed a glance to left and right. On the far bank the Fascists milled around, stamping out their fires, hitching up their horses, swallowing a last hasty bite of food. But none of them were looking *down* into the river. Their gazes were fixed exclusively *upwards* at the bridge.

'*Horoscho*,' he grunted to himself satisfied. He held up three fingers. The next three men behind him rushed forward, boxes bouncing on their white backs. Without hesitation, they took hold of the first white-gleaming girder and started to climb like monkeys, each carrying their freight of death.

The leader allowed himself a quick grin. The Fascists, he told himself, were going to get a nasty pain in the arse soon, very soon . . .

Two kilometres away, equally well hidden, Colonel Bogdan and his *Sotniks* crouched in the snow, their mounts tethered in firs behind them, the orderlies holding their big hands over the horses' muzzles to stop them whinnying and giving their presence away. Down below the bridge was packed, two lanes of horse-drawn traffic running its whole length, while on the other bank the vehicles were eight abreast.

'A perfect target, Comrade Colonel,' the senior *Sotnik* said, lowering his binoculars. 'The Fritzes are packed like sardines.'

'Agreed, Alexei,' Bogdan said, doing the same. He rolled over in the snow and stared at the sky. It still was not clear enough for the dive-bombers. 'But I want a goodly number of the bastards to come across before we strike. You see,' he went on before anyone could interrupt his train of thought, 'let the

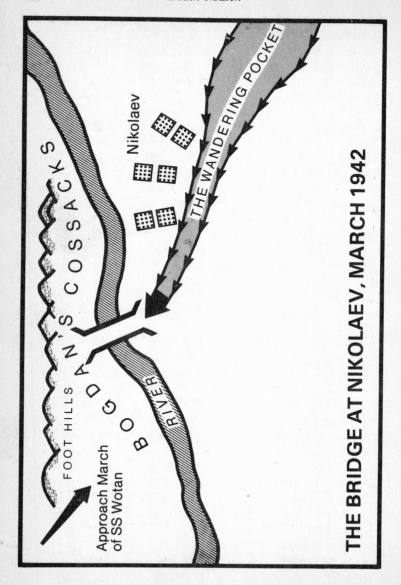

THE BRIDGE AT NIKOLAEV, MARCH 1942

THE WANDERING POCKET

Nikolaev

COSSACKS

BOGDAN'S

FOOT HILLS

RIVER

Approach March
of SS Wotan

Fritzes get three or four hundred across before we blow the bridge and attack and we have them committed.'

'You mean, Comrade Colonel,' another of the *Sotniks* said, 'that the mass of the Fritzes will be committed to attempting to rescuing the ones on our side of the river?'

'Exactly. Like when a monkey puts his paw in a jar to grab an attractive titbit and is trapped, not knowing that by letting go of the nut he can free himself, I hope the Fritzes will not let go. They'll mass and try to help their comrades so that we can slaughter them systematically.' Bogdan's grin was cruel, tough, dare-devil. Instinctively he felt for the little leather sack of holy soil hanging around his neck. 'You are all young men,' he added, 'but you know, whatever your political views, just how much our people have suffered since the Revolution?'

There was a muttered '*da*' from his listeners and their young faces grew suddenly sombre and thoughtful. Most of them had lost close relatives in the purges inflicted on the Cossacks in the twenties and thirties.

'We are not just tackling a German division here,' Bogdan lectured his young officers, 'we are proving something. We are proving the loyalty of the Cossack nation. Old Leather Face' – even such a fearless man as Colonel Bogdan dare not use the name of the Soviet dictator publicly, but preferred the Army nickname for their swarthy, pock-marked tyrant – 'has granted us the honour of being a guards cossack division. But he still does not trust his Cossacks altogether. We bought that last honour in our blood, many hundreds of us dying to achieve it. Now we will buy his total confidence in the Cossacks with our native cunning.' He flashed a glance at one of the five wrist-watches which adorned his brawny arm, all looted from dead Fritzes. 'In thirty minutes we commence, as soon as there are enough of them across. Then, comrades, the slaughter of their wounded commences. Once that is done, we wipe out the Iron Division.'

CHAPTER 7

It was nine in the morning.

At the bridge the massed carts, pulled by the tired nags, urged on by angry, sweating drivers cracking their whips, still jammed the structure from end to end. To the front of the Goulash Cannon Company, spread out in a thin line, there was an uneasy stillness that was a premonition of impending danger. Karl, crouched close to Ami and Polack, felt the need for their closeness, in the tense atmosphere. To another eye, the snow-heavy plain, fringed by the hills beyond, sparkling in the thin hard line of a March morning sun, might have seemed beautiful. But not to Karl. The danger was too tangible.

King Bull came stamping up through the snow, twin jets of grey smoke erupting regularly from his flared nostrils. 'Keep yer eyes peeled, you piss-pansies,' he growled, body hung with pouches of extra ammunition clips, two grenades thrust down the sides of his boots. 'And as soon as I give the word to get moving, move!'

Karl eyed the head cook coldly. They had had many run-ins in the past; he was not frightened of King Bull. 'Pissing yer pants, *Oberfeld*?' he enquired cheekily. 'Why all the hardware?'

Hastily Ami intervened with, 'Do you think there's gonna be trouble, *Oberfeld*?'

'The only trouble is gonna be the tip of my dice-beaker up your fat arses if you keep on being cheeky. Risking a fat lip like that! What do you think them things is?' he demanded pointing a gloved hand at the stars on his shoulders. '*Frigging silver shiteballs?*'

A sudden rumbling, low, eerie, menacing, cut into his angry retort. He swung round immediately, brick-red face puzzled. 'What's that?'

'One of them nags farting,' Ami suggested brightly, but

Karl held up his hand for silence, cocking his head to one side urgently, as the rumbling continued, growing louder and more threatening by the instant.

Down at the bridge, a series of angry blue and red sparks was running the length of the steel structure, giving off strange little popping noises like wire being short-circuited. Here and there, too, small puffs of bright white smoke were erupting from the supporting pillars.

King Bull's mouth opened stupidly. He tried to speak but no sound came. A hundred metres away, Creeping Jesus clapped his hand to his forehead and swayed abruptly, as if about to faint.

'It's the bridge!' Polack blurted. 'They' – and everyone knew who 'they' were – 'have done something to the bridge. Oh, my God . . .'

The whole structure was beginning to swing alarmingly, the noise added to by the screams of the wounded, the furious, suddenly panicked whinnying of the nags. From below, as the smoke clouds rose ever more furiously, the bridge had begun to groan and grind. An awesome frightening rending sound began.

A taut girder snapped. Another fell simply from its support and smashed down into the packed, terrified mob below. '*Save yerself! Everyone save yerself, mates!*' the cry went up. Here and there drivers abandoned their carts and raced first to the left and then to the right, as the bridge swayed and trembled violently. A soldier dived over the side to slap into the ice below and crack it into a glittering silver star. He lay moaning in a crumpled heap.

'What are we gonna do, Karl?' Ami cried wildly, eyes wide and staring with terror.

Karl didn't answer. He couldn't. Like the rest he was mesmerized by the awesome sight, as the bridge, shrouded in dust and smoke in part, oscillated back and forth, terrified drivers clinging to the stanchions for dear life, wondering if they dare jump; while the wounded, screaming and frightened beyond all measure attempted to crawl, dragging their blood-stained bandages behind them, up the steep slope which one end of the dying bridge had now become.

A tremendous crack. A loud hollow boom. The supporting girders gave like clipped wire. They scythed through the air, shearing off heads, limbs, dissecting bodies as they went, the metal a sudden bright crimson. A centre pillar began to crumple, the bricks and mortar raining down at an ever-increasing speed.

'Run for it . . . for chrissake *run for it!*' the cries rose on all sides, as the hysterically whinnying horses rose high in the traces, hooves flailing, trying to break the shafts that held them before it was too late. '*COME ON, COMRADES . . . R-U-N F-O-R I-T!*'

There was a sound like a sudden roll of thunder. The bridge trembled like jelly. The men on it clung onto any support they could desperately. Those who hadn't any were flung from side to side, rolling across the track helplessly. Above them the railway line snapped, shot upwards like a snapped matchstick. The noise grew louder and louder, reaching an ear-splitting banshee-howl.

Startlingly the explosion burst forth. A great mess of earth, steel and masonry erupted in the centre of the bridge, followed an instant later by a giant ball of fire, from which a mushroom of dark smoke sailed upwards. With absolute, total finality, the middle span rose, then started to tumble to the ice below, bearing a cargo of screaming soldiers and wounded, splattering them on the ice, plunging them deep into the freezing water as the ice cracked and broke in a dozen places.

Karl stared aghast at the terrible scene of death and destruction. The drum roll seemed to go on and on forever, circling the surrounding hills before being thrown back onto the plain again; and the blast slapped his ashen face, making him gasp for air and blink his eyelids rapidly to clear his vision.

When it did, he saw that the middle span of the bridge, now a crazy mess of shattered masonry, tangled and grotesquely twisted girders, was hanging right down to the water, in which men floated silently or splashed frantically, trying to escape to the opposite bank before the icy water drove all feeling from their limbs and they went under for good.

Karl shook himself. 'We've got to do something,' he cried. 'Come on, *los*.' He didn't wait for King Bull or anyone else to give orders. 'Let's go, comrades!' Slinging his rifle, he pelted through the ankle-deep snow, ears already unconsciously taking in the drone of aircraft engines.

The gull-winged Stormoviks, a whole squadron of them, came hurtling down on an invisible slide, plane after plane dropping out of the winter sky at 400 kilometres an hour. The survivors of the bridge disaster flung themselves flat, trying to bury themselves in the frozen earth in a desperate search for cover.

There was none. Time and time again the ugly little anti-personnel bombs came fluttering down from their fish-grey bellies to explode with devasting effect on the crowded steppe below. They couldn't miss. In a flash the steppe was littered with dead and dying wounded, the little carts bearing the wounded being blown apart like matchwood, scattering their cargoes of bandaged, screaming men into the snow, bodies spouting blood from fresh wounds.

Their bombs gone, the bombers soared high into the hard blue morning sky and here and there survivors, shocked and ashen-faced, clambered to their knees, hoping against hope that they had gone for good. But they hadn't. The target was too tempting. All of them, the pilots in red-brown leather jackets, heads burdened by heavy flying helmets made of leather too, knew there would be a week's leave in Moscow for this. There'd be women and vodka and the finest food. The *Stavka* always kept its promises to the 'fly-boys'. They were Stalin's favourite soldiers. They were going to make a thorough job of it. Besides there was no danger. The Fascists had no flak guns.

Once more, spread out low across the steppe in a single line, they came shrieking in, flame rippling the length of their wings as they opened up with their banked machine-guns. Tracer zipped towards those who were foolish enough to get up and make a run for it. The others simply lay and accepted their fate, the slugs ripping their bodies into bloody shreds, the snow all about them staining a bright red.

Then they were gone, flying low towards the east, wiggling their wings, jigging in and out of formation as the Russians always did, as if the pilots were already drunk, leaving behind the bloody carnage.

But the ordeal of the wounded was not over yet – not by a long way. As Karl and his two comrades poked their heads above the edge of a still smoking bomb crater, hardly daring to believe they had survived that maelstrom of steel, a sight met them that most West Europeans would have thought belonged back in the nineteenth century.

Stretched right along the horizon to their front, black against the white mantle of snow, was a long line of horsemen, perfectly still, clearly outlined, making no attempt at cover. It was Bogdan's Cossacks, waiting for the order to attack.

Colonel Bogdan took his time as he trotted the length of his front rank, saluting the Red Flag casually but whipping up a tremendous salute at the old black flag of the Cossack horde. Behind rode the black-clad *Popo*, armed with sabre like the rest, blessing the men. They hastily whipped off their black fur caps for a moment and whispered a hurried prayer to a God forbidden to them these twenty-odd years or more.

Watching, Polack said in a hushed awed voice, 'My God, they're holding a parade!'

But the other two, their faces blackened and smeared with fresh brown earth, didn't hear. They were too intrigued by what was taking place in front of them; they didn't seem to hear. It was as if they didn't realize their imminent danger.

Bogdan reined his white stallion and raised his gleaming sabre in salute to his Cossacks. He jerked his mount round and trotted to the centre of the first rank, between the flags, sabre raised once more. 'Cossacks!' he cried, drawing out the syllables, 'Cossacks will . . . advance . . . *at the walk*!'

As one the massed ranks started to move forward with no sound other than that of the jingle of harness and the soft crunch of many thousands of hooves on the snow.

The Three Rebels were transfixed by this amazing sight. All around them, save for the wounded who moaned and tossed in their agony, nothing stirred either. Even Creeping Jesus, abject coward that he was, remained motionless, gaze fixed on the advancing riders.

Bogdan took his sabre from his right shoulder once more and raising it, cried, 'Cossacks . . . Cossacks will trot. *Trot!*'

Abruptly the crunch-crunch on the snow changed to a steady thunder, as the pace of the horses quickened, those in the front rank tossing and bending their heads, beginning to be touched by the excitement of the whole thing.

Bogdan in front slackened the bit of the stallion, feeling that old, old thrill of good horseflesh between his thighs and a strong sabre in his right fist. They could keep their tanks and airplanes, he told himself, the excitement within him mounting by the instant. What greater sensation was there than this – a good horse carrying a good man into battle!

The state of mesmerized wonder of the watchers started to vanish to be replaced by dread, fear, even unreasoning terror. Those of the wounded who could do so began to crawl and hop back towards the shattered bridge, dragging their blood-stained bandages after them in the snow. *Schwester* Klara, resolute and unafraid, clapped her big hands to her massive hips, standing upright and completely exposed. 'You orderlies,' she bellowed above the rising thunder, 'get those carts back to the river! Move it now. For God's sake, get them back. *Schnell*!'

For his part Creeping Jesus was petrified with fear. Turning a trembling ashen face to King Bull, who, like *Schwester* Klara, stood bolt upright observing this tremendous spectacle, he quavered, '*Oberfeld*, what – what are we going to do?'

King Bull didn't reply. He didn't know. The only way to escape was across what was left of the bridge lying in the water, an escape route already packed with hundreds of terrified men, sick and hearty, tearing and scraping at each other in their fear. Otherwise there was the river itself. But how long could a man survive in its bone-chilling waters?

'*Bulle!*' Creeping Jesus shrieked hysterically, clawing at the big noncom. '*What are we going to do?*' Huge tears of fear now coursed furiously down his cheeks. 'They're almost on top of us. For God's sake, tell me . . .'

Polack swallowed hard, eyes still fixed to his front, the gesture of a man making some overwhelming final decision, and raised his rifle.

Automatically, Karl and Ami did the same. What alternative did they have? There was no way back and certainly no way forward. As one they clicked off their safety catches and jerked back the bolts to check their magazines were full. As an afterthought Karl fumbled awkwardly in his ammunition pouch and placed the yellow, gleaming clips of bullets on the snow in front of them so that they could help themselves. The other two gave him a quick significant glance, but said nothing. Their hearts were too full.

The thunder grew louder. Now the observers could pick out individual riders in that packed mass quite clearly. They jogged up and down in unison, black woolly caps set rakishly at the side of their curled, pomaded hair, some of them smoking long Russian cigarettes in a dare-devil, casual manner; others chanting steadily, as if saying their prayers.

Down at the river incredible scenes were taking place, as mobile towers of black oily smoke rose from exploding gas tanks, riderless horses, some wounded, stampeded back and forth, their manes on fire; and everywhere the wreckage of men, horses and carts lay packed together in jumbled heaps, over which the panic-stricken survivors tried to escape. Others gasped and choked in the water, desperately trying to fight the cold current, as it scooped them up, ripping the ground away from their feet, the icy water stabbing at their lungs like a sharp knife.

'Cossacks!' Bogdan cried, raising himself in his stirrups, barrel chest thrown out proudly, everything forgotten now save that unbearable, almost sexual, excitement of the battle to come, 'will canter. *Canter!*'

Even before his command had died away, the horses jerked their heads furiously, some of them attempting to tear away from the control of the reins, almost as if they, too, were carried away by that same thrill. Furiously the young Cossack riders dug their silver spurs into their mounts' gleaming, glazed sides and fought for mastery, as the horses threatened to break into the gallop prematurely.

Karl raised his rifle and, peering along the barrel, took aim on one of the flag-bearers. Why he did not know, or care. He was quite calm and cool, for he had accepted his fate. There would be no escape from this.

Polack seemed to sense Karl's resignation, for without looking up as he too took aim, he said quietly, 'Good luck, comrades. There have been good times –' His voice broke, but the other two Rebels knew what he meant.

As the Cossacks came on like a wall of black and silver, a series of waves rippling across the snow of the steppe, King Bull woke from his bemused reverie. Flinging aside Creeping Jesus's importuning arm, face flushed a brick-red, consumed by a sudden burning rage, he cried, 'Stand to, you bunch of piss-pansies. *Stand frigging to!*' He brandished his machine pistol. 'I'll blast a hole big enough to run a tank through any shit who tries to take a powder! *Now stand to!*'

'But you're not going to attempt –' Creeping Jesus began, face green with fear, but King Bull was no longer listening.

Standing next to one of the carts, filled with dying men, watching the advancing Cossacks with almost clinical detachment, *Schwester* Klara nodded her approval and then, her face suddenly glowing with pride, she wrenched off one of the cart's shafts and measured it for size. It was big enough. She nodded again and then took up her position, great wooden shaft at the ready. The Cossacks wouldn't slaughter her charges without a fight, by God no!

Bogdan waved his sabre above his head, the blade gleaming a bright silver. 'The Guards Cossack Division,' he bellowed above the thunder of those massed hooves, 'the Guards Cossack Division will charge. *CHARGE!*'

'*URRAH!*' The Russian war-cry rose from thousands of hoarse throats, followed an instant by that great bass atavastic roar, '*FOR THE HOMELAND!*' drowned the next instant by a wild drum roll of racing, flying hooves.

'Here they come!' Karl said quite calmly. Almost casually, he started to take first pressure . . .

CHAPTER 8

'*Herr General*,' Colonel von Heinersdorff, commanding what was left of the Fourth Grenadiers, barked with unusual urgency, 'there has been an unmitigated disaster at the bridge near Nikolaev!'

General Sobel was of that school of generals, who affected the utmost calm even in the tightest of situations. As a young cadet at the Prussian military academy he had read how when one of the Duke of Wellington's officers had had his leg shot off at the Iron Duke's side during the Battle of Waterloo and had remarked, 'Damme, sir, I think the Frenchies have gorn and shot orf my leg,' the Duke had replied with equal aplomb, 'Damme, I do think you're right.' It was an anecdote that had firmed his own conception of how a commander should act in desperate circumstances. 'Disaster, *mein lieber Oberst*?' he echoed with a little quiet smile. 'Now then, sit down and tell me all about it.' It was as if he were humouring a slightly hysterical maiden aunt.

Von Heinersdorff frowned and swung his broken sabre in some agitation. 'I prefer to stand, *Herr General*,' he barked, though at that moment of crisis he would dearly have loved to sit down.

'Well, have a drink, man, then,' Sobel said and shoved the bottle of cognac across the kitchen table, the only furniture in the peasant cottage which was his 'headquarters'. Like most of his officers General Sobel was living off cognac and cigarettes.

Gratefully von Heinersdorff took the bottle and drunk straight from the neck. There was no time for the niceties of civilized behaviour. He felt the fiery liquid run down his throat and strike his empty stomach with a satisfying burning smack. He felt better immediately.

'Now then, von Heinersdorff, where's the fire?'

Hastily the CO of the Fourth Grenadiers told him how the bridge the advance party had found across the tributary of the Dnieper had been bombed and shattered and how now the wounded were stalled on both sides of the river. 'The message was garbled at the best. The Ivans were trying to jam it all the time, but that much got through before the beastly thing went dead on us.' Von Heinersdorff mopped his brow with a dirty silk handkerchief. The heat and the stench inside the hut were virtually unbearable. Already his lice were beginning to stir unpleasantly. God, when had he last been able to wash!

Sobel considered the information and then bent over his map. As he did so, von Heinersdorff shuddered. A grey felt louse was beginning to crawl from beneath the General's tight collar up the back of his cropped white hair. Outside the gunfire had commenced again. The Russians were attacking what was left of the Iron Division yet again.

Sobel swung the compass and hastily measured the distance between his division and the river. 'Two days' march at least,' he announced after a moment, 'even if the Ivans don't attack in strength as seems likely they will.'

'*Two days!*' von Heinersdorff echoed aghast. 'Impossible! It will mean the wounded will be wiped out if we cannot defend our side of the river. The Ivans will cross on the ice further up and come in from the flank. Or they'll simply pound the poor swine to pieces with their artillery.'

Sobel held up his hand for silence. 'My dear Colonel, you are jumping ahead of yourself. Please let us consider this matter calmly – *in aller Ruhe*.' He frowned at the map. Outside the whistles shrilled and a coarse voice cried, 'Come on, you shower o' shit, stand to! Stand to! The Popov pricks are coming again!' There was the irate chatter of a Russian machine-gun close by, followed an instant later by the high-pitched hysterical hiss of a German Spandau firing a thousand rounds a minute.

'I tried to raise the SS Corps at dawn, von Heinersdorff,'

the General continued after a moment, 'but like you my signallers experienced terrible jamming. We didn't get much through save that we need help urgently – and I'm sure *General*' – he hesitated over the rank, for like most of the *Wehrmacht's* general officers, he didn't think much of his SS confreres' abilities – 'Dietrich will do his best to help.'

'But what about the wounded, General?' von Heinersdorff cried urgently. 'We can't leave them to be slaughtered. They are defenceless up there at the river.'

Sobel frowned. 'It wasn't my plan to get bogged down in a major fight anywhere, von Heinersdorff. Once the Ivans have got us pinned down, they'll start building up at a tremendous rate. You know what they're like?'

'But we have to do *something, Herr General*?' von Heinersdorff persisted, virtually in tears now. 'The defenceless wounded deserve something better than to be slaughtered on their litters.'

Sobel shrugged with a faint sigh. 'All right, I'll disengage what's left of your Fourth and my own First Fusiliers, poor fellows, they're down to company strength, and *rush* – if that's the word – them to the bridge. In the meantime, my dear Colonel, there is nothing I can do to help the wounded.' His weary face cracked into a sad smile, verging a little on despair. 'Now all that remains is the old motto, which we both know only too well, "March or croak", "*March or croak*" . . .'

Numbly von Heinersdorff nodded, as the grey felt louse started to burrow in the General's white thatch. Outside it had begun to snow again . . .

Crouching low over the flying manes of their mounts, sabres held low and dangerous, points to the racing forelegs of their horses, the Cossacks came in in a solid black mass.

'*Fire!*' King Bull cried and fired a savage burst at them from his machine pistol.

Everywhere the ragged fire erupted, as the desperate men of the Goulash Cannon Company obeyed the order. Cossacks and horses went down everywhere, piling up in a confused mess of dying men, riderless mounts and wounded horses. Slugs hissed through the morning air like heavy tropical rain. Relentlessly the defenders poured it into them. Cossack after Cossack went down. Terrified riderless horses galloped off to the rear, plunging through the oncoming ranks, rearing and tossing, snorting with wide-nostriled, unreasoning fear.

For a moment the front rank, great gaps torn in the line, seemed to recoil and hesitate. But the pressure from behind was too great. They couldn't back off from the murderous fire. They came on again, carried forward by the mindless momentum of the wild charge. The whole front was filled with the savage, black-coated horsemen: a crazy panorama of screaming men, slashing silver sabres, galloping hooves, waving flags, as the defenders fought back knowing that there was only one way out for them now – kill or be killed.

A Cossack reared up directly in front of Karl. He tugged the bit back cruelly. The horse whinnied, red eyes crazy with pain, its forelegs clawing the air. The Cossack laughed and shouted something. He raised his sabre high above his fur-capped head. It gleamed in the thin sun. Next instant he would bring it down, cleaving Karl's head in two. The latter was quicker. He rolled to one side and shot from the hip as he did so. The Cossack's swarthy face was an instant red mess, as the shot slammed him right out of the saddle.

Another Cossack sprang like an acrobat from his dying mount as it sank to its knees, a great gaping scarlet wound on its left flank. He ran forward screaming obscenities. Polack fired. The Cossack stopped in mid-stride, a length of steaming grey-purple entrails slipping out of the sudden wound in his guts like a sinister snake. He staggered forward a few paces, dragging his intestines behind him in a bloody trail on the scuffed snow, then he pitched face-forward and died without a single moan.

The second rank of charging Cossacks wrenched desperately at their bits, the steel glistening in the white froth of the crazed animals. They slithered and skidded in the snow, right into the dead and dying men and mounts to their front. Riders were flung out of their saddles. Others went head first over the necks of their mounts. But in spite of their awesome casualties they still came on. Everywhere, the ranks of the Cossacks were breaking into little groups, seeking and slaughtering their prey in the wild blood-fever of combat.

They flung themselves on the Fritzes, fit and sick alike. They gave no quarter. All their Cossack pride found release in a wild savage orgy of slaughter. Sabres rose and fell, the blades gleaming with blood up to the hilts. They fought like a bunch of mad butchers and rode down those who attempted to escape, murdering the wounded as they lay strapped helplessly to the stretchers.

Alone, save for her wounded, *Schwester* Klara wielded her pole like a drill instructor in bayonet-fighting, parrying blow after blow, slamming unwary Cossacks from their saddles, not even feeling the sabre slashes which had turned her bare, brawny arms into a mass of oozing cuts.

But even *Schwester* Klara had to succumb in the end. One Cossack rode straight at her, thrashing his sabre from left to right, screaming at the top of his voice. She raised her pole, its length hacked and chipped. The Cossack laughed uproariously, as if he had been expecting it. Expertly he tossed the sabre from his right hand to his left. She reacted a moment too late. The terrible slash caught her right across her massive chest. The apron opened in a welter of red gore to reveal her mighty breasts, milky white and blue-veined but already flushing with blood, as they flopped down onto her stomach. She sank to her knees, suddenly nerveless.

'*Boshe moi!*' the Cossack who had felled her cried in amazement when he saw those enormous dugs flap down. In a bound he was down from his horse, fumbling with his flies. 'Woman!' he yelled in delight. '*Fritz woman, comrades!*'

'*FRITZ WOMAN!*' The cry was taken up by half a dozen throats. All around men started to drop from their mounts, the battle suddenly forgotten, as the first man flung himself on a dying Klara, who fought to the last, as she felt her drawers ripped cruelly from her loins and those greedy fingers penetrating her virginity at last . . .

Now there were few Germans left. Here and there the Cossacks still hacked at the already dead sprawled in their own blood on the stretchers. Half a dozen yelling and crying riders milled around an unfortunate cook as they forced him to his knees under their sadistic blows. Finally he fell under the flailing hooves of their excited horses and they rode away, whooping in triumph, to search for their next victim.

Creeping Jesus ran this way and that in mindless panic. Twice he was almost ridden down but saved at the last moment when the hunters changed direction, perhaps spotting an easier victim. Once a monster of a Cossack loomed out of the smoke of battle, sabre already raised. Jibbering, feeling himself evacuating his bowels with unreasoning fear, Creeping Jesus fell to his knees, raising his hands in the classic gesture of supplication. But the killing blow did not come. A shot rang out from somewhere. The Cossack flopped forward over the mane of his horse. The horse bolted and charged away, carrying its dead master with it. Creeping Jesus stumbled on.

King Bull fought mightily. He had long used up his ammunition. Now he flailed a butcher's cleaver he had picked up from one of his dead hash-slingers, hacking and slashing at the horses and riders milling all around him, using his enormous strength to pull Cossacks from their mounts. Once he actually smashed a white horse in the snout and sent it bucking and snorting onto its hindlegs so that its rider, caught by surprise, fell off only to be kicked into unconsciousness by one kick from King Bull's dice-beaker. But he was only one against many. Now his luck ran out, too.

A rider towered above him, carbine raised, aiming straight

at the massive head cook. Desperately King Bull lunged for it. Together with the rider, dragged off his horse by the surprise move, he tumbled to his knees in the same instant that he felt a tremendous whack across his neck.

Red stars exploded before his eyes. A black mist threatened to engulf him. There was a rushing noise in his ears. The sounds of the battle all around grew ever more distant. But he refused to go down. Another awesome whack. It felt as if his whole head had been severed. The pain was agonizing. He groaned once and fell face forward into the confused mass of dead men and horses, lying there two and three deep.

The sounds of the battle were petering out. On the little hillock where Bogdan and his staff had taken up their stand to observe the end of the massacre, for such it was, the whistles started to shrill and the bugles began to sound recall. Bogdan knew his Cossacks. There were some of them already racing down to the bank of the river, sabreing down the running fugitives, springing from their mounts at the gallop in order to loot the Fritz dead lying everywhere in the snow and the mud. If he didn't stop them soon, they'd be wading the river on horseback, carried away by the Cossack's primitive bloodlust, and he didn't want that. He wanted the Fritzes to have some men left alive to signal the others what had happened. His radio jammers would allow them to get that message through before they started jamming with recordings of Soviet massed brass bands once more. He had to have the Fritzes concentrated here if his plans were to succeed.

Bogdan cupped his hands about his mouth and shouted above the dying snap-and-crackle of small-arms fire, the shrieks of the wounded, the thunder of horses' hooves and all the dread noise of battle, 'There is a hundred grams for each man . . . a hundred grams!'* He grinned and suddenly felt tired. That would do the trick. Women and vodka – his Cossacks would give their souls for them.

---

* In Russia vodka is 'weighed' in grams.

Karl and the other Rebels crouched in the mud of the river bank, surrounded by dead men, their faces, smeared with mud deliberately, barely visible. The sound of firing was dying away. Those Cossacks who had threaded their way along the river bank on their horses looking for the last victims had already begun to turn, presumably in answer to the bugles and whistles, and were urging their mounts to return to the main body. Slowly the firing was giving way to single shots and by the sound Karl could tell these were not from German weapons. They were Popov. The Russians were finishing off the rest of the wounded with a shot to the back of the base of the skull.

Karl breathed hard and wiped some of the dirt from his face. Then he looked at the others. 'Now what do you make of that, comrades?' he asked in weary bewilderment, as more and more of the black-coated riders trotted to the rear, leaving the field to the dead and dying.

Polack said, 'They'll come again. Why should they call a halt now when they've got us nearly down for the count?'

Ami nodded his agreement and said with renewed energy, 'The question now, Karl, is what are *we* going to do? There ain't much time left. Do we go back across the river?' He indicated the other side where already hundreds of heads were beginning to poke up from holes and shell craters now that the Cossack attack had ceased.

Karl tugged the end of his frozen nose and told himself he would have given his right arm at this moment for a canteen of piping hot nigger sweat laced with a good slug of firewater. 'Don't really know. I don't fancy that river, but I suppose we could get across the bridge debris. But what then?'

'They'll be slaughtered just like these poor swine.' Polack extended his arm – it was bleeding from a sabre slash – to encompass the still piles of dead, stacked like logs. 'It's only a matter of time. As soon as they've filled their bellies with rot-gut, they'll come again.'

Slowly Karl started to make up his mind. He thought of Pill and his sacrifice for the wounded, even that enormous nursing sister, the feared *Schwester* Klara, who had given her life in the defence of her patients (he had seen her disappear under the mass of Cossacks, powerless to help). 'Ami . . . Polack,' he asked, 'what have we got left?'

'Left?' they echoed.

'Yes. Food, ammo.'

Polack scrabbled inside his ammunition pouch and brought out two clips of bullets – ten in all. Then he touched his bread bag. 'One loaf,' he growled, 'and that's as frigging hard as a sergeant-major's heart.'

Karl laughed softly and turned to Ami. 'Five clips,' the latter said, 'but no rifle. One loaf of bread and – *this*!' From inside his bread bag, producing it like a conjuror does a white rabbit for the delight of his audience of children, he brought out a whole ring of sausage. 'Now what do you say to that, Karl?'

Karl slapped him across his skinny shoulders. 'A feast, a veritable feast, we can have from that. Now, I've got a rifle, a clip of ammo, one loaf and a tin of sardines –'

'In tomato sauce?' Polack enquired greedily, licking his parched lips in anticipation.

'In tomato sauce,' Karl said patiently.

'Now what is all this?' Ami snapped a little angrily. 'You practising to be a frigging quartermaster or something, Karl, eh?' he demanded.

Karl shook his head, still wondering if they could do it. The odds against them were so great. They'd be braving the Cossacks, a shortage of food and that great pitiless Russian steppe, probably bare of any human habitation, for all he knew.

'Well, Karl?' Ami persisted. 'Spit it!'

Karl hesitated no longer. 'Listen, those poor shits over there,' he indicated the other side of the river, 'are going nowhere, are they?'

'Nowhere, but the knacker's yard,' Ami agreed miserably.

'So why throw in our lot with the poor shits and wait to be slaughtered like tame sheep?'

Polack whistled softly through his front teeth. He had already guessed what his handsome young friend had in mind. 'It's gonna be one hell of a risk, Karl, one helluva risk!' he said.

Karl nodded. 'I know, but we can try. If we succeed we save ourselves and,' he added significantly, 'we can perhaps help the others, the wounded and the rest of the mob. Surely we can convince our people to send help before the Popovs finish them off?'

Polack and Ami remained silent, as if they weren't altogether convinced.

Karl left them to think about it for a moment while he surveyed the Cossack positions carefully. Most of the riders had returned to the main body. In the hills where they were grouping great bonfires had already been lit, as if to celebrate the slaughter of the wounded and the poor bloody Goulash Cannon Company, and Karl could hear the muted sound of song and laughter. Were they already hitting the firewater? If so, why? Why didn't they attack across the river and have done with it?

Polack broke into his troubled reverie. 'Karl,' he said.

'Yes?'

'There's not much of an alternative, is there?'

Karl shook his head.

Polack rose to his feet cautiously and shook the snow and mud from his big body, saying, 'Well, what are we waiting for?'

'Remember, I don't know how far it is, where our lines are – don't even have a frigging compass.' Karl gave his two old friends a last warning, as Ami rose too, new determination in his skinny little face.

'It's over there to the west,' Polack growled and shouldered his rifle, 'isn't it, away from them frigging Cossacks. Besides,' he said, with a sudden grin, 'since when has the poor bleeding infantry ever worried about distances, eh?'

Now it was Karl's and Ami's turn to grin. Karl slapped Polack on the shoulder. 'Right, you're on, you Slavic shit! You, too, Ami. March or croak,' he cried, unwittingly echoing General Sobel's grim motto.

'*March or croak*, it is!' the other two cried in an odd mixture of despair and hope.

BOOK THREE

Wotan to the Rescue

CHAPTER 1

'*Los, Los!*' Colonel Grier,* known as the Vulture on account
of his name and great beak of a nose set in a rapacious face,
commanded urgently, as his giant SS men pelted forward
through the snow. To their front the *isba*, in which they had
trapped the partisans was already beginning to stream forth
brilliant white smoke. A trooper paused in mid-stride and
hurled another phosphorus grenade. It exploded with a burst
of harsh, incandescent light on the roof, showering lethal
white pellets everywhere.

'*Kapital!*' the Vulture rasped, screwing his monocle more
firmly in his right eye and thrusting his pistol back in its
holster. The little fire-fight was virtually over now. Once
again the partisans had suffered a bloody nose, as they always
did when they came up against SS Assault Battalion Wotan.
He was not going to tolerate any of their damned underhand
Popov tricks behind his lines.

Corporal Schulze raced to the right of the *isba*, firing from
the hip as he ran, ignoring the lead stitching the snow at his
flying feet. He slammed into a stone watering trough as a
burst of fire ripped the length of it, showering his helmeted
head with splinters. He shook his big head like a bull trying to
shoo off importuning flies and yelled over his shoulder, 'All
right, Matzi, you little overflowing piss-pot, move it. It's safe
now!'

Lance-Corporal Matz, his undersized running mate,
cursed and took a hefty swig out of his flatman, then he, too,
raced forward zig-zagging expertly, the enemy bullets
striking home to left and right of his feet.

Standing next to the Vulture, the company commander,

* *Geier* is the German for 'vulture'.

Captain von Dodenburg, placed his pistol into its holster as well, knowing that with those two rogues, Schulze and Matz, coming up to the rear of the *isba*, it was virtually over now. They might well be the worse garrison soldiers in the whole of Wotan, always behind 'Swedish curtains',* but they certainly were the Battalion's finest combat fighting men.

A moment later the two of them proved it. Like a wizened monkey, Matz clambered up onto Schulze's broad shoulders and crawled onto the smoking roof of the *isba*, ignoring the bullets being fired up through it by the desperate trapped partisans. Hurriedly he drew his bayonet, while Schulze stood guard, and began cutting away at the mud and wattle, cursing furiously to himself for reasons only he knew.

'Hurry up, you perverted little banana-sucker!' Schulze called. 'I've got a date with a hot piece of Popov pussy at zero fifteen hundred – and I don't wanna be late, just 'cos you can't get yer frigging finger out!'

Matz paused, his face glazed with blackened sweat and stuck up his thumb wordlessly.

'Can't,' Schulze shouted back without rancour. 'Got a double-decker bus up there already, plush-ears!'

Von Dodenburg shook his head.

Next moment Matz had disappeared through the hole in the roof and Schulze was racing round to the front of the peasant hut, machine pistol chattering frantically . . .

Five minutes later it was all over. From the sagging door, from which now streamed thick smoke, the coughing spluttering partisans emerged at the double, hands raised high in the air, being prodded forward by Matz's bayonet, as he yelled, '*Davai. Davai. Davai it up*, you Popov pricks!'

Von Dodenburg looked at the Vulture, his harshly handsome face worried.

The Vulture read the look. He slapped the side of his ludicrously too large riding breeches, which he still affected

* German slang for prison bars.

though he had long left the *Wehrmacht*'s cavalry to transfer to
the SS and its quicker promotion, and rasped, 'My dear
young friend, where is that SS hardness? You know, as tough
as Krupp steel and all that stuff?' He smiled cynically. 'What
else can we do with them –' He didn't finish his words. Instead
he stuck out one gloved finger, as if it were a pistol barrel and
made a clicking sound. 'Eliminate them. After all, they are
only Bolshevik scum, as our dear Herr Himmler is always
assuring us.'

'They might have information –' von Dodenburg began,
noting that one of the captured partisans who had been
sniping and sabotaging behind Wotan's lines these last two
weeks was a girl. She looked hardly older than sixteen.

'Peasants,' the Vulture interrupted him roughly. 'What do
they know? The price of cow shit on the local market.' He
dismissed them with a wave of his hand and the remark,
'Make it quick. We're wanted back at our beloved *Obergruppenführer*'s HQ' – he grinned cynically – 'at fifteen
hundred hours sharp.' And with that he strode back to the
waiting command car and left von Dodenburg to it, as if
bored with the whole business.

What was left of SS Assault Battalion Wotan had been out
of the line for over two weeks now, billeted in a large
abandoned *Kolkhoz* – a Soviet collective farm. The surviving
'old hares' rested and took their ease, while the Battalion
absorbed hundreds of recruits – 'green-beaks' – straight from
the Reich. As Schulze commented more than once to his
running mate Matz, 'Holy strawsack, Matzi, they must be
shitting well robbing the kindergartens these days!'

Green they might have been, but they were fanatics,
products of the Hitler Youth and nearly ten years of
indoctrination in the National Socialist creed, burning to go
into the steppe and fight the 'red Bolshevik scum'. The old
hares had other ideas. They spent their time sleeping,
drinking and visiting the local army brothels where the
admission price was one log of wood (to heat the brothel's

fires) and a 'Parisian', as they called contraceptives, to avoid disease. For now in an army rapidly running out of cannon-fodder, the punishment for contracting VD was the firing squad.

A few of the lucky ones, like Corporals Schulze and Matz, naturally, had managed to get their feet under the table, as they called it happily. They had each found a Popov *devochka*, one of the big-bosomed, strong peasant girls who had not fled the *Kolkhoz* with the rest when the *nmetski* had come. The two of them provided the corporals with bed and board in one of the outlying barns in return for food and chocolate and what a gleeful Schulze was always proclaiming proudly was the 'biggest piece of German salami in the whole of the shitting SS!'

Only the Vulture, and naturally Captain von Dodenburg, of the old hares disliked this time out of war. The Vulture wanted fresh action; for battle brought casualties among officers and fresh promotion – and it was promotion and handsome boys that filled his dreams exclusively. Von Dodenburg's motive was very different. He hated the kind of dirty war in the shadows fought behind the front: these sneaking attacks on lone German soldiers made by the partisans who committed awful atrocities, which always resulted in bloody, terrible retribution by his own side. He preferred the cleaner air of the front, where the enemy was clear and visible; where it was soldier fighting soldier in honest combat.

Now, as he strode slightly behind the Vulture, as military protocol demanded, into Dietrich's HQ, past the rigid giants of guards standing at the present, heads following the officers' progress as if worked by clockwork, he hoped the summons meant the prospect of clear-cut military action. He did not want to have to shoot any more civilian prisoners.

'*Meine Herren – Kameraden.*' *Obergruppenführer* Sepp Dietrich, dwarfed by the assembled officers, got down to business immediately. They had all been offered the usual schnapps and cigar. But now the little Bavarian bully-boy who had fought the Reds in Munich back in the twenties with the Führer wanted to get down to business. 'Schnapps is schnapps and duty is duty,' he had proclaimed and then led them straight into the operations room, its walls lined with maps, criss-crossed with tapes and markings in china pencil. 'You don't need me to tell you what a bunch o' crap the Corps front is. We're holding it with the proverbial man and boy. I daren't even allow the wounded to be evacuated. If a man can hold a rifle, he can fill out the line.'

Von Dodenburg smiled. 'Sepp', as they all called him behind his back, was a card: a typical ex-NCO, who still retained the speech and mannerisms of a non-commissioned officer. The Vulture, for his part, smiled superciliously. It was said the Bavarian bully-boy couldn't even read a map properly; his chief of staff had to do it for him.

'Now, there's talk of some frigging *Wehrmacht* division being cut off around here.' He indicated the map vaguely, and his smooth, clever chief of staff Kraemer whispered something urgently in his ear. 'All right,' he retorted, 'I'm not that dumb! Anyway, between the Dnieper and the tributary – here!'

Von Dodenburg craned his neck forward and stared at the map. His experienced eye told him the distance between this 'frigging *Wehrmacht* division' and their own front was at least a hundred kilometres. A helluva long way in Russia in the depths of winter!

Sepp Dietrich licked his thick lips beneath the toothbrush moustache he wore in imitation of the Führer's. 'Now, there is also some talk of my Corps doing something about carving this *Wehrmacht* division out of the shit it finds itself in. As always, comrades, the SS gets the shitting end of the stick, otherwise the gentlemen of the Army have no time for us. Upstarts we are. *Pfui!*'

The older officers who, like the Vulture, had been transferred from the *Wehrmacht* refrained from any comment, but the younger ones who had come straight into the SS murmured angrily and someone said, 'Damn it, *Obergruppen-führer*, why doesn't the Army pull its own hot chestnuts out of the fire?'

'Exactly,' Dietrich agreed hotly. 'My thinking entirely, Witt!'

Von Dodenburg did not join in the protest of the younger officers. In a way he belonged to the group of older officers; his background was the same as theirs. Wasn't his father an army general, retired, of the old school? All the same he believed in the National Socialist cause fervently. It had come along just at the right time when Europe had begun to sink into complete decadence. Now there was a new spirit abroad, not only in the Reich, but in the rest of Europe, too. There was new hope for the youth of the Old Continent; a belief that things *could* be changed for the better, as long as there was a leader with imagination, energy and an eye for greatness. He kept his peace and wondered where all this was leading.

'But what are we supposed to do?' Dietrich continued. 'Where are the necessary armoured vehicles, the ambulances –'

'*Obergruppenführer*.' Von Dodenburg's cold, precise Prussian voice cut into the thick Bavarian accent like a sharp knife.

'Yes. Oh, it's you, von Dodenburg. Well, what do you want?'

'Is there a mission, sir?' von Dodenburg snapped, knowing that Dietrich thought him an arrogant swine and not giving a damn about it. 'Is that what the High Command is proposing?'

'Well, if you must know, von Dodenburg, not exactly. It's what those gentlemen call grandly a feasibility study. It is not an order, but a question. Not "we shall", but "can we"?' He gave the tall aristocratic officer one of his dark moody Bavarian looks which would have said to any normal officer, 'Well, that's enough. Now shut up!'

But Kuno von Dodenburg was not an ordinary young

officer. He was afraid of neither rank nor responsibility. So he didn't shut up. Instead he said, 'Well, can we, sir?'

Dietrich's sallow broad face flushed. 'Von Dodenburg,' he cried in exasperation like a man who is being sorely tried, 'you know the shitting state of the Corps? Most battalions have got more than a dozen runners.* And where in three devils' name are we supposed to get the half-tracks we would need to bring out that number of wounded. Pray tell me that, *my dear young friend*?' He emphasized the words as if to say that von Dodenburg wouldn't be his 'dear young friend' much longer if he persisted in this matter.

But von Dodenburg did exactly that. 'My company has half a dozen runners, sir,' he retorted boldly, 'and the General Field Hospital has umpteen medical half-tracks –'

The Vulture threw his subordinate a warning glance, as Dietrich snorted, 'General Field Hospital! You haven't got all your cups in the cupboard, von Dodenburg! Those fat-arsed base stallions are a lot of bed-pan jockeys who'd have their periods if you asked them to go within sniffing distance of the firing line!'

'One could *order* them, sir,' von Dodenburg began, but Dietrich held up his hand for silence.

'Now I've been tolerant with you for long enough, *Hauptsturm* von Dodenburg. That's enough. The matter is now closed. Let us pass on to the next matter.'

The Vulture grinned maliciously and whispered out of the side of his mouth, 'Well, my dear von Dodenburg, I'm afraid you're not going to cure your throatache on that one, what?'

A red-faced, embarrassed von Dodenburg could have struck him right on his monstrous beak of a nose. He was not the slightest bit interested in winning the Knight's Cross and 'curing his throatache', as the Vulture inferred. Nor was he particularly concerned with the fate of the trapped *Wehrmacht* division – this winter a lot of army divisions were cut off and

---

* Armoured vehicles capable of moving.

wandering about in pockets trying to escape from the trap. It was just that he wanted to be in action again, to feel the sensation of freedom that came with being operational, master of his own fate. Abruptly he thought of the girl with the partisans they had shot that morning. She had gone down on her knees in front of him in the snow, wringing her hands, pleading, calling him '*Gospodin*', 'sir', begging him not to have her shot. But he had. He'd had her shot all right and afterwards he had been sick in the officers' crapper.

God, how heartily sick he was of this war in the shadows, this time out of action! Fervently, as Dietrich droned on and on about the new tank the Corps would be soon receiving from the Reich, he prayed for battle.

Two kilometres away back at the *Kolkhoz*, Corporals Schulze and Matz were well content to be out of combat for the time being. Sprawled in the hay next to the glowing stove, the warmest place in the barn, watched enviously by the green-beaks, they were frying looted eggs on the blades of their entrenching tools, glowing bayonets already inserted in two pots of bubbling beer, mulling it for the meal to come. 'Delicate guts I've got,' Schulze had just declared to the green-beaks shivering in the outer regions of the barn as the wind howled outside. 'I should have been downgraded years ago.' To which Matz, his skinny running-mate had commented scornfully, '*Downgraded*, they should have flogged yer to the knacker's yard for frigging glue, like horse hooves!' This, in its turn, had brought the retort from Schulze, 'Hold yer piss, *Lance*-Corporal, or yer'll have *my* horse-hoof right up yer jacksy!'

Now however, in anticipation of the feast to come, all was sweetness and light between the two old comrades, though Schulze was assailed by the slightest of nagging doubts at the thought of the officers' conference, to which the Vulture and the company commander, his beloved Captain von

Dodenburg, had been called. 'You know that shitty Vulture,' he remarked to Matz, whose face glowed in the heat from the stove, as he jiggled the spade so that all six of the eggs which bubbled and spat merrily on its blade were equally well done. 'If there's any chance of winning a bit o' tin,* he's the shit who'll go after it?'

Matz nodded happily, not taking his greedy little eyes off the eggs for one moment. 'German soldiers, folk comrades,' Matz aped the Vulture's high-pitching rasping manner of speech for the benefit of the green-beaks, 'you now have the honour of belonging to SS Assault Battalion Wotan, the SS's premier formation. Wotan has fought in Poland, in France, in Holland, in Greece –'

'Even in the frigging knocking shops of Hamburg – and that certainly takes outstanding courage,' Schulze chortled in high good humour, and reaching over, sprinkled some more salt on his eggs happily.

'In Jugoslavia, wherever the fuck that is, in Russia. And, my dear young folk comrades, Wotan has not yet once been defeated. Now I ask you. *Why?*' He bent stiffly, still holding the shovel, as the Vulture often did from his tightly corsetted waist. Matz formed a circle with the fingers of his free hand and gazed at the amused green-beaks through it, just as the Vulture was wont to peer through his monocle, as if his soldiers were something which had just crept out of the woodwork. 'I shall tell you why. Because the men of the Wotan know that I and my officers demand one hundred per cent blind, unquestioning obedience from them. You have one duty only, to sacrifice your miserable lives glady for Wotan so that I can win a drawerful of tin and retire a general –'

The words died abruptly on his lips as the barn door was suddenly rudely flung open to admit a freezing blast of ice-cold air. There stood the object of his parody. Legs in his gleaming riding boots well braced apart, hands imperiously

---

* SS slang for 'decorations'.

on his broad hips, he peered through his monocle at the unfortunate little corporal. Behind him, a newly happy von Dodenburg grinned at Matz's discomfiture, as the latter swallowed hard and went a brick-red.

'Exactly right, my dear Corporal Matz, exactly right!' the Vulture rasped. 'That is all I ask from you – to sacrifice your miserable lives gladly – *so that I can win a drawerful of tin and retire a general*! Now I'm going to give you the opportunity to do exactly that for me.'

'Bollocks!' Schulze groaned mournfully, guessing what was coming. Sadly he let the red-hot shovel sink. Slowly but inevitably the precious fried eggs began to slip into the roaring fire.

CHAPTER 2

It was unearthly cold. At eighty kilometres an hour a terrible freezing wind, straight from Siberia, raced across the snowbound steppe. It lashed millions of razor-sharp particles of snow against their poor sunken faces. Icicles hung from their eyebrows and nostrils. Every single breath cut their aching gasping lungs like a slash from a sharp knife. Shoulders bent, like those of very old men, they stumbled across the never-ending plain.

Only habit, discipline, and the flickering, ever-weakening desire to keep alive, kept them going, with Karl bullying, cajoling, pleading with the other two all the time. The snow looked so soft and tempting. Karl felt it, too. One would only need to close one's eyes and sink gratefully into its soft embrace and simply sleep, sleep, sleep. Oh, my God, how he would love just to sleep!

But he knew that would be fatal. They *had* to keep on going, trailing through this vast empty landscape like insignificant human ants. The very countryside breathed hostility. Here and there they spotted a road, a lower level of snow than the rest of the steppe, marked by crooked telegraph posts. But they knew they couldn't take them. If the Popovs were out there somewhere it would be on the roads. So they continued to plod miserably through the knee-deep snow, while ever more poured down from the grey sullen sky, as if God himself wanted to eradicate them from the cruel, war-torn landscape.

It was two days since they had set out. Now all their bread was gone. Indeed that morning they had turned out their bread bags and had greedily consumed the crumbs they had found there, as if they were some great delicacy. Now Karl tried to keep himself going, as they stumbled on, strung out in single file, with visions of food: meals he had taken in the past. The huge pan of fried potatoes and bubbling, spluttering eggs on the top of the white enamel stove, which his mother had kept waiting for him and his father on a winter evening. King Bull's huge urns of rich green pea-soup – his proverbial 'fart-cannon mix' – complete with a hefty chunk of *bockwurst*. The three steaks and mountain of *pommes frites*, washed down with litres of weak foaming beer, he had consumed on his first leave in Paris back in 1940. And all the time his stomach rumbled and rumbled so strongly that he was sure that if there were marauding Cossacks in the area, they would hear the rebellious murmurings of his gastric juices a good kilometre away.

Surprisingly enough, though Karl bringing up the rear was so preoccupied with food, it was Polack at the front who first smelled the delicious odour of something roasting. Suddenly he came to an abrupt halt so that Ami stumbled blindly into him and mumbled a curse. 'What the frig –' he began, but Polack held up his hand for silence.

While the other two stared at him as if he had suddenly gone crazy, Polack turned his head into the snow-heavy wind and sniffed, his broad nostrils twitching. There was no mistaking it. Somewhere something was cooking! In anticipation two thin streams of saliva started to trickle down the sides of his bearded chin. His stomach rolled noisily and abruptly he felt faint at the thought of food. He swayed alarmingly.

'What is it, Polack?' Karl groaned.

Polack wiped the saliva from his chin with the back of his hand. '*Fodder*. I can smell fodder being cooked!' He turned, his nose twitching like an antennae, surveying the awesome snowy waste, covering every hillock, every depression, every patch of snow-heavy firs. 'There!' he croaked. 'Over there, comrades. Look!'

The other two turned their heads slowly, as if they were

worked by rusty springs. 'Where?' Ami asked dully.

'There, at three o'clock,' Polack replied, new energy coursing through his emaciated body. 'Beyond them trees. Can't yer see?'

'Holy strawsack, *smoke!*' Karl exclaimed.

There was no mistaking it. A thin wisp of grey smoke was being driven furiously to one side by the howling wind, dispersing almost immediately, but undeniably smoke all the same. A moment later Karl too caught a whiff of food or something hot and succulent being cooked. 'Popovs!' He cautioned, bringing up his rifle.

'So what!' Ami hissed, crouching a little all the same. 'I could eat one of them too as long as he had salt on his tail.'

It wasn't very funny but it was better than nothing and Karl realized there was still life in his two old comrades after all. 'Shall we risk it?' he whispered.

Polack shrugged. 'Why not? What have we to lose?'

'You're right,' Ami agreed. 'We're gonna croak it out here as it is if we don't get some warmth and fodder inside us soon. Yer, I'm for risking it, Karl.'

Karl held up his finger in warning. 'Let's not go at it like a bull at a red rag. You know what they say – caution is the mother of the china cabinet. There are people out there and we're not exactly well armed, are we? So quietly does it. Follow me, comrades.'

Five minutes later they were breaking out of the firs, the snow still pelting down in a steady white stream. But now they had forgotten the wind and the snow altogether. Their attention was concentrated exclusively on the smoke and the smell of cooking.

'I'm sure it's a roast,' Polack whispered, as they crept forward like silent white ghosts. 'Certainly smells like it. Roast pig and tatties! My God, my guts are doing back flips already!'

'Keep yer mind on the business in hand,' Karl warned severely, gripping his rifle, while Ami followed him, armed now with a sturdy tree branch, his only weapon. 'Off you go to the right, Polack. Me and Ami'll come in from the left.' Taking a deep breath, Karl advanced another few paces, grateful now for the storm, for it covered any sound he and Ami might make. He paused again and then removed a branch, heavy with snow, to his immediate front and crouched, rifle pressed tightly to his right hip, heart beating furiously.

Half a dozen men were squatting around a roaring fire set in the trail next to a shattered cart obviously left by some retreating German column. They were in rough, undressed furs and wore the long peaked caps of Russian peasants. Next to them were their neatly stacked rifles.

'Partisans!' Karl hissed to Ami, pressing his mouth close to his comrade's ear.

'Don't worry me,' Ami whispered back cheerfully, 'they're partisans with fodder!'

'Yer, but let's take it nice and easy –' He stopped short. Christ, he told himself in alarm, what a frigging racket Polack is making. They'll hear –

They already had. As one the heads of the men eating shot up, strips of meat hanging from their greasy lips, suddenly tense and expectant, ears cocked against the raging storm. Someone was coming down the trail they had taken, following the retreating Germans until they had come across the abandoned Fritz cart.

Noiselessly Karl slipped off his safety catch, cursing Polack for having alarmed the Popovs too damned soon. 'I'll count up to three and then we're going in, Ami,' he hissed urgently. 'The ugly big shit has gone –'

He stopped short. Another huge man, with a familiar face, supporting another man, had appeared at the end of the trail. But it wasn't Polack. '*Himmelherrje*,' he cried in surprise, 'it's frigging King Bull and the Adjutant!'

Next moment things happened fast.

King Bull let Creeping Jesus fall into the snow. In the

same instant he fired without aiming. The partisan getting up to grab his rifle from the stack fell screaming. Polack burst out of the bushes firing too, yelling his head off. A partisan ripped an egg grenade from his pocket and flung it in the moment that Polack's slug tore his face away. A crump and Polack fell groaning to the ground.

Karl sprang into the open to the rear of the partisans. '*Ruki verhk!*' he called in Russian, but the partisans weren't waiting to put their hands up. They broke up and bolted, dropping their meat. Karl fired but missed. Seconds later the partisans had vanished into the trees, leaving their comrade bleeding to death in the snow and Polack cursing angrily, holding his bloody leg.

For a few moments – to them it seemed like an age – the five of them stayed in position, like actors at the end of some bloodthirsty melodrama waiting for the curtain to go down. Then King Bull growled, 'So it's you three, is it? Thought if anybody was going to do it, it'd be you three shits. All right, don't just stand there like wet farts waiting to hit the side of the thundermug, come over and gimme a hand with this piss-pansy.' He gestured contemptuously at Creeping Jesus who lay at his feet.

'You just help him, Ami,' Karl said. 'I'll see just how bad Polack is. Off you go.'

Fortunately their comrade hadn't been hit badly, though the wound was bleeding heavily and it looked worse than it was. Swiftly Karl slapped on a shell-dressing, while Polack held the pressure point, grumbling, 'Come on, Karl, hurry up. My chin water is running down on my vest with hunger. Let's get at it before them greedy sods scoff it all up.' He indicated the others who were now coming up the forest trail.

'Hold on . . . I'm doing my best. All right. Try it now,' Karl said and Polack let go. The red jet of blood ceased and was reduced to a steady ooze. The bandage had done the trick.

Polack waited no longer. As best he could he hobbled after
the others, past the dead partisan towards the fire, still
crackling away merrily, from whence there came the
beautiful smell of roasted meat, crying. 'Don't scoff it all. I
smelled it first.'

But there was to be no roast for an excited Polack this day,
or for the others either for that matter. Just as Creeping Jesus,
who seemingly had now recovered his strength, was about to
head for the nearest twig with a piece of meat speared on its
end, Ami cried in thick-voiced horror, 'For God's sake, don't.
Don't touch it! Listen to me – *don't touch* –' Suddenly he turned
to one side and began to retch violently, his skinny shoulders
shaking with the effort.

'What the frig has got into you,' King Bull began. Then he
too saw what had caused Ami's sudden cry of alarm.

Lying in the snow, not far from where the partisans had
been cooking their 'roast' over the log fire, there was a leg, still
clad in a German dice-beaker, with the stump at the top
clearly visible, the flesh sawn off raggedly and heavy with
congealed black blood. A little further on there was a human
rump, the shirt thrown up to reveal two great fleshy wounds
where the buttocks should have been.

'Oh, my God –' King Bull clapped his hand to his mouth and
began to retch. He tossed his own piece of meat hurriedly into
the bushes.

Karl fought back the hot vomit that had flooded his throat,
trying not to smell the 'roast', which now seemed so sweet, so
cloying, eyes filled with stupefied horror. 'Jesus,' he whispered
thickly, 'how can people be like –'

'Food!' It was Creeping Jesus. He staggered by Karl, hand
outstretched like a blind man feeling his way. 'I must have
food. I'm starving. *Food*!'

He stumbled to a stop next to the fire and reached for one of
the spits, the meat at its end charred but still smoking. Hastily
he put it to his mouth, the saliva dripping from his mouth
with total greed.

'No!' Karl screamed hysterically. 'Don't eat it. You can't eat it!'

The adjutant stared at him open-mouthed. 'What . . . can't eat it? Why?'

'Because it's human flesh!' Karl cried desperately, while Ami and King Bull continued to vomit helplessly. 'The Russians were committing cannibalism. Don't you see, they were eating *one of our dead*!'

Creeping Jesus stared at him dully, as if he were finding it very hard to take in Karl's words, the saliva still dripping down his chin. 'Cannibalism,' he stuttered. 'But I'm starving . . .' He swallowed hard. 'Don't you see, if we don't eat, we die. People have done it before. We've got to eat.' He raised the spit, mouth open, teeth bared, ready to bite deep into the charred flesh.

Karl whipped up his rifle and ripped back the bolt. 'Drop it!' he commanded through gritted teeth, fighting hard to overcome his revulsion, the temptation to shoot this monster opposite without mercy. 'I said – drop it!'

'Karl!' Polack protested.

But Karl wasn't listening. His eyes blazed a crazy red. He was preparing to kill the adjutant.

'I must eat!'

The ragged volley of shots from the trees cut suddenly into the adjutant's defiant words. A bullet struck the spit and tore it from his hand. He whirled round with the shock of it.

'It's the partisans,' Polack cried and fired wildly into the firs. 'Come on, let's get the hell outa here. *Quick!*'

Abruptly Creeping Jesus realized the danger, as the sound of running feet crunching across the snow grew ever louder in the trees. 'God in Heaven,' he faltered, the food forgotten now, 'they'll slaughter us. What are we going –'

Karl grabbed him by the arm. 'Ami,' he yelled, 'give Polack a hand. Bulle, move it. You stick close to me, *sir*!'

'Oh, my God, yes,' Creeping Jesus quavered. 'Please don't leave me . . .'

And then they were running for their lives, blundering heavily through the trees, the fir branches cruelly ripping and tearing at their terrified faces, leaving that scene of barbarity behind them.

CHAPTER 3

The valley below was awesome and brooding. It stank of death and destruction. For over two hundred metres straight ahead along the forest trail there were shattered trucks, tanks and carts – German to judge from the insignia – mostly covered by snow but still recognizable for what they had once been.

It was now half an hour since they had had their last contact with the pursuing partisans. But now they were too exhausted and too hungry to care whether they were still being chased or not. Their sole thought was to rest and eat.

'What do you think, Karl?' Polack asked. He was limping badly now, as his wound stiffened, and even his giant strength was about spent.

Karl didn't reply for an instant. He stared down at the shattered convoy, probably caught by some marauding Stormoviks as it had emerged from the forest and prior to reaching the cover of the next stretch of snow-heavy firs. His eyes were fixed on the ghastly tableau below, with here and there a frozen, waxen hand protruding from the snow, as if the owner might still be alive and was pleading for help.

But Polack was not the only one waiting for Karl's decision on what to do next. Creeping Jesus and King Bull were too. Now rank counted for nothing. All that counted was determination and the ability to make a decision; and for the last six gruelling hours Karl had been making all the decisions.

Finally he broke his heavy silence. 'We can't lose anything,' he said slowly, realizing suddenly just how goddam tired he was. 'Like you, I'm so damned hungry, I could eat steamed dog-shit at this very moment. Let's see if they've got any food on them.'

'It'd mean robbing our own dead,' Polack began to protest. Then he saw the light in Karl's eyes and stopped suddenly.

In single file, they limped and slipped their way down the slope into the valley of death, heavy with its atmosphere of brooding menace. Almost immediately they were down, Creeping Jesus collapsed in the lee of a shattered truck and sighed, 'I can't go another step. I can't go –'

'Shut your fucking hole,' King Bull cut him off brutally. He turned to Karl, ignoring the adjutant completely, 'Carstens, where do we start?'

'Try that tank. The grave robbers, if there were any,' he frowned at the thought of those starving partisans who had sunk to cannibalism, 'might not have got into it. You, Polack, stay guard here. Ami, come with me.'

Obediently the others followed his orders; even King Bull started to clear away the snow from the Mark III's turret without demur, as if it was quite normal for a senior non-commissioned officer to take orders from a twenty-year-old private, first class.

Grimly Karl and Ami stomped through the knee-deep snow, the snow crunching beneath their boots, searching the dead for food in the awesome, trance-like silence. It wasn't pleasant, but Karl knew it had to be done if they weren't to starve to death. He steeled himself against his stomach-churning own revulsion as he worked his way through a lorry-load of panzer grenadiers sitting bolt upright in their seats in their burnt-out truck like rotting cabbage stalks in an abandoned winter allotment.

In the end, their hands stinking from searching bodies with the viscera swelling out of shattered guts like giant pink sea-anemones, they had found a few pathetic frozen morsels: a couple of hunks of solid army bread, ends of salami, a few slices of salted bacon, an already rusting tin of *Sauerkraut und Speck*, at which Polack hammered desperately with his bayonet, almost in tears when it refused to open.

They squatted in the snow, gobbling down the carefully

rationed out food, trying to avoid the accusing look in the eyes of a dead grenadier, standing frozen rigid and bolt upright, a look of passionate eloquence on his green face.

Slowly, as the odd pieces entered their systems, new energy started to flood their emaciated bodies and even Creeping Jesus's dazed, bewildered look vanished, though he remained silent and kept his council to himself as the others began to chat in a desultory sort of way.

At first it was about the food and whether it would be safe enough to light a fire – they had found a few grains of ersatz coffee in a dead grenadier's pack. They decided against it and washed down the hard dry food with handfuls of snow. Then the conversation changed to what they should do next. All of them knew that the partisans would catch up with them again, and if not the ones who had pursued them originally, then others. The countryside was obviously controlled by them. They would have to keep going.

Karl tried to reassure them. 'One thing is certain, wherever you find plenty of partisans, you'll find our own people too. After all, why are the Popov pigs there, if not to harass our supply lines and service troops?'

King Bull nodded his agreement, as he chewed away greedily at a crust of frozen black bread.

'So that means we can't be *that* far from our own lines.' Karl hesitated an optimistic guess. 'Fifty kilometres, say.'

Ami sniffed, but said nothing.

'So,' Karl continued, 'there's nothing for it but to keep on going.'

Polack winced a little with pain as he moved his leg, which had grown very stiff, but he too said nothing.

'Now,' Karl said, 'once we've eaten and rested a little while, we're gonna do something about our armament. We must be able to frighten off the partisans if nothing else, and with the stuff we've got . . . Well, it's not very impressive.'

'Where we gonna get new weapons, Karl?' Polack asked.

'The column. There's a MG 38 in that tank back there and

we'll check the truck with the panzer grenadiers for machine pistols. They carry machine pistols, some of them. And one thing, comrades, something that might be a bit encouraging. Did you notice their helmets?'

Ami finished the last of his bone-dry sausage and snorted. 'Frankly, Karl, I was trying to look the other way. They're in a mess, the poor shits.'

Karl frowned momentarily and then said, 'I know, I know, Ami. Well, I'll tell you. All their helmets had the swastika on them. That means they are, *were*, SS.' He frowned again. 'It might mean something . . . it might mean nothing. But it was to Dietrich's SS Corps that we were trying to break through, wasn't it?' He looked at Creeping Jesus and omitted the 'sir'.

The adjutant was passed caring about the courtesies of military life. 'Yes,' he said with sudden eagerness. 'That's right, Carstens. So you think – ?'

'I don't think nothing,' Karl interrupted coldly. 'But it just might mean we're getting closer, that's all.' He rose to his feet wearily. 'Right, let's get on with it and be on our way.' He looked at the sky. 'It'll be dark in an hour and by then we've got to be under cover somewhere or other and well protected . . .'

The same thought animated von Dodenburg as he led his little column of tanks and armoured cars across the white waste. The going had been murderous all day, with the snow sweeping in thick flurries, virtually blinding the purple-faced look-outs in their leather masks and the tank commanders standing upright in the open turrets. Time and time again the treads slipped and skidded on the slick trail, with the cursing sweating drivers fighting the controls, desperately trying not to go off into the drainage ditches on both sides. Sometimes a tank would hover on the edge of the damned ditch, engines roaring, see-sawing back and forth as the furious driver tried to save the thirty-ton monster. Then the grenadiers would be turfed out of their half-tracks to begin the back-breaking, time-consuming chore of getting the monster back on the trail. Kilometre after kilometre the Wotan column had fought the road, which was often little better than a treacherous skating rink.

Now, however, von Dodenburg, who was leading this 'reconnaissance', as the Vulture had carefully phrased it so as not to occasion Sepp Dietrich's wrath ('If you find 'em, von Dodenburg, it's glory all around for Wotan. If you don't, well you were just on a routine recce'), knew it was almost time to laager up for the night. The darkness was increasing by the minute and with it would come the biting night cold that could cause frostbite within half an hour. Besides, in the darkness his armoured vehicles were completely vulnerable. Any peasant armed with a grenade could rush a Mark III at night and easily knock it out.

Next to him, Corporal Schulze, manning the turret machine-gun – just in case – growled, 'Got to get 'em under cover soon, sir.' It was as if he had read his CO's thoughts. 'These frigging Christmas tree soldiers ain't used to a bit of damp weather.' He sniffed. 'Christ, ain't they just wet behind the frigging spoons!'

Despite his mood, von Dodenburg grinned. Schulze, the big rogue, *would* call this arctic storm 'a bit of damp weather'. 'Have you got the hot and cold running maids laid on for them, Schulze?' he joked.

'Shit on the shingle, sir,' he moaned, 'I wouldn't frigging well know what to do with it if there was a big piece of juicy gash opening up right in front of me glassy orbs –' He stopped suddenly as an eerie howl, the first of many of that evening, echoed across the snowy waste, making the small hairs at the back of his shaven skull stand erect with apprehension. 'What the fuck was that, sir?' he exclaimed. 'Did you hear that frigging howl?'

From down below came Matz's disembodied voice from

the driving seat of the tank. 'Was that a shitting wolf, sir?' he demanded.

Von Dodenburg pressed his throat-mike and snapped urgently, 'You watch your, er, *shitting* driving, Corporal!' before he turned to an abruptly shocked Schulze and said, 'Are there wolves in this part of Russia, Corporal?'

Schulze shrugged, eyeing the white gloom apprehensively. 'Search me, sir. Anything's possible in this arsehole of a frigging country.' He bent forward, his eyes narrowed to slits against the driving, snow-laden wind. 'But I didn't think they had wolves just around this part.'

'Well,' von Dodenburg demanded, searching the gloom uneasily himself, 'what was it then?'

To that question, Schulze, who always knew everything, for once had no answer.

It was half an hour later, as they were slowly approaching a low huddle of dark buildings on the snowy ridge to their front, the armoured cars already churning ahead of the column through the powder snow to reconnoitre the place, that they heard the eerie howl repeated close by. This time there was no mistaking it for what it was, the savage cry of some wild beast of the canine family. It was only a matter of metres away, somewhere to the left of von Dodenburg's command tank.

Together he and Schulze spun in that direction, feeling an icy finger of unreasoning fear trace its way slowly down their spines. 'It's coming from just over there,' von Dodenburg hissed, keeping his voice low for some reason he couldn't explain.

Suddenly, taking the two of them completely by surprise, a dark shape hurtled across the snowfield at a tremendous rate and disappeared beneath the leading armoured car heading for the buildings to their front. It happened so quickly that von Dodenburg couldn't quite believe he had seen the dark shape racing across the snow.

There was a muffled crump and a burst of bright white

smoke. The leading armoured car rocked alarmingly as a ball of angry yellow flame exploded beneath it. Slowly, very slowly, the whole five tons of the vehicle rose into the air before their eyes and came crashing down again with a resounding smack. Both rear wheels burst and the engine caught fire. With flames pouring from the cowling, the crew, already ablaze, clambered frantically out of the escape hatches, fighting themselves free with hands turning into charred claws in the tremendous heat.

Von Dodenburg cowered back, shielding his face and eyes against the hot glare. 'What in God's name was –'

'Look, sir!' Schulze cut him short with a cry of rage. 'Over there at ten o'clock!'

Von Dodenburg swung round to the right. He peered through the gloom. Another dark shape was racing across the snow towards one of the armoured cars. For a moment he couldn't believe the evidence of his own eyes. 'Heaven, arse and cloudburst,' he exclaimed, 'it's . . . *a dog!*'

'Yes, sir, and do you make out what it's carrying on its back?'

Von Dodenburg narrowed his eyes against the wind. A box-like shape was strapped to the big dog's back with something attached to it whipping back and forth in bursts of dull silver. 'A box . . . and a kind of aerial!' he cried.

'Mines, sir!' Schulze exclaimed. 'The Popov pricks are using mine-dogs. Don't you see. That box is full of high explosive and they've been trained to sniff out our armoured vehicles –'

'And that aerial thing is the contact which detonates the explosive once they've got underneath –' Hurriedly he pressed his throat-mike. '*Kuno One to all,*' he cried urgently, 'Kuno One to all, the Ivans are using dogs laden with mines. Do you read me?'

The rest of his words were drowned as a frantic Schulze pressed the trigger of the turret machine-gun and poured a stream of urgent tracer towards the dog racing for an unsuspecting armoured car, groaning as he missed time and time again.

'Kuno One to Kuno Five,' von Dodenburg cried, eyes filled with horror, as the racing dog, tongue hanging out, ears clipped to its long sloping head grew ever closer, 'for chrissake look out.' He abandoned all radio procedure. 'Hanno, there's a frigging dog just about to shove an explosive charge up your rear passage. For God's sake hit the tube.'

A burst of machine-gun fire from the armoured car's turret told him that his message had been heard. Madly the armoured car driver swung his vehicle round and pressed his foot down. The eight wheels bit into the snow, flinging up a white whirling wake behind the cumbersome vehicle.

But the mine-dog held on grimly. It changed direction and set off on a new course, pelting towards the German vehicle, going all out, ignoring the lead stitching the area all about it. It was as if it took a fiendish pleasure in sacrificing itself to rid the world of yet another bunch of the hated Fritzes.

Cursing fluently, Schulze aimed and ripped off another burst. The dog suddenly leapt in the air, as if a red-hot poker had been thrust into its side. Legs flailing wildly, it fell into a heap in the snow fifty metres away from the second armoured car. The aerial of steel hit the ground. There was a tremendous explosion. The hound disintegrated. More hounds of death were already streaming from the nearby forest and pelting across the steppe, intent on destruction.

'Kuno One to all,' von Dodenburg yelled over the R/T, 'close in, close in on me, for God's sake! Gunners, pick them off now! Don't let them get within range!' He gasped with horror as a third dog sneaked from the right and almost joyfully buried itself beneath the hurrying wheels of the second armoured car, which thought it had escaped. In the same instant that the heavy wheels crushed the life out of the dog, its explosive charge went off right beneath the vehicle. The turret, weighing all of a ton, sailed majestically into the white gloom and all eight wheels burst. The armoured car came to a sudden smoking halt. No one got out.

The vehicles had now drawn up into a circle, guns blazing as the dogs charged time and time again. Others circled the ring of steel like wary Red Indians trying to find a loophole in the pioneers' defences.

Von Dodenburg raged, knowing they had walked into a trap. The killer dogs, were not alone. There were also their masters, out there in the forest – and it was getting ever darker by the second. *Almost before they had started, his little reconnaissance group had walked straight into a trap!*

CHAPTER 4

'In all my life,' Creeping Jesus quavered, 'I've never been so cold!' He shuddered dramatically, as he squatted with his back to the ruined wall. Around him the others also pressed themselves against the walls of the abandoned forester's hut, trying not to feel the icy night wind that whistled through every crack and the holed, ancient roof. An hour ago they had all drunk one cup of lukewarm water (Karl had ordered the fire put out as soon as it had grown completely dark) and finished off the last crumbs of the food they had looted from the dead men of the column. Now those not on guard tried to get some sleep. But it was too cold. Weary as they were, sleep was impossible in that freezing cold.

Karl looked contemptuously at Creeping Jesus's craven face, just visible in the faint silver light of the stars coming from the holes in the roof. 'You get yer share of the cold,' he snapped. 'Now stop bitching and let's rest.' He yawned and cowered a little lower in the collar of his greatcoat, breathing out hard so that his warm breath heated the tip of his frozen nose.

As he squatted there shivering, listening to the others shiver all around him, Karl knew that they had reached the end of the road again. Another day like today and they would be dead. He had seen it happen before in Russia: men, who appeared quite healthy, suddenly keeling over and dying for no other apparent reason than extreme cold and exhaustion. They needed good food and warmth urgently.

He stared at the dim outlines of their faces in the silver gloom and wondered at the cruel irony of it all. This was how they were, perhaps, to spend their last night on, earth. Thousands of kilometres away, back in the Homeland, there was a totally different world, where people slept in wonderfully soft, warm beds and could eat as much as they wished. Today was Saturday, he realized abruptly, and so there would be big capable women busy feeding their men and then spoiling them afterwards in those warm beds. After all it was Saturday night, wasn't it?

It didn't seem fair, Karl told himself, sudden tears of cold self-pity rolling down his sunken cheeks. Why should they have to die? They hadn't even begun to live. Why? Slowly he drifted off into an uncomfortable, restless doze, the awesome, biting cold forgotten for a little while, his dream mind full of hot, steaming food and big-bosomed gentle women who carried him into a bed piled high with down *Federdecken* as if he were a little child once more. It was blissful, heavenly. As he dozed there, his poor hungry face, the tears already freezing on his pale, sunken cheeks, twisted into a parody of a faint smile . . .

'*Karl!*'

He awoke with a start, feeling Polack's heavy paw clamping down on his shoulder urgently.

'What . . . what is it?' he asked thickly, blinking his eyes rapidly, the beautiful visions of food, warm beds and big-bosomed women vanishing. Next to him the others still snored softly and the cold hard silver light still came filtering through the holed roof.

'Listen,' Polack whispered tensely. 'Listen hard!'

Karl did so, straining hard. But there seemed nothing out there but the soft hush of the wind in the firs and the hiss as it blew the surface of the snow into dancing snow devils. 'I can't hear –'

'There it is again!' Polack interrupted urgently.

Karl held his breath. Then he heard it too. A low muted eerie howl a very long way off. 'Wolves?' he queried.

Polack shook his head. 'There's something else as well,' he said. 'Listen.'

Again Karl strained his ears. Again there was that spine-chilling canine howl, but this time it was followed by the unmistakable thump of explosive. Karl's heart leapt. Suddenly he felt his nerves tingling electrically. 'That was an explosion,' he exclaimed.

'Yes,' Polack hissed excitedly, new hope suddenly in his bearded weary face, 'and you know what that means?'

'There's somebody out there.'

'More.'

'What, Polack?'

'If there's an explosion, there's fighting, and where there's fighting, one of the two parties is going to be our lot.'

'What?' Karl stared at him dully, mouth gaping like some village yokel. 'What did you say?'

'Our people are out there – *somewhere*?' Polack didn't attempt to lower his voice in his excitement. Next to him the others stirred and Ami said thickly, 'Eh?'

Polack repeated what he had just said and cried joyfully, 'We've got a chance, comrades. *We've got a frigging chance after all!*'

Another of the devilish dark furry shapes came slinking out of the trees. In the silver light Schulze could see it quite clearly, muzzle up, long ears erect, moving forward on its belly with a queer kind of slither. A moment later another appeared, and then another.

The first one raised its hideous muzzle to the sky and gave a long low howl that turned Matz's legs to water as he squatted in the driver's seat below. The others took up the howl. They tilted back their sloping heads and in unison set up a hellish eerie baying. 'Aching arseholes,' Matz moaned, 'won't they ever shut up. They want to make me piss mesen!'

Schulze growled an oath and concentrated on bringing the turret machine-gun round. Next to him Kuno von Dodenburg whispered softly into the throat-mike, 'Kuno One to all, they're up to something again. Stand by!'

It was over an hour now since the last attack, which they had beaten off successfully at the cost of a third armoured car. Von Dodenburg, cradling a machine pistol next to Schulze, told himself that the unseen enemy was about to launch another assault, and somehow he knew that this would be an all-out one. Even the partisan masters of these terrible killer hounds could not stand the cold in the open much longer. It was hellish, even in the cover of the vehicles with the engines running. They dared not turn them off; they'd never start again in this murderous cold.

The hounds continued to howl at the sky, as if they would never stop. The terrible keening went on, making the waiting sentries twitch with nervousness until their eyes were wide with fear and they were virtually at the end of their tether.

'Christ on a crutch,' Matz moaned yet again, 'won't they ever put a frigging sock in it!'

With startling suddenness, as if in response to Matz's empassioned plea, the keening ceased. It was followed by a reverberating silence. Schulze's eyes narrowed to slits, a nerve ticking at the side of his face from pent-up tension. Then the killer dogs came. This time they weren't pelting across the snow. Now the low, furry shapes were crawling, flat wicked heads down, moving from side to side as if sniffing out their prey.

Schulze felt the sweat beginning to drip from his forehead. He had seen many horrors in this war, but never anything like this before. 'Christ,' he cried in exasperation to no one in particular, 'it oughtn't to be fucking allowed!'

'*Schnauze!*' von Dodenburg rasped. 'Keep yer eyes peeled. We don't want to lose 'em!'

'Peeled like tinned tomatoes they are, sir,' Schulze answered promptly and von Dodenburg forced a wan grin. He could always rely on old hares like Schulze and Matz in a tricky situation. And this was definitely a tricky one. Here were the dogs, but where were the Popov partisans? A sixth sense told him they were out there somewhere? *But where?*

*

Sonja pushed back the hood of her white camouflage cape and knelt next to Elinka in the snow. Even the bulky clothes and the camouflage gear could not quite hide Comrade Elinka's wonderful figure and resolute beautiful face. Sonja felt a shiver of desire. How dearly she would have loved to take the commander of the 'Hounds of Hell' commando in her big arms and press her to her own ample bosom. Instead she whispered, as the hounds shuffled ever closer to the Fritzes' tanks, standing there in the snow like stalled metal monsters, 'All is well, *Tovaritsch Doktor*. The Fascist pigs haven't seen the fire squad yet.' She meant the fifty women crawling through the trees on the opposite side of the valley, each one of them armed with a home-made Molotov cocktail.

Elinka Vassiloya, who in another life had been the chief district surgeon, a professional woman devoted to saving humankind and not destroying it so cruelly, nodded her head. 'You have done well, Sonja,' she whispered.

Sonja could have swooned. Any faint bit of praise from the woman she loved secretly made her dizzy, although she always did her best to conceal it. Neither Elinka nor any other of the tough women who made up this elite female commando had the faintest inkling that Comrade Sonja, who had twice strangled a Fritz with her bare hands, harboured such feelings beneath her tough hulking exterior. But how difficult it was to suppress them, when night after night, lying in their rough-and-ready quarters in barns, abandoned *isbas* and the like, it would have been *so* easy just to stretch out a hand and caress the object of her love and desire.

Elinka Vassiloya had been raped by a whole line of SS men the day they had conquered the capital of the province on that horrible, hot June day. They had lined up, with their camouflaged pants around their ankles, not overly excited, indeed some of them had even seemed bored, waiting their turn to have her on her own operating table, with the dead patient and the murdered male nurses lying crumpled all around the theatre. After a while she had accepted them inside her, willing herself not to tense up and fight back – that would only cause more damage – letting them rut.

Later that night, when they had all been drunk out of this world, perhaps even already dead, because they had consumed medical spirits straight from the big jars without even attempting to dilute the stuff with water, she had crept into the ward where they had snored in their drunken sleep. While a dying Alexei had covered her with one of their own machine pistols, she had slipped from bed to bed and neatly emasculated each and every one of them with a neat cut of the scalpel until her hand was wet and slippery with blood right up to the wrist and she had grown weary of the whole rotten business.

Two days later she had slipped into the woods, crowded with runaways like herself, rogues, deserters, Jews – all of those who for one reason or other had not wanted to remain behind in the capital (of course, the Party officials had been warned beforehand and had escaped in style). For weeks, months, they had all lived from hand to mouth, existing little better than the bandits who had once terrorized this area, shunned by their own people even, who in the villages and towns at least had come to be able to live with the Fritzes – hadn't the *nmetski* given them back the land Stalin had taken away in the twenties?

Slowly, however, the peasants and the small shopkeeper class, which had sprung up again under a fairly benevolent German occupation, had begun to turn against the Germans – and the partisans had been born. In a small way at first, but as the war in the shadows had escalated, with German reprisals mounting as the partisan attacks mounted, more and more had fled to the forests and the partisans – 'to Comrade Forest', as the townsfolk had phrased it. Now the forests were full of such groups, but there was nothing to match the 'Hounds of Hell', which had made a speciality of their trained dogs. Why, what other partisan group could claim to have destroyed twenty Fritz tanks in one day? The killer dogs, each laden with anti-tank mines, had emerged from a flock of sheep blocking the column's way to carry out their work of destruction.

'*Tovaritsch Doktor*', as she was known far and wide, even in Moscow, was proud of her girls and dogs, though deep down in her innermost self she was troubled by two things: one, that she had lost her vocation to heal – now she preferred to kill; and two, she was no longer attracted to men. She rationalized that it was because of the terrible thing the SS men had done to her when the provincial capital had been captured. But in those troubled moments at three o'clock in the morning when one cannot sleep and one makes one's assessment of life and the world, she knew it was something else. She had become like poor helpless Comrade Sonja with her moustache, itchy hands and sheepdog-like, devoted eyes. She was turning into one of *those*!

But at this moment such problems were far from her mind. She was concerned solely with the destruction of this German column, which she guessed was searching for the Fritzes trapped back at the river. Comrade Colonel Bogdan – what an arrogant male stallion he was, always fingering the flies of his britches, as if he were only waiting her signal to rip them open and mount – had warned her to inform him immediately she spotted such a column. The big handsome Cossack would find out about the column after *she* had destroyed it.

She grinned at the thought in the glowing silvery darkness and said, 'All right, Sonja. We shall give the attack squad fifteen more minutes. The "Hounds of Hell" will run in soon. Once the Fritzes are occupied with them – the poor beasts – we move in.' She patted her signal pistol and added, 'One red flare, that's the signal – and then we go in for the kill.'

'*Horoscho!*' the burly second-in-command growled in her deep bass.

Elinka took pity on her. *Boshe moi*, what a terrible sex life she must have led with that damned moustache! She reached across and squeezed her big paw with her own delicate gloved hand. 'Thank you, my dear,' she whispered.

Sonja felt her whole body turn to water. She caught herself just in time before she fainted with the sheer delight of it all. The 'Comrade Doctor' had actually squeezed *her* hand!

A kilometre away, Karl raised his hand and the four men strung out behind him came to a weary halt. Already their energy was beginning to flag again, after the initial excitement of Polack's discovery had pumped new life into them, and Creeping Jesus, bringing up the rear of the little column, was weaving like a punchdrunk boxer. 'Listen,' he commanded, as the fast *burr-burr* of a machine-gun sounded again to their right beyond the trees. 'You know what that is?'

No one responded; they were too weary even for hope, it seemed. Karl pushed by the others to Creeping Jesus, their weakest link. He grabbed him roughly by the collar. 'Did you hear that?' he rasped.

The adjutant stared at him blankly. Strange animal sounds came from his throat.

Karl shook him. 'Listen, you – and listen all of you,' he hissed malevolently, eyes gleaming crazily in the silver light. 'We've nearly done it. We're virtually saved. All we need to do is to hang on a little longer. Not only for ourselves,' his voice came through gritted teeth, as if he were very angry with himself, restraining himself by sheer will-power, 'but the others too. You must remember them.'

'Yes,' Polack croaked, 'we remember them, Karl.'

King Bull, shaking his head like an animal troubled by flies, said thickly, 'Let's get on – get it done with, Carstens.'

'Then act like damned soldiers!' Karl snapped. 'Unsling your weapons. We're going to have to do something up there – God knows what. But we must do *something*!' He grabbed the rifle taken from the dead he had forced Creeping Jesus to carry. He unslung it and slapped it into the adjutant's hands. 'Take off the safety! Come on now – do as I say!'

Clumsily, Creeping Jesus clicked off the weapon's safety catch.

'Now jerk back the bolt – check the magazine. *Los!*' He spun round on the others, eyes blazing furiously, his thin face full of fury. 'The rest of you, too!'

Numbly they did as he commanded.

He waited till they had finished before crying, 'Now you're beginning to act like real soldiers. All right, follow me. We're going to help whoever's out there any way we can – and woe betide any of you bastards who let me down!' With that he set off, crunching through the snow at a tremendous pace.

Polack shook his head in disbelief. 'A week ago, we were wondering how we were gonna do a bunk,' he grunted.

Ami nodded sourly. 'Yer, and now he's acting like a frigging fire-eating field-marshal. It's a frigging funny old world.' He stared at Karl in the silver gloom, stamping towards the sound of the firing, rifle at the ready, and shook his head too, as if he simply couldn't believe what he saw. Then, with a muffled curse, he started after Karl.

Reluctantly the others followed. The chatter of the machine-guns began to grow in intensity . . .

CHAPTER 5

Yet another of the damned hounds came creeping in, clinging to the snow with its furry belly. Schulze, his tense nerves vibrating like fiddle strings, yelled a warning as he swung the turret gun round. Too late! The hound of hell sprang clean into the air and the burst of tracer zipped by it harmlessly. Von Dodenburg jerked up his machine pistol. It chattered into violent, frenetic activity. The animal yelped with unbearable agony as it was hit. Next moment there was a tremendous explosion.

The tank rocked back on its rear bogies with the impact. Von Dodenburg ducked, feeling the blast lash him savagely across his shocked face. Gory pieces of the shattered animal fell on the deck of the tank like scarlet rain. A head slammed into the side of the turret and down below Matz cried, 'And now they're frigging well throwing dogs' heads at us!' Von Dodenburg retched.

Now the animals were everywhere, while the Wotan troopers blazed away at them furiously, more afraid of these hellish hounds than they had ever been of their masters. There was something fiendish and uncanny about the way they came running in, intent on suicide, totally unafraid, dying for something they knew absolutely nothing about.

Once one of the dogs collapsed, writhing in the snow, its hind leg severed by a burst of machine-gun fire. It gave an almost human shriek as it twisted and turned in its mortal agony, splattering blood on all sides. In a flash half a dozen of the other hounds of hell sprang upon it. Grunting and growling, snapping at each other, with their yellow fangs bared, they fell on the other beast, ripping great chunks of red-dripping flesh and fur from the still living animal.

For a few moments the sickened men of the Wotan were too shocked, too nauseated, to act. They stared aghast at the spectacle, weapons idle in their hands until Schulze, with a great oath, swung the turret machine-gun round and rattled off a whole belt, sending the dogs yelping and dropping with pain, as an instant later the first of their deadly cargo exploded, filling the air with great lumps of severed flesh.

The others joined in again, blazing away at the dogs, too concerned with the horror of the sight to notice the other dark shapes – human this time, – sneaking out of the trees . . .

Karl saw the bulky white-clad figure first. He stopped in his tracks and, pressing himself against a tree, hissed an urgent warning to the others.

They halted at once, hardly daring to breathe as the unsuspecting figure moved slowly through the firs, a bottle-like object in hand. Karl's mind raced furiously. Was the lone person a German or –

'Popov,' Polack whispered gently into his right ear, solving the problem for him.

'How do you know?'

'Smell him,' Polack replied. 'Trust me.'

Karl did. Polack, the country boy, did have the keenest sense of smell of them all. He nodded his understanding and slung his rifle swiftly.

'What you gonna do, Karl?'

'Nobble him. Keep me covered.' Silently he drew his bayonet and gripped it more firmly in the rags which had once been gloves.

Polack started to protest, but already his comrade was rushing forward, any sound he made covered by the wind, bayonet raised, ready for the kill.

Polack held his breath. Now Karl was five metres away from the stooped white-clad figure.

Suddenly the crouched figure tensed. Polack gasped. He could see by the way the Russian abruptly hunched his shoulder that he had sensed something. In a moment he

would turn and then all would be lost. But Karl didn't wait to
be discovered. He dived forward, with a great grunt. In that
same instant, his cruel bayonet rose and fell. It caught the
Russian right between the shoulders. It went in with a great
sucking noise, as if its tip had already punctured the victim's
lungs. The Russian screamed, as Karl drew out the red-
shining blade and slashed it down savagely – a high,
hysterical and utterly, unmistakably feminine cry.

Polack's mouth dropped open. 'Great God,' he gasped,
'*he's a – a woman!*'

'*Alarm, alarm!*' someone shouted urgently, as that uncanny
woman's scream shrilled out of the trees close to where the
tanks had finally beaten off the attack of the hounds of hell.
'They're in the trees . . . *everywhere*!' There was the excited
burr-burr of a machine pistol firing all out and a white-clad
figure running towards the nearest armoured car came to an
abrupt stop. For a moment the figure poised there. Then the
Molotov cocktail fell to the snow and exploded in a sudden
blinding sheet of violent blue flame, which turned the figure
in a flash into a writhing screaming human torch.

'*Ten o'clock!*' von Dodenburg cried swiftly as the white-clad
figures came running awkwardly towards the column,
Molotov cocktails already raised to throw. 'Fire at will. Keep
them at their distance!' He fired himself and another one of
the women went writhing and screaming to the snow to be
enveloped in those cruel blue flames an instant later.

A massacre commenced. There was no other word for it.
The women partisans were unarmed save for the petrol-filled
bottles. They had no way of defending themselves and as soon
as they were spotted by the Wotan troopers darting forward
to throw their deadly cocktails, they were mown down
mercilessly. The SS men knew what their fate would be if they
fell into the partisans' hands. First there would be torture and
then they would be shot out of hand. SS men were never

taken prisoner by the Popovs. And all of them knew that the women partisans were the cruellest of them all. They played very nasty tricks with their male SS prisoners before they allowed them the release of death.

'Keep them at a distance,' von Dodenburg cried desperately, as a bottle came whizzing through the air to explode in an instant blaze only metres away from his command tank. 'For chrissake don't let them get too close – or we're finished!' He ripped off another burst from the hip and sent another of their attackers down on her knees in the snow, fighting desperately to remain upright, but failing miserably. A moment later she too went up in a burst of cruel, all-consuming flame . . .

Even Creeping Jesus seemed to have regained his strength, as they burst in among the surprised women, crouching in the trees, watching the massacre of their comrades. Taken completely off guard, the women had no time to grab their weapons. They went down under the weight of the German attack, men and women grappling in a mess of flailing limbs in the snow and undergrowth.

King Bull rammed his shoulder brutally into Elinka's face. She yelped with pain as her nose broke and flooded her face with her own hot blood. King Bull laughed triumphantly and grabbed the wrist of her hand with which she had drawn a knife from her boot. He grunted and with a cruel twist snapped her thin wrist in two. The 'Comrade Doctor' would never be able to operate again.

Sonja shrieked with rage when she saw the two of them writhing in the snow. A powerless Elinka was trying to escape the importuning hands already ripping at her clothes. The sudden hardness in the Fritz's loins appalled her. *The man was finding sexual pleasure in this savage attack!* 'Swine!' she gasped in German and after hawking she spat right into King Bull's face.

He laughed crazily. 'Keep at it, hell cat,' he chortled with delight, 'I like a woman to be lively. Now let me get them tits . . .'

He gasped as the whole of Sonja's weight plumped down on his big back. Caught by surprise, he did nothing as Sonja straddled him and started pounding at him with her clenched fists. 'Wriggle out, Comrade Doctor,' she pleaded. 'Quick. I can't hold him much longer. *Davai.*' Furiously she held on as King Bull started to exert his massive strength.

Elinka, choking and weeping with pain, her hand useless, started to crawl away, heading for the cover of the thick firs a few metres away.

But that wasn't to be.

Creeping Jesus's boot lashed out. The brutally shod riding boot caught her in the face. She felt her chin crack. Silver stars exploded in front of her eyes. Blood spurted from her head and ears. A wave of agony shot through her beautiful body and then she was sinking into a deep scarlet mist, while at her side, watched by a crazily grinning Creeping Jesus, King Bull thrust himself into Sonja, laughing like someone demented.

It was thus that *Hauptsturmbannführer* von Dodenburg caught them, as he strode through the trees filled with dead and dying women, some of them charred and petrified like ancient burnt trees, limbs sticking straight upwards. He raised his machine pistol and fired an angry burst into the air and bellowed at the top of his voice, 'Will you cease this piggery!' He spat in disgust and next to him Schulze strode forward and planted a hearty kick on King Bull's naked rump, crying, 'Far too good for you miserable stubble-hoppers! Get off the frigging nest, man!'

Startled King Bull rolled to one side, while von Dodenburg took in the scene: the dying woman, whose face looked as if someone had thrown a handful of strawberry jam at it; the raped woman, eyes full of hate; a crazy officer presiding over it all, grinning inanely; while a ragged handsome young soldier glared at him, fists clenched, face full of impotent rage. 'What in three devils' name is going on here?' he demanded, iron in his voice. 'Who are you people?'

Karl looked at Creeping Jesus, the old habits of respect and military discipline reasserting themselves in the presence of this tough-looking, arrogant young officer, whose cap he now saw bore the hated skull and crossbones of the SS.

Creeping Jesus did not respond. He continued to grin inanely. On the ground a crestfallen King Bull, face still suffused with passion, sheepishly did up his flies, mumbling to himself.

Ami and Polack looked at Karl and the latter nodded encouragingly, although he too had recognized that tarnished insignia. He cleared his throat and said, 'Sir.'

Von Dodenburg shot the ragged young soldier with the intelligent face a hard look, somehow sizing up the situation, knowing that he was looking at the real leader of these ragged stragglers. 'Who are you?' he demanded.

Karl tried wearily to click to attention, but von Dodenburg waved for him to desist. 'Grenadier Carstens, sir,' he reported. 'Of the Fourth Grenadier Regiment.'

Von Dodenburg's face lit up. 'Fourth Grenadiers, eh? So you were with the Iron Division, Grenadier?'

'*Jawohl, Hauptsturm,*' Karl snapped back, realizing suddenly that here might be the help they sought to aid those poor wounded swine suffering still back at the bridge. 'We managed to get through, but there are –'

Von Dodenburg waved for him to be silent and Karl's face fell as he stopped speaking. He watched gloomily, as the SS officer walked off a few paces, face thoughtful. What was going through his head?

The big SS corporal pulled his flatman out of his back pocket, took a mighty swig himself and handed the bottle to Karl. 'Here, son,' he said, 'knock one of these down behind yer front collar stud – and yer comrades as well.' He indicated Polack and Ami. 'Make yer eyes sparkle.' He waited till Karl had taken a drink and handed the flask to Ami before saying, with a nod at von Dodenburg's back, 'There's not much more than a company of us, you know, son. And them shitting dogs has already done for half a dozen of us. Besides, our orders is to make a recce – no more.'

'Thanks for the drink,' Karl said. 'But, you know, Corporal, there are hundreds, perhaps thousands of wounded back at the bridge. They won't be able to last much longer in –'

'What did the opposition look like, Grenadier?' von Dodenburg cut into Karl's excited flow of words.

'Cavalry, sir. Cossack cavalry.' Hastily Karl explained how the Goulash Cannon Company had been attacked by massed Soviet cavalry and been virtually wiped out save for himself and the other four, including the regimental adjutant. He indicated Creeping Jesus who was still staring at Sonja, as she lay there, breasts exposed, eyes burning with hatred.

'Could be a division,' von Dodenburg said, pursing his lips. 'A whole Popov division against one company of SS,' he mused, with a faint arrogant smile on his lips. 'The odds are not too bad, are they?'

Loyally Schulze snorted, 'We'll be through them Soviet shite-shovellers in zero comma nothing seconds, sir! What can they do with them penknives o' theirn against Wotan's armour?' He spat contemptuously in the snow at his feet. 'Fascist pigs!'

They started. It was the woman lying in the snow, eyes full of hate and pride, and totally unafraid. 'You'll die here in Mother Russia,' she spat out the words venomously. 'You have signed your death warrant simply by being German.' Her accent was thick, but her German was perfect. '*Jawohl*, here you will die!'

Suddenly Creeping Jesus raised his rifle. Karl gasped. Ami opened his mouth to protest. But von Dodenburg beat him to it. 'No,' he commanded. Then he looked down at the woman quizzically. 'Madam,' he said gravely, as if he had given the matter some consideration, 'you may be right that some of us will die here.' He laughed suddenly. 'But not yet. *No.*' His voice rose confidently. 'Not yet by a long chalk. We've a job to do here first!'

Karl's heart leapt. 'You mean, sir – ?'

'Yes, I do!' von Dodenburg cut him short and immediately forgot the woman. He had made up his mind.

'You, Grenadier, you and you, too,' he indicated Ami and Polack, 'will come with me in the command tank.' Without another word, he turned and stamped back through the crisp snow to his vehicle. A moment afterwards, the Three Rebels, escorted by the men wearing the same badge as those who had tortured and persecuted their families, followed . . .

Sonja watched them go, all energy drained from her body now, as if someone had opened an invisible tap. She felt a sudden sense of overwhelming fatigue, helplessness, despair. It wasn't because of her poor women who had been slaughtered so cruelly, though she had been spared. As partisans they had all subconsciously expected to die sooner or later; it was the nature of the war in the shadows.

No, it was the sight of that handsome young arrogant German officer that occasioned her mood. There was something . . . something unstoppable, indestructible about him, which made her feel that poor Mother Russia could never survive against him and his kind.

She watched as he stood bolt-upright in the turret of his tank jerking his balled fist up and down smartly, indicating his drivers should prepare to move off, the great engines already roaring impatiently. What thoughts were going through his head? Did he hear Wagner as he prepared to lead his own damned Valkyries into battle? Did he see himself as a kind of latterday Teutonic Knight, once again carrying the banner of German conquest into the heart of Mother Russia as his forefathers had done centuries before? What thoughts did he and all the rest of his kind have, as they prepared to fight the might of Russia, a mere handful of men against Bogdan's thousands of Cossacks? How could that arrogant Fritz swine with his cropped blond hair be so damned confident? Suddenly she started to sob.

CHAPTER 6

The winter sky shimmered.

Already the sun was sinking low over the river and its rays shone horizontally, illuminating the whole far side of the river in its cold yellow light. It had, von Dodenburg thought, as he surveyed it with his binoculars, that chill, suspended-in-time deadened atmosphere of ground that had just been recently fought over. Everywhere the steppe was pitted with shell craters, the trees stripped to the bark, branches hanging down like severed limbs, with the crumpled bodies of the dead lying like stiffly frozen bundles of rags.

The living were everywhere too. The far bank was packed with little carts, ancient Russian lorries, vehicles of all kinds, and in between them the wounded and now the advanced elements of the Iron Division and the Fourth Grenadiers too squatted helplessly in holes, the smoke of their poor little fires trickling slowly into the golden air. At a quick estimate there had to be at least three thousand men trapped down there, von Dodenburg told himself and wondered why the Russians had not attacked before and wiped them out. It would not be too difficult for cavalry to cross the river and attack, even where the ice was broken.

To his right there was a roar like that of an infuriated beast, a dull moaning keening, which rose to a startling crescendo and then died away in a long whining. Von Dodenburg ducked instinctively in the turret as six fingers of smoke roared up into the yellow sky. The salvo of red-tailed rockets, trailing spluttering angry sparks behind them, slammed down on the far bank of the river, making the very ground beneath the tank tremble. Huge mushrooms of smoke erupted and men fell on all sides or ran desperately to find some cover.

Next to the SS officer, Karl groaned and bit his bottom lip. One of the infernal Soviet rockets had landed right in the centre of a group of carts bearing the wounded. They were tossed into the air like broken toys and now lay still – dead or dying, slaughtered impersonally without a chance.

Von Dodenburg shook his head, 'A bad business . . . very bad.' He frowned and swung his glasses round to where the mortars had now ceased firing. 'They're masters of camouflage, the Popovs,' he said, focusing his glasses, 'but they're there all right. No doubt about that.'

'Is there nothing we can do, sir?' Karl asked desperately, following the direction of the SS officer's gaze as he surveyed the white hillsides, where presumably the Cossack division lay hidden. 'Those poor shits won't be able to stand much more of this.'

Von Dodenburg lowered his glasses slowly. 'Of course we will do something. But first we must deal with the Popovs. The minute we attempt to start bringing your people across the river, all hell will be let loose. Indeed, the more I think of it, the more I am inclined to believe that your people are being used to bait a trap.'

'Bait a trap, sir?' Karl echoed in bewilderment.

'Yes. Those Cossacks could have dealt with them days ago. So why didn't they? Because I think they wanted massive German forces to move up, especially armour like us which would be stalled on the opposite bank so that they could cut it up with their guns and planes at their leisure.'

'I see, sir,' Karl answered and realized that the SS officer was right. 'So what do we do, sir?'

Von Dodenburg paused. 'Even a hairy-arsed stubble-hopper like you, Carstens, to use the words of my dear Corporal Schulze here,' he indicated the giant NCO standing next to him in the turret and Schulze grinned, 'must know that even in the SS it is not customary for a company to attack a division. Militarily speaking it is a no-win situation.'

Karl looked from the officer to the corporal and wondered

if his leg was being slightly pulled. From their looks he suspected it was somehow. But he said aloud, 'No, sir, I am sure you're right.'

'Of course. So far the Popovs haven't spotted that we're here. That's one point in our favour, don't you think?'

Again Karl, feeling very stupid, said, 'Yes . . . yes, of course, sir.'

'You asked what do we do? Well, Schulze, what *do* we do?'

Schulze whipped a dewdrop from the end of his big Hamburg nose and flicked it expertly over the side of the tank. 'What do we do, sir?' he echoed. 'Why, we do what the frigging Wotan has always done in situations like this . . . *we frigging well attack*!'

Von Dodenburg smiled softly at Karl. 'There you are. You have the words from the mouth of a humble SS man. We frigging well attack! That's what we do . . .'

'Useful thing that, having a window in yer eyehole, eh, sir,' Schulze commented cheerfully, as Creeping Jesus, slowly reasserting himself as an officer once more, peered down into the valley with the rest of them. 'Controls the face muscles, they tell me. Hides the emotions.'

Karl kept himself from laughing at the massive SS corporal's comments, while Creeping Jesus stared at Schulze somewhat bewildered. Was the man serious or was he somehow making fun of him?

'Now me,' Schulze went on mercilessly, 'I wish I could wear a piece of glass like that up my arsehole – if you'll forgive my French, *Herr Hauptmann*? 'Cos my emotions have a way of turning into the thin shits at a time like this.' He indicated the thousands of horses packed together below in the valley, some tethered, but most of them just standing morosely, wondering probably when they were going to be fed again. 'Now if I had a piece of glass –'

'*Schulze!*' von Dodenburg barked warningly.

Schulze grinned and shut up, as von Dodenburg turned to them. 'Cavalry without their mounts are not very effective,' he commented.

There was a murmur of agreement from his listeners.

'They have no heavy weapons normally, no anti-tank guns and things of that nature, just their side-arms, rifles and mortars, which are ineffective against armour. Now you are all jumping ahead of me, thinking that I am going to propose stampeding those horses down there and putting the Cossacks on their two flat feet, their mobility gone.' He gave them all an arrogant smile.

Karl told himself that if Hitler had an army of clever bastards like von Dodenburg he would have won the war long ago, and he and the other two Rebels would be now safely tucked away in a concentration camp. Still, he couldn't help admiring the SS officer; he was head and shoulders above the bumbling, old-fashioned officers of the Fourth Grenadiers.

'But it isn't as easy as that,' von Dodenburg warned. 'You think perhaps I could have a couple of shells fired over the heads of those nags down there and they would panic, stampede, break loose.' He shook his head. 'But they wouldn't. They are trained cavalry horses, *Cossack* cavalry mounts. They are used to the sound of shot and shell. Indeed, they are trained not to bolt when they hear guns fire. To stampede that lot, other measures will be necessary.'

Karl and the others frowned. Creeping Jesus even looked afraid. He too had thought it was going to be easy. Frighten off the horses, immobilize the Cossacks and then get on bringing the Iron Division and the Fourth across the river. No danger at all. Now it seemed it wasn't going to be that easy. He shivered dramatically.

Von Dodenburg gave them the benefit of his arrogant grin once more. 'But there is one thing that will frighten all horses into stampeding, even those tough old nags down there. *And that is fire!*'

Schulze grinned too and Karl snorted angrily. 'But where

can we get a fire going in this goddamn snow waste, *Hauptsturm*? Nothing will burn on the steppe!'

'And that is just where you are wrong, Grenadier,' von Dodenburg said easily. He pulled out his whistle and shrilled a swift blast on it. There was the crash of gears and the whine of a powerful engine. There was the rumble of armour and the crunch of heavy tyres on the snow. A moment later one of the remaining eight-wheel armoured cars swung round the trail, grinding along in low gear. But the crew standing in the turret were dressed differently from the rest of the Wotan troopers. The black panzer uniforms had been replaced by heavy leather jackets, gloves and face masks, and all of them wore black goggles so that they looked to Karl like sinister denizens of another world.

King Bull gasped and Ami snorted, 'What the hell is that?'

Von Dodenburg raised his hand and obediently the driver halted. Pleased with the success of his surprise, von Dodenburg waved his hand round his head three times, the signal for action. To their front the long, peculiar-shaped, thin cannon of the armoured car swung round to point away from them in the direction of a grove of thin firs, heavily laden with snow and ice.

'Watch,' he commanded.

They did so.

Abruptly there was a sudden vicious hiss. Out of the cannon's ugly nozzle, a thick burning yellow rod of flame erupted with a noise like someone wielding a heavy leather strap. Suddenly the line of flying flame curved downwards. *Smack!* Burning gobs of oil splattered everywhere, making the snow steam and hiss frantically, as it slapped against the firs. The flame spread at once, leaping up the branches, along the trunks, into the fronds. In a second the trees were a raging inferno, the trunks being consumed like matchwood, falling and cracking almost instantly. Then the terrible rod of flame vanished, leaving behind the cloying stench of oil and the smell of burning resin.

Karl wiped the sudden sweat from his forehead and narrowed his eyes against the glare, as von Dodenburg said simply, face very serious now, 'That is how we are going to stampede the horses – and then it's down to the river to start getting those poor wretches across.' He flashed a glance at his watch. '*Meine Herren*, we attack in exactly fifteen minutes . . .'

For the first time since he had set the trap for the Fritzes, Colonel Bogdan was worried. The Fascists were not reacting in the manner he had anticipated. He knew already from his spies on the other side of the Dnieper that a small German armoured force had crossed the great river and had been heading roughly in his direction. The women partisans had also reported that they had spotted them and that the enemy was still heading in the same general direction. But then there had been no other word from the damned women. Had something happened or was their radio out of action? Such things did happen. But the really worrying thing was that the Fritzes were not making any major attempt to concentrate and rescue the survivors of their Iron Division.

As he surveyed the trapped Germans on the opposite side of the river, he asked himself whether the next German move depended upon what their reconnaissance party reported, wherever it might be? He lowered his glasses and unconsciously fingered the little leather bag around his neck, as he always did when he was worried, like now.

Should he wait any longer? The beaten Fritzes on the other side of the river were his for the taking. A flanking movement under the cover of darkness to left and right of the bridge and he would roll them up without difficulty. But by doing so, he would have eaten up the bait with which he had hoped to attract even larger German formations into the trap, ripe for the slaughter. Old Leather Face up there in the Kremlin would not be impressed by the liquidation of one under-strength, virtually beaten Fritz division. Perhaps, although he had his murderous fingers in so many pies in Moscow, the *Stavka* would not even inform him. What was he to do?

Colonel Bogdan crunched slowly over the frozen snow, followed by his senior *Sotnik*, Serge Alexei, who like most of his Cossacks simply burned for action. Considerations of strategy and politics played no role inside his handsome head. All he was concerned with was the thrill of combat and the pleasure battle gave him. He wanted to charge into battle and lop off heads, it really didn't matter much whose.

The *Sotnik* finally broke the heavy silence. 'What do you think, Comrade Colonel? Do we wait any longer? They *are* such a juicy target. Plenty of fine Fritz guts to be ripped open. Perhaps there will even be women, plump Fascist pigeons to be bedded.' He chuckled heartily, black Cossack eyes sparkling merrily at the thought.

Bogdan laughed with him. He had once been like that, simply concerned with combat and women. 'Patience, my dear *Sotnik*,' he cried, 'patience. There'll be killing enough –'

The sudden crackle-and-snap of small-arms fire cut startlingly into his words. The two of them swung round. Over the hills where the division rested and waited, faint puffs of smoke were rising and Bogdan could hear the rusty rattle of tracks. He cursed a great oath and slapped his thigh angrily. 'The horse lines, *Sotnik*. They're into the damned horse lines!'

The *Sotnik* did not need to be told who 'they' were. Even as he drew his sabre, as if he half-expected the Fritzes to appear on all sides, Bogdan was running for his stallion, knowing with the absolute certainty of a vision that his plan had failed. The Fritzes were already attacking and he wasn't ready for them . . .

The handful of armoured vehicles raced towards the horses in a tight 'V', the 'Blow Torch', as the SS called the flame-throwing armoured car, in its centre, protected by the tanks on both sides. They advanced at a tremendous pace, aerials whipping the snow being churned up in a wild white wake behind them, the slugs of the startled picquets howling off their metal sides harmlessly.

The Three Rebels squatting on the deck of von Dodenburg's command tank clung on desperately, as the little driver Matz took every pothole and bump in the steppe at top speed.

'Crazy . . . crazy!' Ami called above the tremendous roar, carried away by that wild mad charge. 'Absolutely fuckin' crazy – and I love it!'

A group of Cossack riflemen came firing out of a thicket, desperate men, knowing how precious their mounts were. Blow Torch's gunners did not hesitate. The streak of flame shot from the cannon's muzzle. All about the Cossacks, the trees burst into flame at once, the snow on their branches melting and sizzling and dropping in a heavy rain. The cruel sheet of sudden death engulfed the helpless Russians. They twisted and turned violently, electrically, like puppets in the hands of a suddenly crazy puppet-master, then they dropped writhing and already charring into grotesque cinders in the steaming snow. The 'V' raced on.

The tethered mounts scented the fire. They bucked and whinnied, tugging at their halters, trying to bite themselves free of their traces. Everywhere there was panic and confusion, with desperate Cossacks racing down the lines, braving the flailing hooves, trying in vain to calm the horses.

A stone cottage loomed up, From one of its shattered windows, a machine-gun opened fire. Tracer hissed towards the tanks. Next to Karl, King Bull yelped with pain and clapped a hand to his shoulder, bright blood already oozing between tight-pressed fingers. Creeping Jesus hid his face in his hands like a frightened child, while Bulle cursed angrily.

Again Blow Torch went into action. Flames gushed from the muzzle of that frightening cannon. They lashed the cottage time and time again, curling their way round it in violet anger until the very stones glowed and the hard steel of the machine-gun's muzzle poking out of the window started to melt. From inside there came muffled screams, terrible screams, like those of a trapped animal; then there was silence and they rattled on.

The Cossacks' horses had begun to break away from their halters and traces, ripping them loose in their unreasoning panic. Scores were already galloping madly across the steppe, ignoring the vain attempts of the Russians, arms outstretched, waving their fur caps, whooping crazily, to stop them. Daring riders that they were, some of the Cossacks vaulted into the saddles of their escaping mounts and tried to halt them, tugging furiously, savagely, at the bits. To no avail. Others disappeared underneath flailing hooves. The stampede grew ever larger. It wouldn't be long before all of them broke loose . . .

Bogdan sized up the situation at once. He saw he would be unable to stop the horses bolting. Brain racing furiously, he tried to outguess the Fritzes. Once they had stampeded his horses, what would they do? He guessed correctly. They would wheel down to the river, assuming his Cossacks would be immobilized without their mounts, and attempt a crossing – or at least to bring the other Fritzes across. Time was of the essence if he was going to stop them. '*Sotnik*,' he bellowed to Sergei Alexei above the roar of the massed hooves. 'Get on to the rockets. Tell the commander to fire at the Fritzes . . . stop them somehow for a little while at least. You . . . you and you,' he yelled to the other *Sotniks* close by, 'start pulling your men back to the river –'

'But Cossacks need their horses,' a big one-eyed ruffian with an eye-patch began to protest.

'Need nothing. Move back, I said,' Bogdan snarled. 'At the double now. *Davai. Davai.* While there's still time.' His voice rose to a bellow above the ever-increasing thunder of hooves. '*MOVE! NOW!*'

The *Sotniks* moved.

*

The armoured 'V' was careering madly across the steppe, herding the panic-stricken horses before it. From both flanks the Cossacks fired at them, bullets hammering at their sides like heavy tropical rain on a tin roof. The men didn't seem to notice. Panzer grenadiers, hanging on for their life on the swaying decks, whipped grenades from their boots and flung them like snowballs at the Russians who milled around in absolute confusion, faces crazed with fear, as that great mass of flying tanks bore down upon them.

Some of them had dug themselves in and braved the armoured attack. But the SS had no mercy on them and a wildly excited Karl could see why the black guards had attained their fearsome reputation. Tank after tank crashed into the holes, swirling round and round with whirling tracks in a great cloud of snow and earth, until the foxholes gave way and were turned into horrific coffins filled with bloody pulp.

Once a Soviet anti-tank took up the challenge, David facing Goliath. A white-glowing solid AP* shell howled through the air and it struck the tank to the right of von Dodenburg's a resounding blow. The tank reeled back on its rear bogies like a wild mustang being put to the saddle for the first time. The screaming panzer grenadiers on its deck were scythed off, it came to an abrupt halt and almost immediately thick white smoke started to pour from its shattered engine.

Von Dodenburg groaned and yelled to Schulze behind the big 75 mm cannon, 'Target ten o'clock. Range four hundred metres!'

With amazing speed for such a big man, Schulze whirled the controls, squinting down the sight, and Karl tensed for the crash of the cannon opening fire. The 75 mm roared. Karl

* AP Armour-piercing.

gasped as the blast whipped his face and tore the air from his lungs. The solid AP shot seared flatly across the steppe. There was the hollow boom of metal striking metal. The gun disappeared in a ball of angry red fire. Bits of metal, human bodies and one solitary intact wheel soared slowly through the golden air. The attack 'V' roared on victoriously.

Virtually all the Cossack Division's horses had now broken loose from the horse lines. Thousands of terrified animals, tossing their heads, eyes wide and wild with fear, were thundering across the steppe, their flying hooves lost in a cloud of snow. Beyond, the mass of the Division, all on foot save for a few officers, were streaming away in complete confusion, or so von Dodenburg thought. Bolt upright in the turret he surveyed the scene to his front, marvelling once again how a handful of brave determined men could always win over the mass, especially if that mass had no real leaders and no *corps d'esprit*.

To his front the horizon erupted abruptly with flame, as if the doors of a dozen giant blast furnaces had just been opened. There was a familiar blood-curdling howl like that of a poorly tuned church organ. Black fingers of smoke poked their way furiously into the sky. '*Stalin organs!*' King Bull screamed excitedly above that tremendous racket. The salvo of rockets hushed from the sky and landed with a tremendous thud that made the very earth quake and shiver. The tanks shook. The hot acrid blast wind of the explosions swept over them. What looked like a series of gigantic mole-heaps, brown and steaming with smoke, appearing in front of the flying 'V', as if by magic. One of the armoured cars to the right simply disappeared in a flash of vivid red, leaving nothing behind save what appeared to be a giant smoke ring ascending slowly to the sky.

Von Dodenburg saw immediately what the Russians were about. They were attempting to stop his bold charge with their electric mortars, while the mass of the Cossacks streaming to the east on foot would be turned by their officers on horseback to head for the river. There the armoured thrust would have to end and then it would be the turn of the Cossacks acting as infantry. If that happened the handful of SS men from Wotan wouldn't have a cat's chance in hell of breaking through to the trapped Iron Division.

He reacted immediately. By now the stampeding horses were out of reach of 'Blow Torch' – its range was a mere eighty or ninety metres. They were now charging to the west, gathering speed by the instant, outdistancing the tanks and the handful of Cossacks still attempting to catch up with them. He pressed his throat-mike urgently and rasped above the thunder of hooves and the roar of the tanks' huge Maybach engines, 'Kuno One to all.' Even as he spoke he guessed the range, '*Kuno One to all. Fire star shells – all you've got – eleven o'clock. Range five hundred metres! Ende!*'

In the same moment that he ended his order, Schulze, grunting heavily, swung open the breech of the 75 mm and ripped out the heavy armour-piercing shell as if it were a child's toy. In its place he inserted a star shell. It clattered into the breech and Schulze swiftly slammed down the breach lever. He peered through the sight, guessing instinctively what the CO wanted. Schulze needed no orders. He aimed and fired in almost the same instant. The cannon shuddered. The shell flew from the muzzle and soared into the sky, while on either side of them the other Wotan gunners did the same.

The tank and armoured car commanders waited tensely. To their front the horses still thundered on, tightly packed together, terrified and lathered with sweat, while the Cossacks hurried to the river, the mounted *Sotniks* now lashing out with their evil knouts to force them into greater speed.

Crack . . . crack . . . crack! One after another a dozen star shells exploded in rapid succession to the immediate front of the mass of horses. The sky was flooded instantly with a burning, brilliant white incandescent light. Karl shielded his eyes against the sudden glare. He had never seen anything like it before, save once as a child on New Year's Eve.* The whole horizon seemed to burn with that awesome glowing light. Next to him an awed Polack gasped, '*Boshe moi*, it's like the end of the world,' while von Dodenburg waited tensely, his knuckles gripping the turret a bright white, wondering if his plan would work.

The leading horses rose high in the air, flailing their forelegs, snorting wildly from distended nostrils, terrified by the tremendous glare of the burning white light.

Von Dodenburg willed them to turn. 'Move,' he cursed, '*move!*'

Suddenly the leaders could stand it no more, as yet another salvo of star shells exploded low in the sky to their front, this time only a hundred metres away – the heat must have been terrific. They broke and swung to the east. Von Dodenburg could have cheered out loud. The great mass behind, equally terrified, followed them in a huge whirling wake of snow. In a flash thousands of horses, packed tightly together, were bolting for the river in an attempt to escape that frightening light and a relieved von Dodenburg, feeling as weak as a baby, was calling through his throat-mike, 'Cease fire. Cease firing. Reload HE! *Cease fire!*'

Instinctively Bogdan knew what the Fritzes intended as the first star shells started to explode in front of the divisional horses. In a flash he took in the situation: the panicked horses, the Fritz tanks changing direction and his own sweating cursing Cossacks desperately trying to reach the river, as from the other side came the first weak volleys from the trapped Fascists. 'Keep them moving. In the name of the Black Virgin, keep them moving!' he yelled at a senior *Sotnik* and dug his spurs into the gleaming sides of his mount.

* Germans celebrate with fireworks on New Year's Eve.

'Comrade Colonel – *no*!' the other Cossack yelled desperately. '*NO!*'

Already it was too late. Bogdan, bent low over the flying mane of the stallion, was racing forward, heading straight for the massed horses, who, in their panic, were now beginning to turn and head for his men. He felt no fear as that solid mass of horseflesh bore down upon him, his ears deafened by the thunder of their hooves. He had been brought up with horses; his father the *Hetman* had made him learn to ride even before he could really walk. To him it didn't seem crazy for one lone man to attempt to avert or deflect the stampede of thousands of panic-stricken horses. Expertly he flung the reins between his teeth in true Cossack fashion, so that his hands were free. Beneath him, he felt his good loyal horse falter, as it too realized what was about to descend upon him. He pressed his muscular thighs into its lathered sides reassuringly and the stallion picked up the stride once more.

The lone horseman flew across the steppe at a tremendous rate, bound on a collision course with the stampede. The gap between the two narrowed by the instant. *Three hundred metres . . . two fifty . . . two hundred . . . one hundred and fifty . . .* Bogdan's eyes narrowed to slits as he peered at the flying mass, attempting to pick out the leaders – for even in a stampede there were leaders.

He spotted one. A great black beast with bared yellow teeth and flying jet-black mane, its eyes red and wild with fear. He hesitated no longer. He didn't have much space left before it was too late. Urgently he dug his knees into the stallion's sides and relaxed the reins held between his teeth. He fumbled for his sabre and ripped it from the scabbard, not taking his eyes off the black horse for a moment. Now it had got a little ahead of the rest. Ideal, he told himself as he took a firmer grip of the sabre in a hand that was beginning to sweat. Suddenly he realized he was as nervous as he had been back in his first battle as a sixteen-year-old ensign charging the Poles back in 1920.

Fifty metres. To his immediate front there was a solid wall of sweating glittering horseflesh. He would have only one chance to deflect their charge. He bent even lower over the flying mane of his mount, loving the stallion for not panicking, as they charged forward on this terrible collision course. He held his breath. It wouldn't be long now.

Twenty metres! The black horse had spotted him. Even in its unreasoning panic, it realized that he was heading straight for it. Its pace slackened. It would shy in a moment, exactly as he hoped it would. Then with a swing of his silver sabre, he would frighten it, make it swerve to the right. With a bit of luck the rest would follow. In a panic horses were like sheep. They would blindly follow a leader without thinking.

Ten metres!

He raised his sabre. It was now or never. The animal saw the gleam of silver. It was a cavalry horse. It had been in battle before. It knew what that sudden light meant. Something was going to hurt. It shied, breaking pace. Bogdan laughed triumphantly. *It was working!* He prepared to bring the curved sword down hard right across the black beast's snout! That would complete the process.

'Take that my fine –' he began to chortle. Abruptly the stallion stumbled. The reins were wrenched from his teeth. He screamed as the mount went down on its knees and he was hurtled right over its suddenly bent head, right into the path of the charging horses. The sword flew from his hand. Frantically he grabbed for the precious sack of earth around his neck. Next moment the first of those cruel flailing hooves crashed into his inert body and then he was submerged by them, the bag of earth bursting in his lifeless fingers. The horses swept on – to the river . . .

Envoi

'*Hurrah . . . hurrah . . . hurrah!*' the hoarse bass cry of welcome rose from hundreds of throats, as the first of what was left from von Dodenburg's 'reconnaissance' force started to rattle across the bridge over the Dnieper. Everywhere the engineers, the anti-aircraft gunners, the panzer grenadiers of Dietrich's SS Corps rose from their holes and slit-trenches to cheer the handful of ragged weary men. From mouth to mouth the excited words flew, half in envy, half in admiration. '*That frigging Wotan's done it agen.* They've brought back what's left of a whole frigging division of stubble-hoppers. *Wotan's gone and done it a frigging agen!*'

This brilliant winter morning, *Obergruppenführer* Sepp Dietrich himself, surrounded by his staff officers and elegant flunkies, was present to welcome them back. He had been against the operation right from the start admittedly. But now that it had succeeded – without his permission – he wanted to be party to the triumph.

Already the UFA* camera people were in position, ready to record the event for Goebbels's *Tonende Wochenschau.*† Next week or so, he told himself joyfully, his ugly old mug would be seen in every cinema throughout the length and breadth of the Reich. Oh yes, he couldn't afford to miss an occasion like this whatever he thought privately of von Dodenburg's arrogant flouting of his order, the aristocratic young swine.

In due course, he'd ensure that von Dodenburg paid for his insubordination. That young man needed his knuckles rapping very firmly. But for the time being, while the world – and the Führer – thought the sunshine shone from his arrogant, upper-class arse, he would have to be praised.

---

* A German film company.
† German newsreel company.

Corps commander Dietrich cast a glance at the Wotan's CO, preening himself at the edge of the group of the high-ranking staff officers, enjoying the reflected glory. Obviously, Dietrich thought sourly, that ugly warm brother, pervert that he was, would be wanting a share of whatever 'tin' was going – and the Führer had promised a whole shitting crateful of the stuff. Sometimes Adolf was just too soft, too good-hearted with these Johnny-come-latelies who had joined the Armed SS solely for the goodies – quick promotion and plenty of decorations.

He forgot the ugly colonel with his great beak of a nose. Instead he turned his gaze on the bridge and as the cheering rose from the bridge to the little hillock upon which he and the rest stood, overlooking the Dnieper, he joined in half-heartedly. As the battered armoured vehicles, their sides blackened and scarred, drew ever closer, Sepp Dietrich braced himself to put a good face on it and say the right words. After all, it wasn't every day that a corps commander was featured on the newsreels.

But in the event, Sepp Dietrich did not have to play the hypocrite, a role which didn't become him, on that bright morning in the first week of April 1942. Suddenly the cheering on the bridge was beginning to falter, to be replaced by gasps of surprise, even moans. Preceded by a heavy cloying stench which reminded the corps commander of the monkey cages at Munich Zoo before the war, came the survivors of the Iron Division.

Noiselessly, like sleep-walkers, the survivors made their slow pitiful progress across the bridge. Most were without weapons. Some used their rifles as crutches. Others hopped on feet bound up in bundles of stinking rags; and all showed only one emotion; a pathetic animal-like fear of being left behind on the other side of the Dnieper.

Rank after rank they dragged themselves by the suddenly awed and silenced SS men. None of them spoke, even the few who were unwounded. They were numb, gaze fixed on the west and safety. They could have been dead men. Without a glance to left or right at the awe-struck SS, they passed on their way, leaving behind a trail of blood and pus which glistened loathsomely in the thin rays of the sun.

'My God!' the Vulture exclaimed and his monocle popped out of his eye.

'It's Beresina all over again,'* another staff officer said in a hushed tone.

Behind them the director of the camera crew bellowed urgently, 'Stop them shitting cameras! For chrissake *don't* record this! Goebbels'll have our hides if we do. *STOP!*'

Sepp Dietrich had also seen enough. '*Meine Herren,*' he rapped in his thick Bavarian accent, swarthy face very serious and sober now, 'I think we'd better go.' He flashed a glance at the far horizon, automatically noting the muted flashes there which meant *they* were coming. 'There soon will be work to be done – urgent work!'

Silently his staff nodded their agreement, all of their well-fed, normally ruddy confident faces pale and serious after what they had just seen. Without a word they started to file behind the corps commander to the waiting staff cars . . .

Kuno von Dodenburg smiled bitterly, as he watched the retreat of the staff officers behind Dietrich's squat figure. He guessed why they were departing and why the camera crews were already packing up their gear without having filmed the passing survivors. Those complacent, well-fed, self-satisfied 'golden pheasants'† who ran things back in the Reich wanted to know nothing of the harsh realities of the war in Russia.

'It seems,' he mused aloud to no one in particular as they all relaxed in the thin rays of the sun on the deck of his battered tank, 'that retreats are not particularly popular with the rear echelon swine. It always has to be victories for home consumption.'

---

* A catastrophic part of Napoleon's great retreat from Moscow in 1812.
† Nickname for Party officials, due to their love of finery and gold braid.

'Roses, roses, roses all the way, sir,' Schulze agreed, taking in the elegant staff officers in their well-cut uniforms and highly polished boots who were staring at the passing survivors from the Iron Division as if they were creatures from another world.

'Yes, I suppose you're right,' von Dodenburg said easily, enjoying the thin warmth of the April sun. For a moment he stared at the weather-beaten stubble-hoppers in their tattered uniforms. Below the radio sprang into life once again. Suddenly he proffered his hand to Karl, who was lounging against the turret, wrapped in his own thoughts. 'Grenadier, you did a fine job of work. If it is in my power to do so, I shall see you and your two comrades' – he indicated Ami and Polack, who were gnawing hunks of black bread – 'receive some sort of decoration. You richly deserve it.'

Karl hesitated to take the hand. Didn't its owner wear the silver insignia of death and repression?

Von Dodenburg saw the hesitation in the shabby soldier's handsome intelligent face and said softly, using the soldier's phrase, 'We're in this crap right up to our hooters *together*, you know. Rank and regiment mean just nothing now. We're all front swine.'

'Yes, sir, we're all front swine,' Karl agreed and took the hand.

Ami and Polack followed.

'Take their names and particulars, Schulze,' von Dodenburg ordered as the chatter of the radio below became more insistent, 'you know the usual shit needed for a piece of tin.' Then he was gone, sliding into the turret.

A minute later what was left of von Dodenburg's 'reconnaissance' group was rolling back across the Dnieper the way it had come. Sepp Dietrich was already taking his revenge upon the 'arrogant young swine'.

For a while the Three Rebels watched them roll by, waving now and then in a half-hearted sort of a way for they knew they'd never see von Dodenburg and his tough young men ever again. The greedy maw of the war in Russia would soon swallow them up for good.

'Shaking hands with an SS officer,' Polack said thoughtfully.

'We've got to find the regiment,' Ami said, 'I'm hungry.'

Karl said nothing, but he mused to himself, 'Front swine, sitting in the winter sun, licking their wounds – till the next time.' Then he rose wearily and limped into the traffic, followed by the others, to search for quarters for the night. A few moments later they too had gone, as if they had never even existed . . .

To the east, the heavy guns started to rumble.